SNAKES AND LADDERS

JOHN WILLINS

Copyright © 2018 by John Willins

Cover and Interior Design by David Provolo

Published by:

WAS Books
PO Box #4803
Wilmington, Delaware, 19807
United States of America

Hardback ISBN: 978-1-7328590-0-5
Paperback ISBN: 978-1-7328590-1-2
eISBN : 978-1-7328590-2-9

Library of Congress Control Number 2018911753

Lassiter's Hierarchy

Chairman

Chief Executive Officer/President

Executive Vice President

Senior Vice President

Vice President

Executive Director

Director

Employee

CHAPTER LIST

CHAPTER ONE

A Fond Farewell

February 2012

The aerospace center was truly a spectacular location. It housed hundreds of aircraft—ultra-modern fighter jets and historic bombers, early biplanes and gliders, many of which were suspended from the ceiling—an IMAX theater, classrooms, the obligatory gift store, and, its star attraction, a jumbo-sized McDonald's. It was usually the province of weekend family trippers, Guide and Scout troops, overseas tourists, aviation enthusiasts, and military veterans. Backpacks, sneakers, jeans, and baseball caps were the normal dress code.

But occasionally, the museum hosted private functions, cordoning off the most popular exhibits to prepare dining tables and bar areas—smart white linens and wine glass pyramids evoking the early days of luxury air travel as the budget passengers of today were politely yet firmly shepherded out of the doors. The museum guides, mainly retired guys with their "Ask Me" badges and endless tales of aeronautical feats, disappeared to be replaced by a younger, more diverse crew of cool, calm, and collected bartenders and busy, bustling waiters, all very snappy in their black-and-white livery.

Tonight's event promised to be even more upmarket than normal: the platinum package. There were to be five hundred guests—the great and the good, and the not so good yet well connected. The area's business and political elite had been invited to celebrate an illustrious career. A splendid meal, fine wines, entertaining speeches, heartfelt toasts, and an emotional ride out into honorable retirement for the guest of honor were the order of the evening. As well as their "business attire," the guests were expected to wear a great sense of occasion and pride.

■

Through the fog, George Knight approached the brightly lit museum, driving his car at high speed. He took a last check of his invitation before casually tossing it to his traveling companion, his closest friend and counselor, Duncan Ball.

"We all know that this is all a big charade. G-man's retirement party. Nobody cares. The only reason anybody is here is to find out who's getting his job. But what the fuck, Dunc. If the Board wants to throw him a party to celebrate"—Knight grinned—"then who am I to quibble? I like charades. I'm good at them."

The Board of Directors of Lassiter Corporation
requests the pleasure of the company of

Mr. George Knight

at a reception to celebrate the retirement of
Daniel Grauermann
Chairman, Chief Executive Officer and President

7pm February 15th, 2012

Business Attire
RSVP
Sponsored by
QPQ & Drake Devonshire

Waddington
Aerospace
Center

Ball grimaced.

"And believe me, Dunc, I am just as keen as anyone to find out if I'm going to get the job," Knight protested, unconvincingly.

"But you can't just corner the selection panel members and ask them, 'Did I get the job?' can you, George? Wouldn't be . . . you know . . . right, would it?" Ball responded.

"Is that what you think I should do, Dunc? Really?"

"No. As ever, you leave the dirty work to me, mate. You just have a good night. I'll let you know what I find out later," Ball answered, piling on the sarcasm.

They fell silent as the vast white hangars loomed, floodlit in the freezing February fog.

"Impressive-looking place. Is there a seating plan for this thing?" Ball asked impassively as they drew up to the entrance.

"I dunno, mate, maybe we'll find out when we *check in . . . Check in*, get it? We're at a plane place . . ." Knight said with a grin, overplaying the humor card.

"Oh, OK, enough, you win. You're in one of those moods. You're determined to screw around with this, aren't you?" Ball sighed.

Ball's face reddened as he made this earnest assessment. It was unlike him to get angry, but this outburst had been festering away inside for a while, Knight's insouciance finally becoming too much.

"For fuck's sake, just BEHAVE, George. Remember the world is watching now," Ball scolded, increasingly irritated by Knight's exaggerated exuberance.

Climbing out of his car, Knight continued to joke, defying the warning. "Come on, let's join the party. Are we going to be here for more than eight hours? Company travel policy says we can have a business-class seat if we are."

"Sure, George, whatever you say." Ball pulled Knight sharply to one side as they prepared to enter. "Look, mate, you might think you have this all sewn up. But I'm not taking it for granted. I've got a lot of stock vested in George Knight Limited. I reckon there are people here that know if you're getting the job or not, and I'm going to work my backside off tonight to find out. We have to keep on top of this and not find out too late that you've been passed over."

Ball's tone carried the unspoken message that they would both be better off if Knight put in some effort too, if he took things a little more seriously, if he could just look like he meant it.

Sensing that they needed to finish the conversation and not leave things unsaid, they stepped into the gift store, away from the other arriving guests. The two had been close friends for over twenty years, two decades that had brought them from the UK to the United States, from proud Brits to naturalized Americans. Along the way, they'd shared new jobs, new locations, highs and lows, and several narrow escapes, but rarely a cross word between them.

As neither of them wanted to spend the evening brooding over hurt feelings, they instinctively reached for some distracting common ground. For them it was often their clothes. They admired the cut of each other's garb.

Knight, a Senior Vice President at Lassiter Corporation, had brought out his best Ermenegildo Zegna navy suit for the occasion, which he wore with a white shirt and a bold purple paisley tie. Officially five foot eleven, he had a long torso and broad shoulders, a combination that supported his claim to be a six-footer. His appearance featured the telltale signs of his late forties: the frameless glasses over a few crow's feet; his buzz cut offering only a token disguise to his thinning and increasingly gray hair; his irrepressible smile, the face of experience, wisdom and eternal optimism or perhaps a mask of chronic immaturity. He was a man of many contradictions: ambitious yet complacent, insightful yet blinkered, confident yet unsure, his intelligence defined by his ability to feel concurrently both deep dedication and detached disinterest in the same subject.

Ball, a Lassiter Vice President, genuinely a six-footer—six four or more—topped with thick salt-and-pepper hair, wore a somber black Armani. He was without question a few years older than Knight, and almost certainly a lot wiser.

Reassured that they were both looking suitably sharp, they settled their game plan. Using their individual talents—Knight's charm, Ball's menace—they would embark on a full intelligence-gathering mission. Knight would work the room, abandoning his wise-cracking comedy routine to ingratiate himself with the right people: the lawyers and the selection panel. Ball would use his considerable powers of persuasion, "have a word" with some of the hangers-on, possibly pull in a few "favors." He grinned in expectation.

"Tell you what, George. You could do *something* really useful." Ball's emphasis suggested that this would be a rare event, but there was warm humor in his voice. "Get close to your Canadian pal, Jackie whatshername. She was on the panel. See what she knows."

"Crawford. It's Jacquelyn Crawford," Knight replied, suddenly very serious, even startled, disturbed by a fleeting bad memory. "Hey, Dunc, thanks for putting me straight. I'm on it. Good luck." They shared a brisk handshake and headed purposefully off into the venue.

■

The next guests to arrive were Christina Drago and Patsy Myer. As members of Grauermann's inner circle, they were afforded the luxury of a chauffeur-driven company SUV.

Myer brandished her invitation, her face full of disdain, as if she were sucking on a particularly sour lemon drop.

"I'm just not happy about this at all, Christina. It's irrational and frivolous. It's just not necessary."

"Well, it is meant to be a *party*, Patsy," replied Drago with a snarl, her patience wearing thin.

Drago was an Executive Vice President, the leader of one of Lassiter's business units. Her business attire was a pale gray suit with a cream blouse, and pumps with modest heels. She hadn't found the time to apply any makeup. She rarely did, contemptuously dismissing what she considered her sex's overreliance on war paint. For this special occasion, though, she had added a touch of color, with a large lapis lazuli brooch and matching Breguet watch.

Like Knight, Drago was full of contradictions. Her firm body and strong posture, the gains from her regular sessions with a personal trainer, exuded a forceful, energetic, and demanding presence that dominated the car. This was the Christina Drago that everyone knew or thought they did. Her public image was that of an unstoppable, unrelenting executive. And yet, looking closer, her strained eyes reflected weariness. Her pale, drawn face, set hard, suggested angst, perhaps remorse; and her mouth, tight and unsympathetic, spoke of her frustration and a sense of betrayal.

Their argument about the merits of the event had filled most of the early-evening journey from Lassiter HQ. But the spat was only a symptom, a sign of their fear, their deep unease that the source of their power was about to walk out the door, rendering them instantly ordinary, their fate uncertain as Grauermann had failed to secure their futures. Drago had expected smooth passage into the CEO's seat. For a while that had looked assured, but now she was in a dogfight.

Myer, Grauermann's Senior Executive Assistant, a fearsome gatekeeper who screened his calls, prepared his correspondence, managed his diary, and made his travel arrangements, had expected him to reward her loyalty with a generous early-retirement package, or some guaranteed post within Drago's new regime, or at least a hefty return on her years of accumulated stock options. Alas, she had none of these.

As the car drew up, it was Myer who put the cards on the table, bitterness curling every word. "Look, let's stop beating about the bush. The reason we're so pissed about this is because our man Mr. Daniel Grauermann has royally screwed this up and now we are summoned to kiss his ass once more."

Drago rolled her eyes.

"Just tell me, why did we trust him?" Myer answered her own question, "We all thought he had this covered. Now it's just a coin toss, and he doesn't give a shit how it turns out. Why did Daniel let this go, ruining it for everyone?"

Not anticipating a reply, Myer opened her door and began to get out of the car huffily.

But Drago had had enough of the whining. "Wait, Patsy," she ordered. "I don't know what went wrong. And frankly, I'm past caring. I don't give a rat's anymore. He's spent. Screw him. Let's move on."

Myer quietly closed her door again to see out this conversation. They sat in brooding silence for a moment as Drago's blunt message sank in.

Then, after that brief painful moment, Drago smiled, kindling a little warmth. "Look, I've got the most to lose here. And I haven't lost yet. Yes, they brought Knight in, but he's got nothing. He's a lightweight. This whole thing is unnecessary. I WILL get the job and then we can relax. I'll take care of you. Stop the self-pity, OK?"

"Do you *know* you have it, Christina? How come? Why haven't you told me?" Myer eagerly sought confirmation.

Drago paused before replying calmly, "No, Patsy, I don't *know*. I'm just very confident that I'm going to win, that's all."

"Well, Christina, that's all well and good, but we need to find out, for all our sakes. And our families' sakes, and our 401(k)s' sakes, and our pension plans' sakes, and . . . and . . . and . . . soon." The desperation showed in her voice. With a much younger second husband to support and costly appearances to be kept up with occasional aesthetic work, she feared a future without the grown-ups' table's benefits.

Drago took firm charge. "Well, let's calm down and do something useful, shall we, dear? We'll get an answer. Someone here tonight knows the outcome. They have to. Let's see what we can find out. It needs to be subtle. I'll see what I can get from the legal types and the selection panel members. You see if Daniel actually has any idea what's going on. Mill around with Knight's people too. Use your charms, especially with that Duncan Ball guy. You paid a lot for those tits. See if they'll get him to talk. See you back at the car afterward, and we can share what we've learned."

Myer pumped up her bosom with a pout, then she and Drago headed off into the center.

■

Five minutes later, two others arrived at the museum, also passengers in a Lassiter SUV: Robert Livingston, Lassiter's Senior General Counsel, and Chip Chambers, a Partner with the Quinn Payne Qualye law firm. In the half-light of the car, they seemed undistinguished in their ill-fitting black suits—shiny off-the-peg polyester clones lacking style or substance, perfectly paired with their Ecco dress shoes. Livingston, his chubby sprawl the perfect occupant for the SUV's vast expanse of rear seat leather, finished off the last piece from a bucket of fried chicken he'd picked up on the way.

"Do you have your speech ready, Chip?" Livingston asked, spraying only a modest amount of minced meat on the hapless Chambers.

"Yes, Robert. I'm all set, thanks. I have it here." Chambers replied, brandishing his Blackberry. "I've had a group of my associates working on it full-time for the past three months. They've really done a great job."

"That's some impressive productivity, Chip. Great you guys came through with the sponsorship for tonight too," Livingston enthused.

"I hope we get a return on our investment, Robert. We're really worried about the succession. Have you been able to find out who's taking over from Grauermann yet? Is it that serious bitch Drago or that Brit flake Knight? Or hopefully some halfway decent outsider?" Chambers asked.

"I hear you. But I don't have an answer. Sorry, I'm getting nowhere."

Livingston shrugged. "The Board has shut me out of that discussion, and Drake Devonshire are handling the CEO legal work."

"Yeah, I heard Drake Devonshire got in here. Not good news. They're our biggest rivals and, for a top law firm, pretty straight. That means trouble for us. We could be out if the new CEO is close to them, so I really need an answer on this. Let's see what we can find out tonight. Talk to the selection panel members, Drago and Knight, Grauermann's little band of cling-ons. We can compare notes later."

■

The last group to arrive was the Lassiter Cycling Team—twenty young and fit athletes from Europe, Australia, and the US, along with their manager, trainers, and technicians. They had spent the day out in the mountains completing a 180-mile training ride, preparation for the upcoming professional cycling season. After a short break at Lassiter HQ, they had changed into their identical black, red, and white training suits, emblazoned with Lassiter's and other sponsors' logos, and trooped wearily onto the team bus.

The starving cyclists were not a happy crew. They were desperate to eat, craving the heavy carbohydrate intake their regimen demanded. Most were listening to music on their iPods or slumbering. As they pulled into the driveway, from the back of the coach, Dusty Rhodes, the team's Australian star rider and the unofficial team shop steward, stood up and shouted down the aisle, "Why do we have to do this bollocks, Hansi?"

The other riders perked up, silently thanking Dusty for putting so eloquently what they were all thinking.

"It's part of the deal, Dusty. You know how it works." Hansi Olsen, the team's Danish manager, a former Special Forces soldier and a no-nonsense disciplinarian, walked down the aisle and quietly replied in his perfect English, "We turn up, we pose for photos, we talk about the races, the sacrifices, the crashes, the blood, the sweat, the tears . . . and," now glaring at Rhodes, he said with a sudden shout, "WE GET THE FUCKING TEAM SPONSORSHIP RENEWED AGAIN."

"Yeah, yeah, OK, keep your hair on, mate. I get it," Rhodes replied sheepishly.

He was not going to be steamrollered completely, though. He had his pride. Bringing it down to a conspiratorial whisper with Olsen, he said, "So what's the story with this G-man guy? He was the bloke who brought us in, right? And now he's retiring? Aren't we wasting our fucking time? Which one of these high-and-mighty arseholes is going to sign the checks now?"

"Now that, Mr. Rhodes, is a smart question, an existential question. And finding the answer is the real reason why we are at this event tonight."

"Mate, I've no idea what exis-fucking-tentional means, but whatever, I'm sure I can live without it. I do get that the Lassiter dough might be on the line here. Want me to snoop around, see what I can find out?"

"Yes, affirmative. I can use you." Olsen, relieved to be able to share his fears about the future of the team with his top rider, sat beside Rhodes and calmly explained the team's predicament, and potential demise. Corporate sponsors were much harder to come by after all of the sport's drug issues. The Dane was out of options. Without a renewal of the Lassiter sponsorship, the team would have to fold, putting all of them out of work. Some would find roles with other teams; many would not. So with Rhodes in the know, Olsen slowly and methodically spelled out his event orders.

"Be cautious in the opening stages."

"Check."

"Keep in the group. Don't go charging off by yourself until after the speeches."

"Check."

"Report back to me regularly."

"Check."

"As it gets toward the end and they tire after a few drinks, focus on the Sales and Marketing people. They always get loaded."

"Roger-d."

"Steer clear of the financial types. They'll close us down faster than a UCI tester."

"You betcha."

"Use your charm with the bosses' wives."

"You beauty, I'm your man."

"Hear me, Dusty. If it gets sticky with them, pull out and head for the bus. We cannot afford another incident."

The bus pulled up, and the team filed off and wandered into the center, most looking for carbs and a quiet night, only Rhodes and Olsen with a more ambitious agenda.

Most of the early arrivals congregated in the biggest bar area, which was set out next to the *Blackbird*, a Cold War spy plane that still had a futuristic look. The sleek, menacing aircraft added its own sense of manifest destiny to the occasion as the guests danced the "So good to see you! Who are you with these days? May I introduce to you to my wife?" reel that was expected at such events. Polite small talk continued while the servers passed through the crowd with miniature spring rolls, chicken satays, scallops, and shrimp skewers. The bartenders had the standard caterer range of beers, wines, and a few spirits. The Bombay Sapphire was going down very well.

There was a second bar area set a little farther into the center. Most of the guests hadn't spotted it. One small group had formed, though. Daniel Grauermann, the guest of honor for the night, was taking in a cocktail with his wife of almost thirty-five years, Isobel. Grauermann, tall, thickset, with a dense thatch of unruly gray hair and a large white walrus mustache, was slumped over a small drinks table, his watery brown eyes squinting behind his glasses as he peered contemptuously at the growing crowd.

"Here they come. Look at them all. Sponging bunch of gutless pricks," he mumbled under his breath before draining another large scotch.

"God, why do we have to go through with this BULLSHIT?" He waved over the waiter. "Hey, get me another." He blew out his cheeks, running his fingers over his mustache.

Isobel reacted to his raised voice, recognizing her husband's outburst as a symptom typical of his stage fright.

Isobel glanced around, making sure none of the waiters were within earshot, took the glass from her husband's hand, and calmly instructed, "Daniel Grauermann, slow down the drinking and get your act together. You have a role to play, and I'm not going to let you let me down by going to pieces now."

Her tone brokered no room for dissension.

"OK . . . OK, Isobel. I'll be fine." He sighed, sat up from the table, and straightened his back, responding to her instructions. "Just don't see why I have to entertain these people. Watch them knock back the booze and stuff themselves with food while we foot the bill. What did these people ever do for me?" he added, with a lame half-smile.

His wife had asserted her control, a dominance of a parent over a young child, a master over a servant. Now she could build up his confidence, pander to his ego.

"Yes, you're right, Daniel. You did everything for them. They owe it all to you. This is your night to remind them of that and let them know what they'll be missing when you're gone."

Grauermann — an engineer by training and a technologist for most of his career, a career built upon impersonal data and scientific analysis, sharp yet lacking any great ambition, reinvented as a dynamic, decisive general manager, a Chief Executive Office, a metamorphosis in which he initially played little part, triggered as it was by the self-serving schemes of others, but in which he became fully vested as he accumulated the trappings of the C-suite in the twenty-first century, the private jet, the chauffeur, the seven-figure salary, all of which brought the inevitable, cloying admiration of some and the bitter condemnation of others - complied without protest. He ponderously raised himself up from the table, resigned to following his wife's orders yet again.

"Yeah, you're right. I'll show these pricks. It's the last time I'll have to deal with them. Do you have my script?"

"Yes, here you are." Isobel passed her husband a white envelope prominently bearing the Lassiter logo. He pulled out the contents: twelve pages of typing in a very large font. He flicked through them and flinched. "What on earth have you written here? I'll never get through all this. Can't I just give a toast or something?"

"No, you can't. I told you. You have a role to play and you are going to play it. Besides, it'll all be on the teleprompter, so just read it off there. Do you understand?"

"Right, let's face the music. Over there, look. The cycling guys just arrived. I'll just get another drink and then we'll go talk to them."

Grauermann moodily snatched another glass from the impassive bartender.

"I've just spotted Jebby, your . . . my useless nephew," Isobel said.

"Oh great, that's all I need. Why is *he* here?" Grauermann groaned.

"I invited him. And my dear sister. I wanted them to see how well we've done," Isobel replied.

Grauermann's face lost all its color, his eyes bulging, stung by another quaff of scotch. "Is she coming too?"

"No, calm down, of course not." A cruel smile flickered across Isobel's face. "At first she replied yes to the invite, then she sent me an email yesterday telling me she wouldn't be able to make it after all."

"Thank God. What's her excuse this time?"

"She's flown off to Dubai with her latest toy boy. Maybe he's a Gulf sheikh. I don't care," Isobel replied with an exaggerated nonchalance, her instinctive attempt to disguise her disappointment. "Forget about her. She's not going to spoil our event, Daniel. You go talk to your biker gang friends. I'll see you at the table. I need to talk to dear little Jebby first."

■

Isobel left her husband and strolled purposefully into the main hangar. She carried a confident, majestic air as she felt the eyes upon her. It was a special night. It might ostensibly be her husband's event, but she knew that it was really a recognition of what they had achieved together. She had paid no mind to his tenure's premature ending. She was pleased with her husband's career. And she was proud of her part in it, a critical part—no, *the* critical part of his success. She relished the crowd's attention, deserved their recognition, and despised their very existence.

Her nephew had collected a drink from the bar. He was lurking on the fringes, nervously shifting from foot to foot like a freshman at a seniors' party. He was relieved to see a familiar face. She gestured for him to join her farther from the group. She did not want their conversation to be overheard.

"Aunt Isobel, it's good to see you. Thank you for inviting me."

"You're welcome, Jebby. You're sitting by yourself with some Lassiter nobodies, I'm afraid. Your mother was meant to be with you, but she's canceled on us. Something more interesting came up, as ever."

"I don't know what to say. She's always put herself first. I'm sorry, Aunt Isobel."

"Don't apologize, Jebby. I don't really care. It's her loss that she's missing out on tonight. Besides, it's not your fault. She was this way well before you arrived, believe me. Even as a girl, she thought she was a princess."

"I wish you could get along, then again I guess it's too late for that. You're so different. She's still running around like she's seventeen.

She'll never grow up. And you're just so . . . disciplined and organized, Aunt Isobel."

"I can do without the comparison. I've spent my life being compared to her, and I don't need reminding of that tonight."

"Oh, sorry. I really didn't mean to offend you. I won't mention her again."

"Let's talk about something much more important. Thank you for taking care of that business that I asked you about at the school."

"You're welcome, Aunt Isobel. Getting two boys expelled when they'd done nothing wrong wasn't easy."

"Good boy. I was relying on you. I knew you wouldn't let me down."

She began to walk away dismissively.

Ding, dang, dong.

Ding, dang, dong.

Ding, dang, dong.

Isobel paused as one of the catering crew passed by them playing a small xylophone, chiming out an attention-grabbing arpeggio scale to summon everyone to their seats. It gave Jebby a chance to catch her.

"Aunt Isobel, can I ask you something?"

"If you must. Make it quick. What do you want? Another promotion?"

"No, I just want to know what this is all about. Getting these boys expelled. Why did it matter to you? It's only a few years ago that I helped you get them into the school."

"Revenge, Jebby, revenge. Pure and simple. Just like me. Now, let's get to our tables."

■

Fifty circular tables were laid out in neat rows between the aircraft. As the tables filled up, the guests noticed two things. First, as if they hadn't already known, they were reminded that this dinner was all about Grauermann. The napkins were embroidered with his initials. Each seat had a glossy "commemorative brochure" featuring photos of the great moments, an extensive account of his career and achievements. The guests had a raffle ticket to a prize draw for an autographed copy of the brochure too, a future collectors' item no doubt.

The second thing was that . . . well . . . the place was rather empty. Most tables had only two or three people at them. Some were completely deserted. The only ones that appeared full were the two reserved for the cycling team. Scrunched together in their uniform tracksuits, their full complement only served to highlight the empty spaces elsewhere.

There were four at table four. Knight and Ball had been joined by Robin "NASA" Houston, the Senior Vice President of Quality Management, and Jacquelyn Crawford. An influential client, Crawford worked for one of Lassiter's biggest customers and headed the Lassiter Strategic Advisory Council.

Houston finished a scan of the dining tables. He was always good at counting the numbers. "One hundred and twenty-five, one hundred and twenty-six . . . That's it. No, stop the presses, here comes another attorney. One hundred and twenty-seven. Hell's bells."

"At least G-man's got a full house. Look . . . it's the grown-ups' table on a picnic. Bless." Knight pointed to the head table, where Grauermann and his wife had been joined by Myer, Drago, and several other trusted retainers.

"What a joke. One hundred and twenty-seven, and that includes twenty-odd from the bike team too," Houston said to no one in particular. "What a total waste of time."

"Thanks. I'm glad to be so appreciated," Crawford said mockingly, glaring at Houston.

"Oh, um. I'm sorry, Jacquelyn, no offense. Always a pleasure spending time with you."

Around the other tables, similar conversations were had.

"Why so many no-shows?"

"Must be the fog."

"There's a bug going around."

"Maybe some got the dates messed up in their calendars."

One young waitress was even heard to say, "Maybe people just don't like him?"

That was quickly dismissed as immature nonsense.

Over the next hour or so, as the diners worked their way through a goat cheese and beet salad with champagne vinaigrette, a succulent filet mignon wrapped in bacon and served with scallops, and a chocolate mousse with mascarpone and a raspberry coulis, Knight tried to steer the conversation with Crawford around to the CEO decision. Each time, she deftly sidestepped the issue, unwilling to share her inside knowledge. Knight abandoned the attempt. He didn't want to push his luck.

As coffee was served, the emcee rose to his feet. A small stage had been set up with a dais, also bearing the DG initials. The emcee tapped on the microphone to get everyone's attention.

"Ladies and gentlemen . . ." The buzz of conversation started to drop. He tapped again. "Ladies and gentlemen." The room finally quieted. "Thank you. Now that I have your attention, we can get this show on the road. Firstly, let me introduce and thank Chip Chambers and the QPQ team, and Dale Dobbs and Drake Devonshire for cosponsoring tonight's event. Gentlemen, please come up and say a few words."

Chambers came up to the stage first, clutching his indispensable Blackberry. He positioned himself behind the dais, held it out in front of him, seemed to stifle a sneeze, sniffed loudly, and then read his script robotically, his eyes fixed on the device's tiny screen.

"Mr. and Mrs. Grauermann, honored guests, ladies and gentlemen, Quinn Payne Qualye are proud to sponsor this event to celebrate the career of a distinguished business leader. We are grateful for the opportunity to work with the executive team at Lassiter, especially Robert Livingston and the legal group. We look forward to continuing our strong partnership as Daniel enjoys his well-deserved retirement. Thank you and enjoy the evening."

Knight whispered to his tablemates, "Wow, pretty good for QPQ. I counted sixty-eight words and several facts. I wonder how much we paid for that?"

Dale Dobbs followed and, remarkably without the assistance of a smartphone, enthusiastically made his remarks.

"Mr. and Mrs. Grauermann, honored guests, ladies and gentlemen, Drake Devonshire are proud to sponsor this event to celebrate the career of a distinguished business leader. We are grateful for the opportunity to work with the executive team at Lassiter, especially Robert Livingston and the legal group. We look forward to continuing our strong partnership as Daniel enjoys his well-deserved retirement. Thank you and enjoy the evening."

"Wow, thank you, Chip and Dale." Knight applauded ironically. "I guess great legal minds think alike. Or is it fools seldom differ?"

■

Over at the cycling tables, the team had refueled; extra servings of bread and potatoes had been ruthlessly demolished. Now the boys were getting a bit restless.

"Hey, Hansi, I'm off on a bit of a recce. I see someone over there who might have some info for us."

"Ten-four, Dusty. Keep it clean. Remember we have to do that honor guard routine later."

Dusty Rhodes got up from his chair and sauntered confidently across the hangar floor. His path took him close to Jacquelyn Crawford. He slowed his pace, glanced at her, their eyes meeting for the briefest instance, and then continued out of the dining area. A few seconds later, she took her Blackberry from her purse, apparently to answer a call. "Excuse me, George, I must take this call. It's my boss." She slipped away from the table gracefully. "One moment, one moment." She said quietly into her phone, her tone animated and intense.

As soon as she was out of sight of the dining tables, she dropped the phone back into her purse and looked around for the cyclist. A slight cough from the entrance to the now closed gift store alerted her.

"Oi, over here, Jacks."

She headed to the gift store and joined Rhodes in the half-lit entrance. He took her hands and pulled her eagerly into the shadows behind a pillar.

"Well, aren't you a sight for sore eyes, Ms. Crawford," he said, his excitement evident in his bright smile.

"Well, hello, Mr. Rhodes. Long time no see," Crawford purred back, and then kissed him on the mouth.

"Yep, has been a while. Did ya miss me?"

"Oh, of course, my life is not complete without you." Her deep, throaty tone mocked his earnestness. "You're my favorite Australian lover."

"It's good to see you too, babe. You look hot."

She had made an extra special effort with her appearance for the event. Her close-fitting dark purple dress accented her voluptuous figure. Her spiky cropped hair, matching purple eye shadow and lipstick, five-inch stilettos, and black stockings enhanced the impact. She was indeed dressed to kill.

"I don't have any underwear on, Dusty," she whispered in his ear. "You know what that means?"

"Strewth, girl, this is more than I bargained for tonight. I'm game if you are."

They headed a little farther down the corridor, trying doors as they went. Eventually one came open. It was the disabled restroom. They stumbled in. The Aussie went to flick on the light switch, but she stopped him.

"Leave it off. Lock the door."

They kissed passionately, both getting aroused. Then she pulled down his tracksuit pants and pushed him down onto the toilet seat.

"Sit there and get ready to be fucked, biker boy."

Pulling up her dress around her hips, she eased herself onto him and began to ride. As the pace quickened, Rhodes reached behind him to steady his balance. Then . . .

Wee-woo! Wee-woo! Wee-woo! Wee-woo!

Their ears were assaulted, the room lit up, their senses in shock as a flashing strobe light blinded them. Then again:

Wee-woo! Wee-woo! Wee-woo! Wee-woo!

"Oh shit, what the fuck? I've set off the fucking disabled help siren!" he shouted above the noise, a look of sheer terror on his face.

"Pull it again, you idiot," she ordered, still sat astride him, icy calm.

He obliged and the siren ceased.

"Let's get out of here. Olsen will kill me if we get caught again."

"Not so fast. And I'll kill you if you don't finish the job. Stay there. I'll handle this."

They sat quietly for fifteen or twenty seconds before there was a loud bang on the door, the inevitable response of the lugubrious security guard.

"All OK in there? You rang the panic button. Do you need help?"

"No, it's OK, Officer. I'm fine. Sorry. I pulled the cord accidentally. I'll be out in a minute," Crawford replied assuredly.

"Uh-huh, uh-huh, 'K, ma'am. I'll leave you to it then."

The security guard scoffed, then reported, "False alarm," into his walkie-talkie and trundled back to his station, mumbling something to himself about fucking nymphos and how he wished they could just book a room like normal people. He'd seen it all before.

"Right, he's gone. Now, let's get back to business," she ordered, kissing him passionately. "Just keep your hands on me this time."

"You are one cool customer, Jacks. Don't miss a beat, do you?"

She quickly had Rhodes's tracksuit top open and was biting hard on his nipples.

"Ouch. Fucking hungry, are ya?"

"No, just need to get you back in the game, Dusty."

He got his mojo back. She mounted him again. Exhilarated by the alarm, they enjoyed a long, wild, and passionate ride, Dusty's endurance ensuring that Crawford reached a mind-blowing conclusion . . . and another . . . and then ahhhnother!

"Wow, Mr. Rhodes, I forgot just how good you can be. We need to meet more often."

She turned on the light so they could straighten out their appearance. As she fixed her lipstick in the mirror, Rhodes plucked up the courage to ask for his reward for the service he had just rendered. Pulling up his tracksuit pants, he threw out, as casually as he could, "So, Jacks, as one of Lassiter's biggest customers, have they told you anything about the new CEO yet? Who's replacing this G-man guy?"

"Oh yes, Dusty. I know who'll get the job. I helped their Board with their selection process," she replied with a mischievous grin, a teasing, tempting smile of invitation.

"Really . . . like, really? Nah, you're having me on, right?"

"Why ask me if you don't want to believe my answer?"

"OK then. Who is it? Spill the beans."

"Oh, you'll have to try harder than that, Dusty. I'll need some more of your special attention to share that secret." She was ready to return to the dinner. "I'm at the Lake View Plaza, room 1702, for the next couple of nights. Maybe you'd like to 'come up and see me sometime'?"

"Lake View, 1702. I'll see what I can do."

She left first, walking briskly back to her seat while apparently shutting off her Blackberry. She whispered to Knight, "I'm so sorry that took so long. I've dealt with it and turned the phone off now."

The cyclist reentered a little later, smirking, his attempts to be inconspicuous attracting everyone's attention. He had picked up a couple of bottles of beer on his way back to provide a "typical Aussie" cover story.

■

Meanwhile, the emcee had returned to the stage.

"I'm going to draw the raffle now. For the signed copy of tonight's commemorative brochure."

One of the waiters brought over a large glass bowl filled with raffle tickets.

"So, I know you're all desperate to win. I know I am. I have a ticket in there somewhere."

With a flourish, he pulled out a ticket.

"Number 316. Three one six. Anyone claiming it?"

No one had the ticket.

"I guess we'll have to have a redraw," the emcee carried on. "Forty-two."

No claimer. Stony silence.

"Two hundred and ten."

No claimer. Stifled guffaws.

"Nine hundred and sixty. Nine six zero."

"Yep, here. It's my lucky day!"

Finally, a winner was found as Houston raised his hand to claim the prize. Whether he actually had ticket 960 or even 096, or just wanted to bring this embarrassing spectacle to an end, no one knew or cared.

"So, let's wrap it up there, folks. You should all have some champagne in front of you. I'd like you to join me as I raise a toast to Daniel Grauermann and thank him for his wonderful service to Lassiter."

The guests all rose to their feet, a few with enthusiasm, primed for the moment, snapping out their chairs ready to pay homage, most with abject indifference.

"To Daniel," the emcee completed the toast and raised his glass.

"Daniel," the others echoed, and everyone took a large swallow of the Cristal that had just been served.

To their surprise, the emcee did not return to his seat. He stayed at the microphone.

"Folks, we now have a surprise for you all. We'd like you to leave your tables. You can take your drinks and follow the staff, who will show you to the IMAX movie theater. We're going to see a special production."

The guests rose from their seats again and began to shuffle toward the IMAX.

■

"Please fill in from the front," a commanding voice announced through the speaker system.

Once all the guests had taken their seats, the cycling team entered, lining up on each side of the screen. After a short fanfare, the announcer again commanded, "Ladies and gentlemen, please rise for Mr. Daniel Grauermann, his wife, Isobel, and other members of the Grauermann party."

The cyclists came to attention like an honor guard as the Grauermann family entered the room to polite applause, which Grauermann acknowledged with a slight smile and raised hand. Isobel also smiled demurely, quickly taking her seat, followed by her husband.

The lights dimmed, and the enormous screen was filled with a close-up of Grauermann as the title credits began.

Lassiter Productions presents

Daniel Grauermann—A Celebration

The film opened with aerial footage of a large city, before the narrator began, "Daniel Grauermann was born here in Madison, Wisconsin, in . . ."

"So we've been hauled in here to watch a freaking ultra-high-definition documentary on Grauermann? Upon my life, this is too much." Even Knight was tiring of the charade.

"Relax, George. It may be good. Better than listening to him give a speech, right?" Ball countered.

"You have a point there, Dunc."

The film ran for twenty minutes, featuring footage from the places of major significance in Grauermann's life—his high school, his university, the church where he had married Isobel—and interviews with his Lassiter associates and former colleagues from early employers. Isobel also gave a short interview, praising her husband's business skills and thanking him for their wonderful marriage. Grauermann himself was not interviewed, although the film closed with sound bites from his speeches at Lassiter's annual executive retreats over his time as CEO. The movie ended as it had begun, with his close-up filling the screen.

Anticipating—indeed hoping—that was the end of the proceedings, people began chattering with their neighbors as they got to their feet. The announcer quickly told them, "Ladies and gentlemen, please keep your seats. Our program will continue momentarily."

Then, after a few moments while the dais, microphone, and autocue were set up in front of the screen, the announcer declared, "Ladies and gentlemen, the Chairman, CEO, and President of Lassiter, Mr. Daniel Grauermann."

Hesitant, unwilling applause greeted Grauermann as he took to the stage.

"Well"—cough, throat clear—"good"—cough, throat clear—"evening, folks. I hope that you are having a good time tonight," Grauermann began. "I wanted to t-t-take a few minutes to thank a few folks who have helped put this great event"—cough, splutter—"event together tonight."

"He speaks like a nervous robot . . . with allergies." Knight continued to complain.

"I'm sure he'll warm up, George," Ball replied calmly.

"Aw, come off it, Dunc. He may have been a great techie way back when, but he can't give a speech to save his life. He's not going to do any better tonight."

"I . . . huh, hmm . . . owe some of you here a debt of gratitude for the prat—sorry, *part* you have played in my very successful career. Small those contributions may have been to me, I'm sure they represented your best work and meant a lot to you. Many of you have also thanked me for my contribution to your own success over the years. You have overcome mediocrity and a lack of inspiration, and with my leadership, vision, and insight, we have laid gray twins together."

Grauermann paused, expecting applause. Instead he got puzzled looks. He stared hard into the teleprompter screen.

"Sorry"—cough, cough—"we made great things together. I look forward to my retirement and to watching how you all do. I hope that despite my absence, you find a way to continue to succeed at Lassiter. Thank you and good night, *gutted nacht, arriving dirty, bonus notches,* cheers!"

The end of the speech came as a relief to everyone. Isobel joined her husband on the stage, and loyalists went up to shake his hand. Most, though, headed quietly for the exits, anxious to make calls of nature, calls on their Blackberries, or both.

The announcer had one last message. "Ladies and gentlemen, that concludes our event for this evening. Please make sure you take all of your belongings with you. The gift store will now be open for thirty minutes, in which you will be able to purchase mementos from the event. Return valet parking service will begin from the main entrance in five minutes."

CHAPTER TWO

A Montreal Misstep

March 2002

Knight's wife was out of town, so he was home from work a little earlier than usual to take care of his children. With them suitably distracted, he was listening on his laptop to the web cast of the all-important Lassiter's quarterly earnings call. It always impressed people in the office the next day when he was able to quote what Gene Farris, the Lassiter Chairman and Chief Executive, had said about the results and interpret what was really happening. It showed that intelligent-yet-dedicated-to-the-company-cause stuff that he had to be seen to be made of.

At this point in his career, Knight was an Executive Director, just a small fish in the big corporate pond. He managed Lassiter's contract with the Farnsfield Representative Service Corporation, known to the world as FRSC, or to their cynical observers as "farce."

He'd been with Lassiter's UK operation since the late 1980s. He hadn't expected the job to last anything like this long. He'd made a spur-of-the-moment decision to join them over a quick pint in the King's Arms, a tiny little spot that he'd called his local. Duncan Ball, another of the regulars, mentioned that his company was having a walk-in recruitment fair in town the following weekend. He offered to put in a word if Knight was interested. Knight thought, *Sure, why not?* He went along, they offered him a job right there and then, he signed up, and his new friend got a substantial referral fee. Everyone was happy.

Looking back, that had been the most important pint of Knight's life. He was smart, but not ambitious back then—rather lazy really, more intent on having fun than building his career. He soon realized that he could move up the ladder without too much trouble at Lassiter. The UK subsidiary was small, a group composed mostly of techies—typically quiet and intense, happy with their heads in a screen, badly dressed introverts without a lot of personality. In contrast, the big cheeses who came over from the States were all outgoing, stylish, larger-than-life characters, like Lou Mariani, the President of Lassiter's US operations. The Brits would take a back seat and shy away from the limelight, except for Knight, who enjoyed mixing with the Yanks. Seeing his potential, Mariani took Knight under his wing and told him the secret of success at Lassiter: "Get your head up above the parapet, reach out, get your name noticed. You can't rely on just doing good work. The opportunities won't find you. You've got to build your network. Network, network, network."

Knight took this to heart and started to put a little extra effort into his career. It didn't take much. He won some business, volunteered for new assignments, organized some special events, and hey presto, he got a promotion, then another. Then his networking paid off big time with an opportunity in the US. Mariani had called him up out of the blue and asked him if he would be interested in coming over to run the deal with FRSC. Knight, like many before him, had fallen for Mariani's macho-Italian charm. He thought his life in the States was going to be like *The Sopranos*. He'd never seen it but Ball told him that it was terrific. So Knight had thought, *What a great opportunity—Executive Director, expat benefits, and joining the Lassiter Cosa Nostra all at the same time.* He packed his bags and headed for JFK, and was followed a few months later by the rest of the family. His friend Ball also fancied a spell in the States, and Knight was able to repay the favor from years before when he brought Ball across to be part of the team. The Knights and Balls soon settled in to the comfortable expatriate lifestyle.

As the earnings call came to an end, Knight closed his laptop. Almost immediately, his cell phone rang. It was his assistant.

"George, I know you're busy, but it's Jacquelyn Crawford. She says it's very urgent. Do you want to take it?"

"Yes, go ahead. I'm done listening to Farris." He'd always take a call from Crawford. As the Americans would say, she was a piece of work. Brash and bold, subtle and sly, overpowering and undermining—she had it all. Knight wondered what she was up to this time.

Crawford came on the line. "Hello, George. We've got a serious issue up here, and I need you to come up and handle it."

"Oh, I wasn't aware of any problems, Jacquelyn." This wasn't quite true. There were always problems up in Canada. "What's happened?"

"I'd much rather we handle it face-to-face, George. When can you come to Montreal?"

"Well, let's look at my diary." He looked at his calendar on his laptop. "Probably next week, maybe Tuesday or Wednesday. Can you give me at least some idea of what you need from me?"

"There's a host of things, George. Your people up here just don't seem up to the job."

"I'd better plan on being there for a couple of days, then? I'll stay at the usual place downtown. I'll let you know when we've confirmed the flights."

"Thank you, George. I'll see you next week."

The call ended and he went back to his assistant.

"You'd better book me flights to Montreal next week," he told her. "I'll go up on Tuesday, return on Wednesday. We have problems at FRSC Canada again."

■

He had a nasty feeling that this was going to get messy. He tried to put it to the back of his mind and focus on his other challenges, the day-to-day operational grind, which included enduring several lengthy conference calls with his colleague "NASA" Houston—and Houston's Quality Management team. They were working on a new initiative to bring industry best practices to Lassiter's customers. It was intended to demonstrate a commitment to partnership, a value-added service that would strengthen relationships and help Lassiter win further work.

Houston had introduced an approach called "Six Sigma." It was all new to Knight. Up to this point, he'd believed that the name referred to some American college fraternity. His eyes glazed over as Houston's technicians earnestly went through a whole range of metrics—statistical gobbledygook about availability, mean time between failures, mean time to repair, and so on and so on. None of it meant much to Knight. Houston wrote up the actions: he would document forty new sets of metrics, as the ones they had produced hadn't revealed anything significant, and arrange a series of four additional conference calls to review progress on the creation of these metrics. There would also be a call to review the progress on the arrangement of the conference calls. Such attention to detail, no wonder everyone saw Houston as a real driver.

Things did indeed get messy, sooner than Knight had expected. As he boarded the small commuter jet, a very elegantly dressed, attractive young lady caught his eye, her slightly haughty look suggesting "French mademoiselle, *très chic*." Midflight, the aircraft was buffeted by some bad weather, violently pitching, rolling, and yawing in the strong winds, rain, and low clouds. Shaken, but not stirred, Knight came out of a slumber and looked up to see the woman again, closer this time, and not such a pretty sight. She was staggering down the aisle, her face turning green, with a look of immense distress. He realized in a split second that she was about to relieve herself of her lunch and, to make matters worse, his seat was next to the toilet. He was directly in the firing line. He came fully to his senses, realizing that the door was shut and she had no way to open it, both hands clasped to her mouth in a vain attempt to keep in what nature wanted to push out. The plane rolled again. He saw the panic in her eyes, her cheeks bulging, the content about to be launched his way. Then, in the nick of time, with a flick of his right foot that his hero David Beckham would have been proud of, he popped the door open. Her momentum carried her into range, and she projectile vomited about three feet into the toilet. Regrettably for her, and others who may have wanted to use the lavatory later, her aim wasn't great, and the tiny cubicle was splattered. Mademoiselle Très Chic had become Mademoiselle Grande Puke.

He didn't offer help and quickly found another empty seat, well away from the offensive odor. He slept soundly for the rest of the flight, enjoying a blissful dream about the romantic notion of air travel—a private jet, luxury leather seats, a real glass of real champagne, a small china bowl of macadamia nuts and fancy chocolates, and a petite brunette anticipating his every need.

"Bienvenue à Montréal. Nous sommes arrivés à Dorval, où l'heure locale est six heures et demie."

The announcement woke him as the plane taxied into the gate, the attendant's tired and disinterested tone bringing him abruptly back to reality. As always, he became acutely irritated by one of his major frustrations about air travel: the dithering, dawdling waste of time as jumbo-sized passengers pried their oversized suitcases from undersized bins. His mood cheered as he breezed through immigration. Like many in the early expat stage, he still thought of himself as an Englishman abroad, "home" a rose-tinted image of a land across the sea. He placed great significance in his pukka-blue passport, a cherished possession that spoke of pluck and empire, of valor and history, so superior to the latest issue, a flimsy European Union version, a small, standardized, homogenized, metricized maroon manifestation of the tyranny of Brussels. He strode toward the taxi rank proudly, a freeman, scoffing at the long line of smart black Mercedes sedans and their wannabe-European drivers.

■

"Bonjour, Monsieur Knight. Welcome back." The hotel receptionist recognized him from his frequent visits over the past year. Knight completed the check-in formalities and picked up his bag, declining the porter's fawning assistance.

"Mr. Knight, there is a message for you." The clerk handed him an envelope with the hotel crest on the front. Inside was a handwritten note.

"George, please join me for dinner. 9 p.m. Jacquelyn."

Blimey. This must be important, he thought to himself as he headed to his room to change.

After agonizing over a decision whether or not to wear a tie, eventually deciding that the occasion demanded it, Knight took a seat in the bar, shrinking into the corner of a vintage brown chesterfield, a plush leather-clad comfort zone. He was apprehensive and intrigued at what the evening would hold. What did she want? A generous measure of gin and a splash of tonic hit the spot, slipping down very nicely. And then a second, as he kept half an eye out for his dinner companion, spreading himself to occupy the whole sofa, his confidence restored.

Respectfully ten minutes early, he crossed the lobby to the restaurant and was shown to the table reserved for Ms. Crawford. The restaurant was very busy, the midweek business crowd enjoying the French cuisine and expense-account wines. Their animated conversations—in French and English—filled the room. The table, however, was in a secluded corner, insulated from the general hubbub. His nerves returned, his palms getting a little sweaty as he fiddled with his napkin.

Respectably ten minutes late, she entered the restaurant. He heard it first; the conversation level suddenly dropped, words dried up, trains of thought were interrupted by *Wow, who is that?* Then he saw the heads turn, eyes following her in admiration. Always a stylish dresser, Crawford had really gone to town, with a low-cut dark brown satin dress, knee-length brown boots, and a dramatic amber and gold necklace that complemented her auburn hair. The look was breezy and effortless, and yet designed with meticulous intent.

He stood up to greet her at the table, and they exchanged gracious air kisses. She even smelled wonderful. His nervousness receded and was replaced with excitement and desire. He should have read the danger signs.

"My dear George. I'm so pleased you could join me tonight," Jacquelyn started the conversation as the waiter helped them get seated. "I think it's best for business partners to get to know one another personally, away from the office. Don't you?"

"Oh yes, of course, Jacquelyn," he replied suppliantly. *So this is it. Bonding.*

Dinner passed quickly as the conversation and wine flowed freely. Politics, music, food, history—she seemed to know about them all. She ordered the meal, recommending oysters and sautéed skate wings. She picked out a Riesling and then a Sauternes to accompany the delicious cheese plate, all French of course.

The conversation only once turned to work when she asked about his career, his aspirations and ambitions. He answered honestly enough that he didn't really know where his career could go. He would like to keep moving up the corporate ladder, and maybe one day he'd have a chance at one of the top jobs. He'd take things as they came.

"If you really want that, you'll have to work harder to build your network, George. And don't be so passive. You can't take it all for granted. Watch out for your rivals. They'll try to block you. They're unscrupulous."

"I don't think I have any rivals, Jacquelyn. I get along with everyone."

"Don't be so naive, George. You're young, charismatic, handsome, a great leader, and a natural candidate to be a CEO someday—of course you have rivals. And admirers too . . ."

Her flattering assessment, delivered with sparkling eyes and an inviting smile, stroked his vanity and libido in equal measure. This was bonding of the highest quality.

As he nursed the after-dinner Cognac that she had also recommended, she smiled very directly at him and said, "I hope you don't think it too presumptuous, George. I have a room in the hotel tonight."

A thousand thoughts went through his head. *Why would that be presumptuous? She can stay anywhere she wants. Hang on, wait a minute. Is this the reason for the dinner?*

He wasn't totally buying the bonding story. All evening, he'd been expecting her to get to the business issue she wanted his help with, but it had never come. Now he realized that she didn't have a business agenda. She had a personal one. *Blimey, there's nothing in the Lassiter Training Handbook about how to handle this one.* He'd have to use his own judgment, his own innate sense of what was right and wrong, what was appropriate in these unique circumstances, how to respond when being seduced, not exactly unwillingly, by a very attractive woman, who just happened to also be a client.

"Yes, probably a good move, Jacquelyn. Don't want to risk the weather, or drinking and driving?" He played dumb, perhaps hoping for a brief moment that these were the real reasons.

"No, I could have taken a car back home, George," she replied dismissively. "I have one of the suites on the top floor, wonderful views of the city."

She did not ask if he'd like to see it, although he knew that the invitation was there all the same.

"Well, perhaps I should escort you back to your room, make sure that you get there safely, Jacquelyn?"

"Oh, how chivalrous. I would be so grateful, George."

I bet you would. Tally-ho, red leader. Here we go.

She signed off the bill, and he followed her eagerly into the lobby.

"Seventeen please. It's room 1702."

He rode the elevator without speaking, avoiding eye contact, the expectation of pleasures to come excluding any other thought. They reached her floor, and he followed her into the corridor, his pulse quickening, coordinates locked in, his lustful autopilot engaged. As they arrived at her door, she inserted the key card, paused, then turned and smiled, a warm smile of invitation. He could wait no longer. He took his chance to end the dance. He moved closer, turning her toward him, closed his eyes, and went to ki—

SLAP!

Not the moist, welcoming, open mouth he'd expected, but a stinging right palm, a blow that abruptly ended the buzz of the alcohol and brought him back to his senses.

The door had opened, and she stood in the doorway in an angry pose.

"George, I thought better of you," she said calmly. "What are you thinking? That I wanted to sleep with you?"

"No, er, yes. I'm sorry, Jacquelyn. I don't know what came over me," he flustered.

"Well, I am very disappointed and offended. You'd better go."

His part over, he felt suddenly hollow, a shallow fool, miscast. *Oh fuck, what if she tells Mariani? I'll lose my job. Shit.*

"Look, I'm very sorry, Jacquelyn. Must be the jet lag," he tried to joke. "If there is anything I can do to make amends, please tell me. Can we keep this just between us? I really am sorry."

"Go to your room, George. I will see you tomorrow at the office as we arranged," she directed. "Oh, and, George, it will be our secret—for now."

He headed back to his room in a state of shock. He'd begun to sweat profusely. He was angry with himself, angry with her, embarrassed, and ashamed. As his mind raced, he struggled to get to sleep, rehashing the evening's events. What had he misread? He wondered what would happen tomorrow.

The next day, the remorseful Knight took a taxi to the FRSC Canada building. Crawford was out at a meeting. Her assistant showed him enthusiastically into the office.

He tried to relax, sipping his latte, although he was a bag of nerves, absentmindedly leafing through the FRSC Canada company magazine. Famine relief in Africa, a feature on the team behind a new product, plans for their sponsorship of the forthcoming soccer World Cup in Japan and Korea. *That might make a good trip,* he thought.

"Ah, good morning, George. How are you today?" Crawford breezed in. She was back to her normal business attire: flat shoes, black pants, gray jacket, white blouse, and modest makeup. Only the necklace remained, a hint of the previous evening's events, a reminder of his indiscretion. They exchanged air kisses, Crawford with complete comfort, Knight with evident fear.

"Jacquelyn, I'm . . . ," he began.

"George, sit down, please. I have an important business request for you. Something that will impact upon the success of the Lassiter and FRSC relationship, and your career."

She had his undivided attention.

"This is highly confidential. You have to promise me that you will not tell anyone else about this."

"Yes, Jacquelyn. This is our secret," he said slowly, deliberately repeating her words from the night before.

"Good, George. Then I'll get straight to the point. I am one of the three candidates that are being considered for a big promotion, a job at FRSC corporate HQ. I have my interview with the decision board next week."

He knew she was ambitious. This would be a great step up for her.

"I would like you to help me prepare for the interviews."

"I'd be happy to, Jacquelyn. Do you want me to role-play the interviews with you? Who's on the board?"

"No, George. It is nothing as banal as that. I don't need your help to rehearse," she replied sharply, dismissing this irrelevance. "You know that we're a bit behind the times at FRSC. I'm going to change that. Learn from you. You're much more advanced at Lassiter. You have some great technology. We'll always buy from you. It's how you run the business I'm interested in. I'd like to compare metrics on all aspects of our operations with yours. Most important, I want your proposals on how we can modernize FRSC with industry best practices. And an implementation plan for the changes."

"What are you going to do with all this?" he asked.

"Call it my manifesto. Neither of the other two candidates will have anything close," she replied.

"And you need this by when?"

"Next Tuesday. I need you to give me the material and brief me in person. That will give me time to review, put my spin on it, and prepare for the board."

"Well, Jacquelyn, it is a tall order to get all that together in a few days, especially without telling anyone why. But I'll see what I can do." He paused then and, grasping for a reprieve, added, "And if you get the job? What happens then? To me?"

"We'll implement the plan together. FRSC will become a very satisfied customer and a great reference for your other deals. You, George, will go on to bigger and better things. And I will follow your career with great interest and influential support."

■

And that was that. Audience over. Dismissed. Dispatched to prepare a presentation that he would not give yet and that could make a big difference to his career. He resented the setup, although the alternative—to say no—was menaced by her threat of a shaming revelation, so was not a viable alternative at all.

The taxi, airport, flight, and drive home passed in a blur as he pondered the task. How could he get this done in a week? Where would he find these metrics? What would an implementation plan look like? Then, as he neared his house, his cell phone rang.

"George, it's NASA. You got a minute? I'd like to give you an update on where we stand with the SMARTER program."

Oh God, NASA. The man is just never on the right chapter, let alone the same page as me.

There was still a little snow on the ground between the trees as he pulled up the steep drive to his house, the Stars and Stripes and a Union Jack hanging limply from poles at either side of the garage door.

"Yep, OK, NASA. Keep it brief, can you, though? I've just got back from Montreal and have a stack of stuff to do for Mariani," he replied. "By the way, what does SMARTER stand for?"

"Service Metrics and Real-Time Effectiveness Review. The guys have been really digging deep, using Six Sigma. We've been looking at each customer, and I think we have some great information for FRSC. I've got a plan for some fundamental changes to their processes, tools, and organization model to implement best practices and save them a lot of money."

Oh great. The last thing I needed, Six Sigma metrics. I really don't have time for this. I have to get that plan to Jacquelyn or I'm toast.

"OK, NASA. That's terrific work. Well done to you and all of the team. Maybe give them some recognition awards. You know, those giraffe things. I've got to take another call now. Mariani's after me."

"Well, maybe tomor—"

Knight cut off the call, oblivious to the disappointment in Houston's voice.

Home at last. What a twenty-four hours. Better go and be sociable with the family for a bit. I wonder if the kids made any progress convincing Carole to get a dog. They are smart. We need a smart dog, a SMARTER dog. Ha ha. NASA and his acronyms. Hang on. What did he say they were doing? Metrics? Industry best practices? Blimey.

Still in his garage, Knight reached for his cell phone.

"Hi, NASA."

"George, oh, great, thanks for calling back. Thought I'd lost you."

"Sorry about that, you know what Mariani is like. Now the SMART-ER program, let me play back what I heard. You've collected a bunch of meaningful hard metrics on performance, and from those you've created a bunch of ideas on how FRSC can benefit from industry best practices? It needs some work to finish it off, sharpen it up for presentation, but the data is all there?"

"Yes, that's the exec summary, George."

"And we need someone at FRSC to work with on these recommendations?"

"Yes, George. And that's the tough part. From what I hear, no one in the current regime over there is interested in making changes. They're very set in their ways, and getting their attention is harder than Chinese algebra."

Knight had apparently mistaken Houston's statistical bent for a lack of political savvy. They really were on the same page after all.

"And we need someone over there who's sympathetic to a different approach. We need a new leader. Then we'd have a fighting chance to get ourselves some kudos."

"Yep, that's about it, George. A tall order, but nothing a man of your caliber can't arrange, I'm sure."

"Well, NASA, can we get together tomorrow to go over all of this? I guess you have a presentation ready? There may just be a way to pull this off. We shall see."

CHAPTER THREE

Japanese Junk Bonds
June 2002

Following his contribution to Crawford's career coup—a contribution of which he was in equal parts proud; aware that his distillation of Houston's data into an actionable roadmap for FRSC's future had been particularly influential; envious, unable as he was, despite the circumstances, to suppress completely the feeling that he should be the primary beneficiary of his own creativity; and embarrassed, the circumstances still a painful reminder of the temptations of self-deception—Knight felt that he deserved a break.

That was how he justified an extended trip to Japan, a true "seize the day, life's not a rehearsal" escapade. Two weeks that promised a new culture, exciting new experiences, and a lot of soccer. It was the World Cup after all.

Always happy in his own company, he planned it all out as a solo adventure—flights, hotels, countryside trips, and of course the soccer games. Belatedly, a few weeks before the tournament began, Ball decided to join the fun and made his own travel plans.

Knight spent the few days before the trip at Lassiter headquarters with his boss Mariani and the business unit management team in intense business reviews and strategic planning sessions. They brought things to a close with a heavy final night in the hotel bar. The next morning, with only a few hours' sleep, Knight packed and checked out of the hotel in a mad hurry. He loaded his bags on the airport shuttle bus just as it was about to pull away, then slumped into a seat, relieved, and quickly fell asleep. At the airport he summoned up the energy to check in, hoping for upgrades on both of his flights, the short haul to Chicago and then long haul to Tokyo. The airline obliged with first class to Chicago only; he'd remain in coach for the overnight flight. He was a little disappointed as he'd collected a lot of points and a good status with his flying around for Lassiter.

Then, with little time to spare, he was on board. He still had a thumping headache and was ready for some more sleep. His plan was thwarted as Houston got on the plane and took the next seat. Houston was his usual chirpy self.

"Hello, George. You awake now? I was on the shuttle bus with you, but you didn't notice me. The lights were on, but there was no one home."

"Oh, sorry, NASA," Knight replied. *Please, God, leave me alone.*

"I'm going to a Six Sigma conference. A labor of love. Where are you off to, George?"

"I'm headed to Japan to watch the football—sorry, soccer World Cup." Knight was wearing his England shirt. He turned his back to show Houston "7 BECKHAM." Houston seemed puzzled by it.

"No clue, I'm afraid. I'm not much into sports, George. And I really don't know diddly squat about soccer. Is that a big event then? Who is Beckham?"

Wearing the shirt as he'd left the hotel was Knight's idea of being rebellious, sticking two fingers up at corporate authority and executive respectability. That had fallen flat as Houston was the only person to see him wearing it and he didn't understand the gesture. Houston had no concept of soccer fans' peculiar behaviors and subcultures. *Just my luck. Maybe I'm not cut out to be a rebel,* Knight told himself.

"Yeah, it's pretty big, NASA. It's the biggest sporting event in the world. Bigger than the Olympics. And David Beckham, he's the England captain. He got sent off in the last World Cup finals in France and everyone hated him. Then he scored the goal that got England to this year's—"

Knight stopped midsentence, realizing that he'd lost his audience. Houston had fallen asleep. "I guess soccer isn't for everyone."

They both slept the rest of the way. As they got off, Houston wished Knight well on his trip.

"Knock yourself out, George. And sorry I dozed off on you back there, didn't sleep too well. I'm a bit pumped up about my conference."

"Thanks, NASA. I'm sure it will be a quality event. Take care," Knight replied.

∎

After the frenetic start to the trip, Knight had plenty of time to kill at O'Hare Airport. He wandered about rather aimlessly, still feeling the effects of his late night. He decided upon a coffee and a huge muffin at Starbucks to perk himself up, then he got some cash out of the ATM, expecting to exchange it later for Yen. He'd been paid his annual bonus the day before and his account was flush. *Life's been good to me so far,* Knight thought to himself.

In a moment of self-congratulation, he decided to pay for an upgrade to business. He had good reasons. First, coach was going to be full of boisterous Mexicans, also on their way to the World Cup; he couldn't face fourteen hours in that hullaballoo, a cacophony that would only prolong his throbbing headache. Joint second were the seats that didn't lay flat, the crappy food, and the bad movies. It was just too much to face, so he splashed the three thousand dollars needed. Not for the last time on this trip, Knight observed phlegmatically, *It's only money.*

Despite the extra expense, the flight started badly, as the attendant spilled orange juice all over him. She was profusely apologetic, although Knight suspected that she'd done it on purpose, unhappy with the idea of a soccer fan sitting in business class. The seat and the tray table smelled of OJ throughout the flight. His England shirt was now stained a pale orange, the nylon fabric sticking equally to his skin and the leather seat like a piece of Velcro. Ignoring this inconvenience, he got several hours of good sleep before landing in Tokyo. After surviving a longish queue at immigration, a veritable United Nations of soccer fans converging for the tournament, he collected his bag. He was relieved to see the Boston Coach limo driver there with his big sign, "MISTER GORGE NIGHTS."

The driver got the car and they were off to the stadium. Or so Knight thought.

"So, Mr. Knights, we go the hotel now. It will take sixty minutes," he announced in excellent English.

"No, no. That's not what I arranged." England's first game kicked off in three hours. Knight thought that they would have to rush. He had read about all the terrible traffic jams around Tokyo so was very jittery about missing the game.

"I'm in a hurry. I go straight to stadium. You drop me there. Then you take bag to hotel." Knight spoke in English, slowly and loudly, display-ing his excellent language skills and cultural sensitivity.

"OK, Mr. Nights. Stadium, then hotel. This will need more payment. I will complete later. Please sign." He passed a credit card slip. Knight had prepaid around $250, and now this was extra. He signed and had another *It's only money* moment.

Once they were out of the airport, the driver asked, "You would like music?"

"Yes, something in English if you can get it, please?"

He put on the American Forces Network. It was the country and western top forty show. Knight frowned at this selection.

"You want something different?"

"No, it's OK. Really."

"No, you *must* choose. You are the customer," the driver said forcefully, but with a smile.

Choose from what? Knight didn't know what other stations the driver had. It was "Have a nice day" with menace. He decided to stick with country and western.

Knight got a big rush of excitement as the stadium appeared beside the motorway. The journey went smoothly, and Knight was very early. So much for the traffic. He could have easily gone to the hotel first. He sensed that the driver was laughing to himself as he drove away.

He waited around to meet Ball, who had arrived the day before. They knew that their US cell phones would be useless in Japan, so they'd picked a rendezvous point in advance.

"Dude!" They hugged.

"You get here OK?" Knight asked him.

"Yes, very easy. Got in last night direct from JFK, checked into my hotel. Sweet."

The game wasn't great, ending in a 1–1 tie. Knight and Ball enjoyed the singing, which was loud and raucous, especially when the band played. "Ingerlund, Ingerlund, Ingerlund!" "I'm England till I die," and the theme from *The Great Escape*—it was an extensive repertoire.

After the train ride back to the city, Knight checked in to the hotel. His bag had safely arrived, occupying most of his tiny room. Then he and Ball headed into Roppongi and hit a self-proclaimed English pub. It was the crowd they'd expected to see, hard-core England fans from all parts of the country. They met a group of brawny baggage handlers, who proudly boasted in their thick Cockney accents that their hotel was "twenty-six pound a night, mate." Knight's postage stamp room was costing ten times that. *God help them,* he thought.

A few days later, on the way to collect the tickets for the next soccer game, Knight and Ball transited a huge station, an underground labyrinth, the conduit for two million people each day. Knight found it unnerving as a sea of Japanese commuters threatened to envelop them and he felt his first experience of claustrophobia. Once back aboveground, he recovered his composure sufficiently to pick up his own tickets and to also buy four tickets for the opening Japan game. These were in very high demand. He and Ball would go to the game and sell the other two to make a tidy profit. Pleased with his initiative, he treated himself to a haircut. With much pointing and confusion, the barber finally understood "Number one." It looked good. He got a shave too. He always really enjoyed that experience, very luxuriant.

Later, they returned to the pub, savoring the opportunity to have some comfort food. Ball scoffed cheese-and-onion crisps; Knight had the shepherd's pie. They met a group of six England fans, salt-of-the-earth northerners, operating on a shoestring budget. Their "hotel" was a small camper van designed to accommodate four in comfort. They planned to drive the length and breadth of Japan to see each game. Their oft-repeated catchphrase was "bag of shite," a description they applied to anything and everything, perhaps not surprising given their travel arrangements. It made for an entertaining night all round, and Knight and Ball left in high spirits. So far so good; the trip was going without a hitch.

■

That all changed the next morning. Knight woke early and took in a Starbucks coffee, then made a trip to an internet café. He checked his personal account and got a surprise. There was an email from Stewart Pearson, Lassiter's Executive Vice President of Human Resources. *Oh shit, what the heck is this?* he thought. Then he saw the subject line— "WORLD CUP SOCCER"—and it all came flooding back.

In the bar after Mariani's meeting, Knight had talked to Pearson, who took a keen interest in the development of the executives and had come along to meet the team in more "relaxed circumstances." Knight had already known that Pearson was an important, well-connected guy. He'd been around for years and was based in the corporate HQ, his office next to Farris's. He was the CEO's confidante, yet a man with an independent streak too. What Knight had learned that night was that

Pearson was a huge Anglophile; he'd worked in London earlier in his career, and it seemed, culturally at least, he had never left. He was also a born-again soccer fan. He'd been to a few games, then lost touch when he came back to the US. Now that soccer was getting much more prominent in America, his interest had been rekindled. When Knight told him about his trip to Japan, Pearson took a very keen interest. Which games would he see? How had he gotten the tickets? Where would he stay?

In his "relaxed" mood, Knight had maybe slightly overstated the ease of getting the tickets and hyped up his "luxury" accommodation. He had even gone so far as to suggest that Pearson come over and join him for a few games. He'd given him his personal email address too. Knight had not expected for one minute this wealthy, highly respectable executive would take him up on the offer. Pearson's email now told him otherwise. He read it to himself over again.

"George. So excited about the chance to join you and take in some World Cup soccer. Hope you still have those tickets. Arriving Tokyo Monday. Meet me at Four Seasons Hotel (Marunouchi) at 8 p.m. to discuss the plan. Best, Stewart."

Obviously Knight had misjudged him. And overplayed his hand. Just a little. And now Pearson—one of the most powerful people in the company—was already there, expecting him to lay on some kind of luxury Abercrombie & Kent five-star soccer package. This really was a bag of shite.

Knight went back to the hotel and banged frantically on Ball's door to wake him up. A few years older than Knight, Ball enjoyed his rest. Eventually, his friend let him in, and Knight blurted out, "Pearson's fucking coming I must have invited him he thinks we are on an organized trip staying in top-notch places he thinks I can get him best seats, hospitality, oh, Dunc, I'm so fucking screwed—"

"George, GEORGE. Slow down, slow down. Tell me that again."

Knight repeated his account of the email and his recollection of the conversation in the hotel. Ball sat there with a growing smirk. Knight thought he was taking the piss. *Schadenfreude. Bastard.*

When Knight had finished, Ball said, "George, relax. I know Stewart pretty well. I did a few brown envelope jobs for him back in his London days."

"Oh, OK. Good." Knight had no idea what a brown envelope job was. It sounded like it could be important.

"Stewart will travel in style and stay in the best places, but really he's a Billy no mates. He just wants to be one of the lads. Let's face it, he could have paid for the A & K version a hundred times over. He wants authentic."

Knight calmed down, and they hatched a plan on how to handle their predicament.

"We've got the tickets for the Japan game. Shit, that's tonight. I must have had a sixth sense when I got those. I'm hoping that maybe if we take him to that game, it'll satisfy him and he'll head off happily back to the US."

Ball was less sanguine. "No chance, mate. We'll need to do better than that. He'll want to go to more than one game to feel good about his trip over. He needs a few more anecdotes to back up his bona-fide-soccer-guy cred."

"Thanks, pal."

"Hey, don't blame me, sunshine, you talked yourself into this mess. We'll sort something out."

Contacting Pearson was the first challenge. The lack of a cell phone was getting to be a real pain. Knight got the number for his hotel, called it, and, after some confusion, convinced someone to put him through to Mr. Pearson's room. The call went to voicemail. He left a message saying that they'd be there at 5 p.m. and they'd be going to the Japan game. Knight left his hotel and room number in case Pearson needed to get hold of him.

He and Ball braved the Metro again to head to the ticket center to see if they could pick up tickets for any more games. After queuing for ages, they made it to the counter only to be turned away by an agent who held up a handwritten "NO TICKET" sign and gave a disinterested shrug. Then they spent several more hours—and a small fortune—in an Internet café trying to get through to the ticket website, without success. Occasionally they whooped with excitement as they progressed to the credit card screen or encountered some colored balls that meant the order was being processed, then the whole thing would time out again and they were back to square one. Reluctantly, they gave up on getting more match tickets. As they left the café, a BBC reporter came up to Knight.

"Excuse me, would you mind doing an interview for us, mate?"

Although his tone seemed a little overly familiar for a BBC man, Knight decided to see what he wanted.

"Yes, sure. What's up?"

"We're interviewing fans about this ticket fiasco. We'd like to get your views. You up for that, mate?"

Again, what's with the "mate"? Knight thought. He guessed the Beeb assumed everyone in an England shirt needed the common touch.

"Yes, I'd be pleased to."

The reporter summoned the cameraman and sound guy.

"I'm here with George Knight, a die-hard England fan, outside the FIFA ticket office in Tokyo. George, as you know, there's a huge furor brewing about the ticket situation. The fans can't buy them, yet there are thousands of empty seats in the stadiums. How is this affecting your trip of a lifetime? You must be very angry."

"It's frustrating. It seems that no one can get tickets. We spent ages in the ticket office until some job's worth told us that it was more than his job's worth to help us."

"That's absolutely terrible, George. This morning, FIFA has blamed Japan and Korea, the organizing countries. The organizers have blamed FIFA. Who do you think is to blame for this total fiasco?"

"I don't really know. It's all a bit of a shambles. I don't think that they thought it through."

"There we have it. England fans are frustrated and angry in Tokyo.

We shouldn't be surprised if they take that anger out on the streets if this continues."

The cameraman and sound guy shut down.

"Thanks, mate. Good luck on the tickets."

"When will it be on the news in the UK then?" Knight asked him.

"Oh, I doubt we'll use your piece. Sorry, not quite what we were looking for." The reporter walked off to fin d someone else that better fitted h is stereotype. Knight had given him polished and mild respons-es. The story he'd already written needed Mr. Angry, a "Let's go on the rampage" character.

On the way back to town, Ball and Knight successfully bought tick-ets, not for soccer, but for a day trip out to Mount Fuji. They'd planned to do it anyway and Knight thought it might be something for Pearson to enjoy and then hopefully head home.

Knight pulled out his most respectable jeans for their evening with Pearson. He was still apprehensive about the whole thing. Ball reassured him that all would be cool. So they turned up at the Four Seasons at 5 p.m. The American was waiting in the reception area. Also wearing jeans, with a navy blazer and open-neck dress shirt, he appeared neat and urbane—not exactly the average soccer fan, although unlike his fellow countrymen, he didn't have tickets around his neck and an enormous camera. Pearson seemed to know that Ball would be there. Knight must have mentioned that to him too. Pearson had arranged a car to the stadium, so they were spared the pressure of being the three *gaijin* among sixty-three thousand Japanese on the Metro.

The driver, the same unflappable country-music fan who had collected Knight from the airport, dropped them off and arranged the pick-up point. As they walked to the stadium, the Japanese fans around them were all highly excited, making lots of noise blowing whistles or singing.

"There seems to be a lot of police out tonight, Dunc."

"They look a mean—"

Their conversation was interrupted by another bombardment from the loud hailers, a relentless, repetitive tirade.

"—bunch of mothers too," Ball continued.

"Did you understand any of that, Stewart?" Knight asked, trying to get him involved.

"No, George. It sounded sort of militaristic. Maybe that Japanese streak of totalitarian intolerance of the individual is trying to get out. This is quite something. I'm loving it already."

Knight had never thought deeply about a soccer game. But Pearson was right. It was quite an experience.

"The stewards seem under instructions to be welcoming and helpful. Even the food and souvenir sellers are charming. But that squad of goons, they were something else."

As they neared the stadium, they were assailed by another blast on the loud hailer. Knight felt a little unhinged. Maybe it was the policing, or his underlying nervousness about Pearson's presence, or perhaps even his indifference to the outcome of the game—he'd not been to many soccer matches, indeed not been to many sporting events of any kind, where he wasn't supporting one of the teams—he felt acutely self-aware, as though watching himself from a distance. *What am I doing here? What is this all for?*

He snapped out of his sixty-second period of introspection to sell the fourth ticket to a scalper outside the grounds. Typically, he was another Brit. Mr. Stanley Flashman paid face value for the ticket, then probably sold it for a healthy profit. The guy who eventually sat next to them in the stadium seemed a wealthy Japanese businessman type, and they didn't dare ask him how much he'd paid for his seat.

The game was a good one. Japan played very well and ran out comfortable winners. The Japanese fans were really into it. They didn't sing songs like the Europeans did. Instead there was a lot of rhythmical chanting and general brouhaha. Knight and Ball enjoyed it. And their unexpected guest? He had a blast. Much to Knight's surprise, Pearson actually knew a lot about the game. He commented shrewdly on some good plays and the ref's bad calls, and was generally very easygoing. He got the beers, enjoyed a hot dog, nothing fancy. He did buy himself one of those scarves that had both teams on them—one half blue for Japan, one half red for Belgium—always a dead giveaway of a newbie. But Knight and Ball didn't rib him. He seemed to be so pleased with it.

As they drove back to the hotel, they discussed their plans, before Knight popped the sixty-four-thousand-dollar question.

"So, Stewart, how long do you expect to be here?"

"Well, I guess that depends on what you guys have planned for me," Pearson replied.

"In a couple of days, we're going to climb up Mount Fuji. We've got you a ticket for that too," Knight responded enthusiastically.

"That's great, George. I'm definitely up for that."

"And then?" Knight asked, hoping to hear *I'll head back home.*

"Then I'd like to see another game. The next England game. I'll come to Sapporo with you guys."

Bag of shite.

Knight was really in a pickle. The Japan game tickets had fallen into his lap. England v. Argentina - that would be a very different story. Had he promised Pearson a ticket for that one in his drunken bravado?

"Stewart, I have to come clean. We aren't really on an organized trip. It's all improv. Half the time Dunc and I aren't on the same flights, in Sapporo we're not even in the same hotel, and, worst of all, we don't have any access to extra tickets for the England–Argentina game."

To Knight's surprise and great relief, Pearson was perfectly fine with this news.

"Look, George, this isn't my first rodeo. I figured that all out. I'll come to Sapporo—I'll arrange my own flight and hotel. I'll hang out with you, and if we can get a ticket for the game, that'll be a bonus. If not, I'll watch in the hotel and join you afterwards. Just being there for the atmosphere will be something I'll savor."

What a great bloke. They could work with that. Ball winked and gave Knight his smug *I told you so* smile.

■

The Mount Fuji trip was soon upon them. Knight and Ball made an early start out of the hotel for the bus station and their two-hour trip out to the Kawaguchiko Station—"the K place," they called it. As arranged, Pearson met them there. After a short wait, they all transferred to another bus to take them up to the fifth station, about halfway up the mountain. There were a few cafés and souvenir shops. Knight bought, wrote, and posted some postcards to home, work, and his mum while Pearson and Ball grabbed a beer and chatted about old times. Then they all went for a wander up the mountain. It was a steep climb up a loose gravel path. They got some photos, but low clouds rolled in to obscure the view of the snowcapped peak. They huffed and puffed their way up to the seventh station before calling it a day.

The trip was a good idea. The much cooler and fresher air made a pleasant change from the crowded, choking city. It also gave Knight a chance to talk to Pearson on the bus back down. He needed to make sure that Pearson really was cool about things and not harboring some grudge about being there under false pretenses. Pearson assured him that he was "in good shape" and just along for the ride.

"It's great that you enjoy soccer so much, George."

"I'm glad you see it that way, Stewart. Sometimes I think maybe it's a bit . . ." Knight was struggling for the right words. "You know, a bit career limiting in an American company."

"Nonsense, George. Everyone needs a hobby. And you don't play golf every weekend like the rest of us, do you?"

"I do occasionally, although I'm not that keen on it."

"That's something you should work on. Not being an avid golf-er, now that could seriously hold back your career." He smiled, but his message was clear. "We've all noticed how well you've handled things at FRSC. You'll get your VP stripe, and there'll be lots of big opportunities for you to keep moving up the ladder. Seriously, though, George, get some golf lessons. It'll put you in a stronger position."

"Apart from golf, anything else I should be doing to make things come good for me?"

"There's a few things. You'll need to keep producing good results, George. That's important. And develop your network. Maybe do some media events. We can get you some training on that. Eventually, you'll need to get to know one or two of the Board members."

"That's plenty to be working on, then, Stewart. I'll have to get myself organized when I get home."

"There's no great hurry, George. One step at a time. You've really shown what you can do at FRSC. They're big fans of yours. That new leader, Jacquelyn Crawford, has had some great things to say about you. Mariani thinks the world of you too, so you're on our radar. I'm in your corner. Follow my advice, and in a few years' time you'll have a shot at one of the top jobs."

Knight was quite taken aback at his candor.

"Oh, wow, thanks, Stewart. Seems FRSC have done me a favor. Perhaps I'll send Jacquelyn some flowers."

"Oh, I wouldn't go that far, George. She might take it the wrong way." He winked.

Knight wondered what he meant by that. Had she said something to him? Knight was contemplating how he might learn some more when the bus pulled in to the K place, but Pearson's town car was there to meet him and he strode off. Knight lost his chance.

■

After a few days, a low-key, sober period in which they caught up on some much-needed sleep and essential laundry, Knight and Ball took their separate flights to Sapporo, both arriving in the late afternoon. Another quiet night, then it was on to the most memorable day of their Japanese junket.

They collected Pearson from his hotel around noon. He wore a red England shirt with "10 OWEN" on the back.

"Wow, Stewart. I'm well impressed. Have you been out shopping, or did you bring it with you?"

"No, I brought it with me. Got it online before I set off. Cool, eh? So, what's the plan, guys?"

"We're going up to the main park to see if we can get you a ticket. We'll sit up there for a while," Ball replied. "Then we'll find somewhere to get some food. And then on to the game."

Ball and Pearson relaxed in the park while Knight tried in vain to find an extra ticket. He saw the bag-of-shite group again and asked them if they wanted to part with a ticket for some serious cash. He got a hostile response.

"Fuck off. We might be skint, stinking, and starving, but none of us are missing the Argies, sunshine."

Knight made it back to Ball and Pearson, and they spent an hour in the park enjoying a few beers. Then they went in search of somewhere to eat. The threesome found themselves quite by chance in the Sapporo Fish Market. Deep inside, there was a small sushi bar. By happy coincidence, they arrived at the same time as a group of twenty other guys, evidently not locals, all dressed in blazers, ties, and gray pants: the FIFA Oceania Delegation. The two groups quickly engaged in an intense crazy-soccer-fan conversation, and Knight, Ball, and Pearson found a kindred spirit in the representative from Guam, a sort of semi-official American. He became Knight's favorite person in the whole wide world when he casually mentioned that one of the delegation had been taken ill at the last minute. Knight seized the opportunity.

"Oh, that's a shame. I guess he's not going to make it to the game, then?"

"No, he's back at the hotel. He's too sick to come out. A bit of food poisoning we think."

"Oh, that's really dreadful." Knight paused, his pulse quickening. "If it's not a rude question, what have you done with his ticket?"

"Oh, nothing. I have it here. You guys want it? I assumed that you were all set."

"Well, two of us are, but Stewart doesn't have one. It was a last-minute trip for him," Knight added eagerly.

"Stewart, my fellow American, you are welcome to have this one." The Guamanian pulled a ticket from his blazer with a game-show-host flourish.

"That's fantastic. Thank you so much. How much do I owe you for it?"

"Oh, don't worry about that. Call it a gift from the people of the US territory of Guam."

Knight was very relieved. *Thank you, God.* "Drinks all round!" He ordered beers for the whole delegation to celebrate.

Knight was finally convinced that this wasn't going to be a massive mistake. To top it off, he had the best sushi ever. It was fresh, of course—they were in a fish market—and delicious. So good that he, Ball, and Pearson had to have another five pieces each to add to the "boat" they'd already eaten. The sushi chefs stood behind the counter and beamed proudly.

When Knight went to settle the bill, Pearson waved him off with a fist full of yen.

"I've got this, George. I've got this."

Knight had had the best meal of the trip, scalped a ticket—which probably would've sold for millions of yen up the street—had a brilliant experience, and not spent a cent. *Who says Japan is too expensive?*

From the fish market, they got the train to the stadium before splitting up. Ball and Knight headed to the heavily policed England section, Pearson to the VIP entrance, reserved for the FIFA delegates and sponsors. However, once inside, Pearson was desperate to enjoy the real deal and soak up the big match's atmosphere with the England fans, so he slipped away from the men in blazers and joined Ball and Knight. The three of them squeezed into their two seats. Nobody noticed or cared as they were all on their feet for the whole of the game.

The England supporters were out in full force. Owen hit the post, then a penalty; Beckham put it away calmly. Then it was all defense and England held on for 1–0.

■

Knight woke up the following day around noon and would be the first to admit that he'd felt better in the morning. In no order of actual time, he could vaguely recall a bus ride, everyone going berserk; Odori Park; shouts of "Ichiro! Ichiro!"; beer bought from a convenience store, where they'd danced in the aisles; a McDonald's; many bars; dancing in the street; some top boys; okey-cokey boys in their Burberry hats; a song for Stew, "Who's the septic? Who's the septic? Who's the septic over there? Who's the septic over there?"; the "Club Room" with its skinny androgynous strippers; then arriving at the hotel at six thirty in the morning, exhausted and out of cash. It had been quite a celebration.

Fortunately, he'd arranged to meet Ball much later, so he had plenty of time to stage a mini recovery. He also found time to go to an internet café, a tiny little storeroom crammed with PCs and sweaty Brits emailing home. When he opened up his account, there was a message from Pearson.

"George. Just wanted to say thanks for a truly awesome trip. Can't thank you enough. Great game and what a night! You boys certainly know how to have a good time. Okey cokey. Hope you enjoy the rest of the trip. I owe you! Let's go, England. Best, Stewart (Septic)."

Knight hadn't a clue when Pearson had called it a night. He's definitely been on the bus and must have been there for the Ichiro moment.

And the "Septic" chorus. What about the strippers? Anyway, it seemed he was fine. Phew. He'd not been a pain at all. Mucked in, played his part and then disappeared, happy as Larry. And now the company's top HR person owed him. What a turnup.

■

He didn't spend long with Ball after that. Following the euphoria of the England win and his initial excitement at getting Pearson's email, Knight felt deflated and homesick. He could have happily flown home there and then. Although he'd had a great time, he was now feeling guilty about the trip; he'd been away from Carole and the kids for such a long time. When he'd booked this adventure, he hadn't given a second thought to them. He was just too excited and absorbed in the planning. Now it felt very selfish, spending all this time enjoying himself. He'd have to make up for it.

All the career stuff was bothering him too. Pearson's guidance was all well and good, but getting serious about it, doing things that people expected of him was not his style. He wasn't ready to give up some part of himself to climb up the greasy pole. All the pressure and the pretending and the games, the relentless perfection—Knight just couldn't handle it. As he dozed in his room, he decided that when he got back from Japan, he'd go down to HQ and tell Pearson, "Thanks, but no thanks." He'd head back to the UK, move on from Lassiter, do something simpler, closer to home, something more *suitable*.

He woke up the next morning convinced that he should bring the trip to an end, a combination of fatigue, family, and the upcoming Father's Day all playing on his mind. When he called the airline he'd booked with, they offered him an earlier flight with an upgrade all the way. He was sold.

Cheered by this success, he met up with Ball to make their final trip to Starbucks. Their coffee had been a big part of the trip.

"So, dude, been a blast. Did you hear from Stewart, by the way?"

Knight told Ball about his email.

"Didn't I tell you? We did the business for him. He'll be a fan for life now. Strings pulled, doors opened. You're well set, mate."

"Oh, give it a rest, Dunc."

"No, I mean it. George Knight, CEO in training. Just remember your mates."

"No, Dunc, I don't want it." Knight stopped him in his tracks. "I'm going to tell Stewart. He doesn't owe me anything. I think I'm going to give up the American Dream and go back home."

"What utter crap. You don't want it. Fuck off, George."

"No, I don't. Too much like hard work."

"It's not hard work you're afraid of, mate. You're just a snob. You think you're some sort of aristocrat, above all this dirty career stuff. It's beneath you to make a fucking effort."

Knight shuddered at his friend's stinging blast. *Where has this come from?*

"And, George, last time I looked, you don't have a silver spoon in your mouth. Stop being such a tosser and take what you can get. If that means playing along with Stewie boy, so be it."

Knight didn't reply, sullenly slurping his latte.

"I have to head out to the airport now, George. I'll see you in the office on Monday." And with that, Ball left. It seemed an inadequate way to end two fantastic weeks together, but that's all they could muster.

With Ball gone, Knight was anxious to head home. He wanted to check in early to make sure there weren't any last-minute problems with his reservation, the date, the flight numbers, or crucially, the upgrade. Why he thought checking in early would help avoid any problems only he would know. That's the way his addled brain had it figured. So he was number two to check in. He need not have worried. The flights were all as he'd arranged on the phone. It was business to San Francisco, then first class to Chicago and for the last leg home.

He got some sleep on the flight to San Francisco, then started to read a book by an Anglo-Japanese author. Much like the past two weeks, it was surreal and strangely compelling. His flight from O'Hare was delayed by several hours. He sat in another crowded lounge, thoughts of work flittering through his mind. What had happened while he'd been away? How were things with Crawford's new regime at FRSC?

His American visa was near its expiry date, and he only got through immigration with a bit of a grilling. The inspector quizzed him about a form that he had never heard of. In the post-9/11 mood, dealing with the fanatical INS people was going to get more and more difficult. He hoped the Lassiter HR machinery had turned a few gears on getting his documents renewed.

He knew that he was now in Pearson's good books. His panic attack was over. Ball was right of course. He'd be a fool to turn his back on all this. It wouldn't be that hard—it hadn't been so far. There was still not much competition. It was time to swallow his pride and follow someone else's advice for a change. He was ready to move up the ladder. Maybe Pearson would be his passport to fame and fortune. Or maybe it was just talk. He would see.

CHAPTER FOUR

A Gentlemen's Wager

May 2004

The golf carts were arranged in four neat lines outside the clubhouse in the early-afternoon sun, their terra-cotta-colored roofs like the shields of a legion of Roman soldiers preparing for battle. The course attendants made their last checks on the paperwork and began to load up the bags of clubs on the backs of the carts. The contestants were assembling on the patio. The Asians, Australians, and British were relaxed, downing a beer or two, sampling the generous hot buffet of pulled pork, rolls, coleslaw, and baked beans. The Americans were content with a soda, the boxed lunch of a ham-and-cheese sandwich and an apple, and a bag of potato chips for later during the round. A select group, those for whom golf was not a sport, but an obsession, were focused on the intense preparation, using the full bag on the driving range and methodically assessing the effect of the high altitude on their ball striking, before testing their aim on the practice putting green.

Most of the players looked the part in the de facto golfer's uniform, neat and color coordinated. There were also a few sartorially challenged outliers, wearing shorts with black dress socks, or sneakers, not golf shoes; and of course, there was Vadim Barthez from France, who every year claimed he'd lost his luggage and would have to play in his jeans. These oddballs were tolerated as the quirks that made everyone else feel superior in their comfortable anonymity.

This golf tournament was the first big event at the Annual Lassiter Executive Retreat. The company's executives gathered at an upmarket resort each May to celebrate the prior year's achievements and plan for their next triumphs. There was a heavy emphasis on the networking aspect at the conference as it was the only occasion when execs from all parts of the company gathered together. This year, the setting was the Bourne Canyon Hotel in Colorado.

According to the event brochure, the hotel's course was "beautifully designed, featuring wide, forgiving fairways and large greens with spectacular mountain vistas, ideal for a range of skill levels and handicaps." That much was true. The brochure continued: "The tournament gives players of all standards a chance to contribute and enjoy a fun afternoon of networking." That part was not true; that was marketing for the genuinely naive. Everyone knew that this was a fiercely competitive event where networking was on hold and personal success was paramount. The range of that success went from minor bragging rights for bettering a colleague, to recognition in the various on-course competitions, like the longest drive and closest to pin, and ultimately, first place in the event, which guaranteed an invitation to play with the Lassiter CEO, Gene Farris, as his guest at his home course.

The pretournament scheming was worthy of a papal conclave, great significance being put on the four-person teams. Even within the teams, the two-person cart assignment was anxiously awaited and assessed. Some teams had played together for years and were always in the reckoning to take the prizes. The first-timer attendees were put together, unless they registered with a low single-figure handicap, in which case they likely found themselves playing on a team with a Board member or a senior exec.

■

"Right, you guys. I'm ready to rip it up now." Knight finished the last of his sandwich and plopped himself down in the driver's seat. "You ready for this, NASA?" he asked his cart partner, Robin Houston. In recognition of his success at FRSC, Knight had been promoted to Vice President, which brought his first invitation to the retreat.

Houston was an old hand, having been a Senior Vice President for several years. He had picked up the packet of information that had been clipped to the front of the cart and was scanning the order of play. "Yep, I'm ready and able. I hit a few balls on the range, took some putts, and feel good. I see we have Christina Drago and Julie Dreiser teamed with us. It's our lucky day."

"Why's that then, NASA?"

"Oh, duh. You are a newbie, aren't you? They're both good golfers, and their drives really help in this thin air. I played with them last year. They were great. If we play well, we'll be in the hunt." Houston checked the course scorecard, studying it hard, before making a few calculations on his notepad.

"That's why we'll always make a great team, NASA. You bring the data, I'll bring the good looks and charm. High five!" Knight sprang out of the cart again, full of enthusiasm. Houston reluctantly returned the showy gesture as others looked on, wondering what they were so chirpy about.

The photographer came around to take a shot of their group.

"Come on, ladies. Christina, Julie, let's look good for the camera."

Knight gathered the four of them in front of his cart. The photo would become a fixture on his office wall: On the left was Houston, who had opted for a red cap, a dark navy and white striped polo shirt, navy pants, and pristine white golf shoes fresh out of the pro shop. With his white forearms and lobster-red face, he was a human star-spangled banner. In the center, Knight and Drago wore the company uniform: black polos and caps adorned with the red Lassiter logo, and matching golf pants. Neither seemed completely at home. He was holding a beer and a forced grin; she was holding her driver and her temper, intense and eager to get out on the course. On the right, Dreiser looked in her element;

with her relaxed smile, even sun tan, and matching blue cap, polo, and skort, she could be mistaken for a golf pro.

■

In the other carts, the players reintroduced themselves to one another, chatted about the tournament, and admired the spectacular views of the still snowcapped Rockies. The conversation was loud and there was a real buzz of expectation. A couple requests of "Quiet please" from the course pro over the PA system got everyone's attention.

"Ladies and gentlemen, welcome to the Annual Lassiter Executive Retreat Golf Tournament. I am absolutely delighted to welcome you all to the Bourne Canyon Golf Club. We spoke to the man upstairs and arranged this beautiful day for you with us. You have bright sunshine, temperature around seventy degrees, no wind. Tell me, what more could you guys want? Are you going to have fun?"

There were a few weak replies.

The pro had launched hundreds of these events in his time at Bourne Canyon and boomed with the passion of a golf evangelist.

"I said, are you guys going to have fun?"

This time there was a resounding "Yes" from the golfers, and a ripple of conversation about the wonderful weather, the great course, and the awesome views swept around the carts.

"Good. That's more like it. Quiet now, QUIET. I'm going to turn over the microphone to your CEO, Mr. Gene Farris, so he can say a few words, then I'll be back with the tournament rules, then we'll get you out on the course. OK? Right, Mr. Farris."

"Thanks. Well, everyone, it's great to see you all out here again on this beautiful day," Farris warmly greeted his guests. "What a setting."

He smiled broadly and gestured to the mountain panorama that towered over the lush green course.

"You know, this tournament has been going for twenty, maybe thirty years, and is always one of the highlights—no, *the* highlight of our retreat. I hope you enjoy your afternoon. I'm sure I shall."

There was a quick burst of applause. Farris was hugely popular with the Lassiter execs, who respected his success as a big deal maker and his easygoing, affable style.

"Thanks. And, folks . . . may the best team win! I'll see you all in the clubhouse later."

The pro came back on the mic to explain the tournament rules. Then something new.

"This year we've kitted out the carts with a new feature that I'm sure you technology types will appreciate. Turn on the display screen attached to the roof of your cart. Go ahead. It won't bite you."

He paused as they turned on their screens, some with assistance from the course staff.

"We are now using an electronic scoreboard. We've put in all the details—your handicaps, where you're starting, and all that. You just put in the gross score for each player on each hole. Take a look."

Again he paused as the golfers got accustomed to their cart screens.

"Neat, huh? And the best thing is that as everyone enters their score, you'll be able to see the leaderboard as you play. You won't have to wait until you're done to see how your group is doing. Should make things exciting, right?"

The conversation level in the carts sparked up again as the golfers played with this new toy.

"So, there you go, folks. Now, please follow out the two marshals' carts, which will guide you to your starting hole. Have a great round and we'll see you all later. Have fun out there."

The two snakes of carts then wove their way out onto the course, the legion breaking into smaller formations, and eventually leaving two carts at each tee box.

In the most prestigious group, Gene Farris was paired with his heir apparent, Lou Mariani. Their group was completed by Lassiter's longest-standing and most influential Board member, Dalton Hastings, and Daniel Grauermann, the company's Chief Technology Officer.

All the other competitors were a little intimidated by this powerful team, which would definitely be one of the ones to beat, a favorite to win the tournament. They looked ready for battle. Their well-used shoes and bags decorated with tags from many different courses hinted at their golfing prowess. Despite the high time demands of their jobs, they all golfed regularly and were consistent, low-handicap players.

"Here we go again, boss. The good ol' Lassiter Texas Scramble. I guess I must have done something right this year. You put me on your team and in your cart," Mariani remarked proudly as they headed to the first tee.

"Well, you know, Lou, sometimes you've just got to stick with what you know and trust," Farris, about six feet tall, with a gleaming head of thick silver hair and a mild year-round tan that radiated a relaxed Californian confidence, the term *laid-back* apparently invented for him, replied with his calming smile.

"That why we've got Hastings and Grauermann with us too?" Mariani asked, with the inane grin of sarcasm.

"No, that would be more of the 'friends close and enemies closer' approach, Lou."

"Hastings still giving you a lot of trouble, boss?"

"Yes, you could say that, Lou."

"Same issue, that Brit fucker wants the Chairman title off of you?"

"Yes, Lou. That's his goal."

"You can beat that prick, boss. Need any help from me?"

"No, not right now, thanks, Lou. He's playing a clever game, though. I'll give him that. He has exactly half the Board members in his pocket now. Enough to be a nuisance, although I still have the casting vote. His latest ploy is to try to expand the Board. Get another of his buddies on so he can out-vote me."

"Well, just say the word, boss. I'll do for him. You know he's always chasing skirt, don't you? They say he'd fuck a barbershop's floor. I can get photos . . ."

"I don't think it will come to that, Lou. I'll handle him. Let's focus on the golf for now."

After a routine first nine holes, Farris's team parked by the clubhouse. Hastings took a comfort break and Farris made a phone call. One of the young stewards replenished their drinks box as Mariani got steamed up with the long delay.

"Hey, son, stick a few beers in there this time, would you? Can only stomach so much soda and water. Oh yeah, do you have any cigars too? May as well enjoy this sucker," Mariani quipped.

"Yes, certainly, sir."

Mariani slipped him twenty bucks and pocketed a couple of Montecristos.

Meanwhile, Grauermann had entered the team's score on their virtual scorecard and, for the first time, decided to check the leaderboard on the golf cart screen. Once they were all ready to set off again, he called the others over to a take a look.

They were in fourth place, five shots behind the leading group of Dreiser, Drago, Houston, and Knight.

Mariani spoke for all of them. "Fuck me sideways, we're getting creamed. We're a long way behind young Knight, NASA, and the two gals."

"Well, I don't think we're going to be on the winners' podium today, gentlemen. Let's make things a bit more interesting. How about we add a little wager to our round to keep us interested. Daniel and me against you two?" Hastings asked.

"That would be just fine, Dalton. What did you have in mind?" Farris took up the challenge.

"Let's take a little wander and discuss that, Gene," Hastings replied and waved for Farris to follow him to the tee on foot. "You two bring the carts."

Hastings and Farris continued a businesslike conversation on the short walk to the tee. The bet was concluded with a crisp handshake, a hint of rivalry in the air.

■

Fired up by the competition, Mariani played some excellent golf, giving himself and Farris a two-hole advantage.

"The bet looks pretty good, eh, boss?" Mariani's grin was now as broad as the Colorado skyline.

"Yes, well done, Lou. We're in great shape." Farris returned the smile.

"I'm loving this. It's just great to see him getting beat. I feel a bit bad for Grauermann, though. Hastings must be giving him some shit back there. That's his look out. I'm going to have a beer to celebrate." He opened up the cooler and cracked open a can of Heineken. "Ahh, that's good. You want one, Gene?"

"No, thanks, Lou. I'll wait until we get back to the clubhouse."

"I'm having a cigar too. You want one of these? They're good ones. Montecristos."

"Maybe later, Lou."

Mariani quaffed his beer and quickly opened a second as they waited for the other cart to arrive.

In their cart, Hastings was putting Grauermann straight.

"You have got to get your act together here, Daniel. Farris and I are evenly matched. Mariani's playing great, and you're doing the cube root of fuck all to help." Hastings angrily wagged his putter at Grauermann. "Pull your bloody finger out."

"I'm . . . I'm sorry, Dalton. I'm doing my best," Grauermann replied, puzzling over the cube root calculation. "Anyway, I thought you said this wasn't important?"

"Well, I lied. I didn't want you to go all nervous Nellie on me."

"Why would I be nervous? What's the bet?"

"Are you sure you want to know? You can handle the truth? Without peeing your pants?"

"Look, Dalton, I may get a little nervous when I have to give a speech. I'm working on that. Got a coach and a speech therapist and DVDs to watch. Everything. Don't worry. I can handle a little bet on the golf course, OK?"

"Well, you asked for it. We're playing for the right to nominate the next Board member. If Farris wins, I predict he'll make your friend Mariani the COO and put him on the Board. If I win, then you know the plan."

Grauermann went white, gasping for air, looking for all the world as if he were about to faint.

■

Grauermann was still in shock as they pulled alongside Farris and Mariani at the next tee. Mariani drained his beer and asked them, "What's taken you guys so long? Are you thinking of chickening out? Got you on the ropes, don't we?"

"No, we're not beaten that easily. Just a little tactical talk, that's all."

Mariani took the wrapping off his cigar, bit off the end, and went to light it up.

"Shoot, I didn't get any matches. I can't start the fucker up."

"I see Harold Griffith over there. He's smoking a cigar too," Hastings replied.

"Oh, great. Yeah, there's Harry." Harry was an old pal of Mariani's, and they often golfed together.

"Yo, Harry, you dumb fucker, wait there a sec!" he called over the adjoining fairway.

He finished the beer, grabbed another from the cool box, and strode off toward the other group.

"Hey, boys, you having fun?" he greeted Griffith and Stewart Pearson, who was sharing Griffith's cart.

"Yep, it's going well. What a great day for golf. We're about six under. Probably not gonna win anything, but as they say, a bad day on the golf course . . ." Griffith chuckled.

"Beats a great day in the office," Mariani completed the well-worn phrase.

"How's your day going with the big kahunas, Lou?" Griffith asked.

"It's a bit starchy, especially with that Dalton Hastings character. I'm enjoying myself, though," Mariani replied, then raised his beer and took another gulp. "Playing good too."

"Well, if you want to liven it up a little, we've got just the thing here." He passed Mariani an orange Gatorade bottle.

"Gatorade?"

"A nice little cocktail."

Mariani took a swig. "Yowza, that's good, H. What's in there?"

"Well, it's Gatorade . . . plus maybe a little vodka, a little Red Bull. You can keep it. We have a few more in the box."

"Great. Thanks. Can I take another one for the road too?"

"Of course, Lou, help yourself."

Mariani grabbed another "Gatorade" and started to stride back toward his own group.

"Lou, wait. Did you come over for something in particular?"

"Oh yeah, right, I need a light for my cigar, H."

"Sure, here you go." Griffith got out his Zippo lighter, and its big flame soon had Mariani's cigar going.

"Thanks, pal, I owe ya."

Mariani stuck the cigar in his mouth, took a big draw, and headed back across the fairway, Heineken in one hand, two Gatorades in the other. Life was so fucking good.

"Finally, you're back to play some bloody golf. Louis, you won the last hole. You have the honor." Hastings brought them to order.

Mariani finished his latest beer, scrunched up the can, and tossed it into a garbage bin. He took a quick sip of the Gatorade mixture, set his cigar down on the ground, and took his stance with his big driver. His swing was good, although maybe his timing was just a little off. Instead of hitting a solid drive, he caught the ground and topped the ball. It flew off fast and low at about six feet in the air before bouncing on the cart path that crossed fifty yards in front of the tee. The concrete gave it a big bounce forward, and it ended up on the fairway one hundred yards away.

"Well, that wasn't my best one. Can't kill 'em all I guess." He laughed it off.

Grauermann was up next. He hit a nice drive straight up the fairway. Farris and Hastings followed with average drives, and then it was back to Mariani to play his second. He had his driver out and again looked ready to play it off the fairway.

"Lou, are you sure? Wouldn't you be better with a three wood or something?" Farris suggested quietly.

"Nah, Gene. We're two up and I'm going to finish them off. I can put this puppy on the green if I catch it right."

He launched himself at the ball as if it had done him some personal harm, letting loose a roar as he crashed the Big Bertha into the ball. Again his timing was just a split second off. Taking a huge divot behind the ball, he turned the club head over, causing the ball to hook wildly to the left. Left, left, and farther left it flew, just missing another team's cart, before it found a group of fir trees on the other side of the next fairway.

"Crap. Sorry, boss. Guess this one's down to you," Mariani said as he got back in the cart.

Hastings and Grauermann saw Mariani's hook and smiled to each other. "I told you he'd go off the rails, Daniel. Now let's take advantage."

And take advantage they did to win the hole. Farris and Mariani's lead was down to one.

On their next tee, Mariani slurped his Gatorade as they waited to play.

"Hey, boss, these guys ahead of us are slow. I'll be back in a mo."

He half jogged, half walked over to a clump of trees beside the tee box and made a clumsy attempt to hide himself among the foliage. However, the camouflage failed, and his mission became clear as the cloud of pungent steam rising from his giant, grateful, glorious piss gave him away. On the way back, he flagged down another passing cart. As it drew to a stop, he helped himself to a couple more beers from their cool box.

Farris looked up briefly from his phone.

"OK, Lou. Steady up now. We're only one ahead. We don't want to let this slip, do we?"

"No, boss. I'll be good on this next hole."

Farris quickly returned to his call. "They'll definitely put thirty-five on the table for outright control?" he said to the person on the other end of the phone. "What's their timetable? Before the end of June? Right. I'll think about it. I'll call you back in an hour."

Farris snapped his phone shut as Mariani opened another Heineken. "All OK, Gene?"

"Yes, Lou, just a bit of personal business. You back with your A game now?"

"Of course, just a hiccup. What's the game plan here?"

"Let's win this hole and get this over and done with. I need to make a couple of calls as soon as possible."

From the tee, Mariani rediscovered his coordination, sending the ball scorching up the middle of the fairway to land only fifty yards from the green. Match point for Farris and Mariani.

Pleased with himself and relishing his imminent triumph, Mariani decided that the second Gatorade would keep him loose. He cracked it open and took a huge gulp, downing most of the bottle in one go. A loud belch inevitably followed. He wanted a draw from his cigar, and then he realized he'd left it in his makeshift restroom. *Shit, I hope those trees don't catch fire,* he thought to himself.

He followed with a strong chip to find the green and set up a putt, a great chance to take the hole and seal the win.

"Here we go, Lou. Sink this and we've won," Farris encouraged.

Mariani settled for the putt, muttering a prayer under his breath, noticeably unsteady on his feet. He stabbed angrily at the ball. It had a good line, but he'd hit way, way too hard and the ball shot at least twenty feet past the hole.

"Fuck, I'm still up."

He putted again and still didn't find the hole.

Grauermann had shrewdly positioned himself behind Mariani to get a good read of the green. He paced around, took several practice strokes, blowing his nose after each, before sending the ball on its way with a smooth strike. It was a great putt, quietly dropping right in the center of the hole. Plop.

"Bloody marvelous shot, Daniel. You ARE the man." Hastings's delight prompted him to attempt an American accent.

"Thank you, Dalton," Grauermann replied shyly.

They headed to the last. Remarkably, the score in the game was now square. But morale wise, the rival pairs could not be farther apart. Farris was distracted, on his phone constantly. His partner, Mariani, was hopping about like a red-faced, sweaty Energizer Bunny. He was inconsistent, incoherent, and increasingly incontinent. In contrast, Hastings and Grauermann had their tails up. They were focused and confident. Barring an unforeseen turn of events, there was only one pair winning this game and the life-changing bet that went with it.

■

Meanwhile, as the senior executives played their high-stakes game, another significant power struggle was emerging in another of the groups, a festering tension building throughout the round.

The tone was set as Knight made a complete hash of things from the first tee with a swing and a miss, then an ugly shank into the woods, then another on his mulligan.

"Sorry, folks, first-timer nerves. I guess we won't be playing my ball." He grinned without the slightest embarrassment and cheerfully jumped in the cart.

After a nice drive, Dreiser hit a perfect, effortless second shot to within four feet of the pin, setting herself up for an eagle. "That'll do," she said calmly with the air of someone who expected nothing less. The rest of the group was in awe. She was just a natural. Knight pulled out another exuberant high five.

Drago's shot followed. She was tense, prickly, and bristling with an assertive independence as she shut everything out of her mind, determined not to be outdone by her teammate. She found the green, but was farther away than Dreiser. She snapped the club back into her bag and sat down in her cart without a word, annoyed at herself for falling short of her goal.

Houston was next, also very focused. He was just about to play, club in motion, when he was interrupted by a large four-seater golf cart speeding across the fairway toward them. Zach Elliot, the head of Lassiter's Marketing team, was driving. Appropriately, he was attired head to toe in the much-logoed Lassiter golf outfit. The two other men with him were anything but uniform: one slim and dapper, dressed in a navy blazer, a panama hat, and white suede shoes; the other in jeans, sneakers, and a gray T-shirt. The smart guy carried a microphone; the scruffy one had a large video camera perched on his shoulder and wore a battery pack on his back.

"Excuse us, folks. Zach Elliot, for Corporate Communications. As you know, we're filming some little vignettes on the course today to show at the awards banquet on Friday. I wondered if you guys would say a few words for us."

"Yes, sure, count us in. What do you need, Zach?" Knight jumped in, immediately presuming the role of team spokesperson.

"Well, let me introduce Wolf Becker, our interviewer. He's with our media consultancy."

The man in the panama hat waved flamboyantly. "Hi, guys, good to see you. I'm just going to ask you a few questions, easy ones like 'How's it going?' 'What do you enjoy about the event?' You get the idea. My trusty cameraman will get it, warts and all. Then later we'll edit it together to make you all sound like superstars. Any questions? No? Good. Who's first? Mr. Knight, is it?"

"No, not me, no way." Knight shook his head. "You should start with our star performer Julie here. Unlike the rest of us, she knows what she's doing. Then do NASA and Christina. I'll go last."

Dreiser was happy with the plan and ready to record her piece.

"Yes, OK. Thanks, George. I'm all yours, Wolf. What can I tell you?"

Drago remained in her cart. She wasn't impressed. *The only one who knows what she's doing, eh? Speak for yourself, buddy,* she fumed. Then, stepping out and turning to Houston, she said quietly, "Is he always this full of himself?" She flicked her eyes toward Knight.

"Yeah, no doubt about it. He can be a wise guy at times. Don't let him get under your skin, Christina. Don't get bent out of shape," Houston replied.

"Well, if he answers for me or tells me what to do again, he'll hear about it," Drago snarled.

Meanwhile, Dreiser was wrapping up her piece for the camera.

"I love this event, Wolf. You get to play with people you may not know too well, away from work. You can learn a lot about people on a golf course. It's very relaxed out here."

"That's wonderful, Julie." Becker indicated to the cameraman to stop filming. He turned off the mic.

"Nice job, thanks." He beckoned to Houston. "OK, Mr. Nasser, you're up."

Houston plodded over sulkily. He'd been ready to take his shot, felt peeved at being interrupted, and certainly wasn't enamored with the prospect of having a camera shoved in his face.

"It's Houston, not Nasser. Mr. Houston." He was determined to put this Becker guy in his place.

"Oh, I'm sorry. I thought you were Mr. Nasser. That's what your boss said," Becker replied, pointing to Knight.

"He's not my boss. He's only a VP," Houston shot back angrily. "He just thinks he's in charge. And I am Mr. Houston. NASA is just my nickname. NASA Houston? The Apollo program?"

Becker shrugged, evidently not following.

"You know, like 'Houston, we have a problem'?" Houston continued.

Becker shrugged again, looking at him blankly, before attempting to settle his apparently unhinged subject. "Right, right, Mr. Na—Mr. Houston it is, then."

They went ahead with the short interview. Houston responded to questions by citing relevant statistics, all in a monotone voice that would have suited an emergency service broadcast. All this footage would later hit the cutting room floor.

"Thank goodness he's done," Becker whispered to Elliot as Houston returned to his stance, ready to play his shot.

"Sssshhhhh," Drago ordered as she put a finger to her lips.

"Oops." Becker giggled.

"Time out. Come on now, you guys, take a long walk off a short plank, would you? You've interrupted me for the interview, the least you can do is shut up while I play my shot." Houston had stepped away from his ball petulantly.

Becker and Elliot hung their heads solemnly as Houston lined up again. He was uptight after all of the fuss. After a couple of deep breaths, he also hit a good one into the same part of the green as Drago.

"OK if we go ahead with you now, Christina?" Elliot, still somewhat intimidated, tried to keep it flowing.

"Yes, let's get on with it." Drago climbed out of the cart and joined Becker and the cameraman.

In her interview, Drago found a middle ground between Dreiser's cameo as a confident, engaging golf pro and Houston's impression of R2-D2. She worked hard to be warm and engaging . . .

"Yes, I've been looking forward to this all year, Wolf. Such a great day to be out here with my colleagues."

But she couldn't keep her perfectionist instincts completely under wraps . . .

"Practice? Oh yes. I believe practice makes perfect in everything. I've been practicing regularly. I've also been taking lessons to improve all facets of my game. It seems to be paying off quite well so far."

And her competitive nature . . .

"Result? We started really well. Julie, NASA, and I were close last year. I think we have a great chance of winning . . . provided that everyone on the team pulls their weight." The camera caught her eyes as they darted contemptuously toward Knight and then returned to a twinkle with her concluding smile.

"Gorgeous, Christina, you were great. Thank you," Becker flattered, relieved to have things back on track. "Now, Mr. Knight, you can't avoid us any longer."

"Oh yes, I can," Knight replied with a laugh. "I'm going to hit my ball, then we'll do it."

Knight showily dropped his ball close to the spot from where the others had hit theirs. He took a couple of competent-looking practice wafts and then struck his shot. Unfortunately, his lack of concentration told, he lifted his head and topped the ball badly, yanking it to the left. It careered along the ground, then found its way into a concrete drainage ditch that ran beside the fairway.

"Bollocks!" Knight jogged after it, still carrying his club.

Sensing an opportunity for some more memorable material, the video crew hopped into their cart and chased after him.

When they caught up with him, Knight was up to his ankles in the murky water, his shoes and socks tossed on the fairway. Elliot signaled to the cameraman to start filming right away. Knight thrashed at his submerged ball, spraying water over himself. When he finally gave it up as a bad job and picked up his ball, Becker pounced.

"Here's the intrepid George Knight. You look like you're having fun."

Knight mopped his wet face. "Yes, of course, Wolf, always. I hope you caught it."

"Yes, we did, George. Your teammates are confident that you're going to win today. Are you going to be making a contribution?"

"I'm sure I shall at some point, Wolf," Knight replied openly, unaware of the tension brewing with Drago. "I'm going to enjoy myself too. Can't take it too seriously, can we? I've been lucky to be put in this group of great players. And as they say, Wolf, better to be lucky than good." He winked and headed off to find his discarded shoes.

■

Things came to a head on their fifteenth hole. They'd all played their tee shot.

"We've still got a big lead. Well done, team," Knight announced, reading the scoreboard proudly.

He hopped out of the cart and began to open the box. Before he had the chance to pull out a beer, Drago sprang out of her cart angrily and shouted, "Oh no, you don't! Screw that, Knight."

"I'm sorry, Christina?" Knight reeled. "What's up?"

"*You* are what's up, buddy. Yes, we've got a big lead. Some of us are playing well. But you've not contributed a thing. It's down to the three of us. And you've just fucked up another tee shot."

Knight sat back down in his cart as she stood over him, snarling.

"Yes, I'm sorry about that, Christina. I think I need to tee it up a bit higher. I just caught it a bit flat—"

"Bullshit, Knight. Stop the fucking excuses. Your club, your grip, the wind. You're just a crap golfer. You should be with a bunch of high-hand-icap no-hopers. This is an elite group. How did you get to play with us?"

"Heck. I'm not sure. The only person I've talked to about it is Tammy McDonald. I saw her at HQ a few months ago. I told her I'd played a bit. I guess she just assumed I was good at golf because I'm from Britain."

It came back to Knight that he'd perhaps overplayed his hand when he introduced himself to McDonald, Gene Farris's assistant. Mariani had told him that it was Tammy who chose the teams. Knight had stopped by her cube and turned on the charm. He cottoned on immediately to her Scottish roots. He learned about her relatives back in the old country, and shared stories of his visits to her homeland. And golf. Golf! In Scotland, nothing to beat it. He had played such wonderful courses there. By the time he'd left, she could have believed he was born in St. Andrews with a mashie niblick in his hand.

Drago brought him back to earth. "A good golfer. You wish," she continued to fume.

"Why are you so concerned anyway? We're winning."

"Because you're going to lose us the whole fucking thing. You know in the rules we have to count three tee shots for each of us. We've not be able to use any of yours as they've gone all over the place. Now, we have to use your shots for all of the last three holes. If you fuck up like you've done so far, everything the rest of us have done will be worthless."

"Oh yes, I'm sorry. I clean forgot about that rule. I'm—"

"That's bullshit too, George. I've reminded you three or four times. You just didn't take any notice. Just my two cents." Houston piled on the agony.

"Look, Knight, I don't mind people making mistakes, as long they work hard and give everything. Hard work. I'm used to it. I thrive on it. It seems you just screw around, making wise cracks and acting like you're in charge. Maybe if you'd done something, anything, for the team . . . but you've been a total deadweight. I'm fucking done with you."

"She's right, George. It's probably too late now, but you've got to learn your lesson and take things more seriously. Play your part." Houston was now firmly in the Drago camp.

"Evidently, NASA, evidently." Knight had listened to enough. "And there was me thinking that this was a fun afternoon with some friendly colleagues. More fool me. Just tell me one thing, you two. Why does it mean so much to you? Winning? Winning the bloody Lassiter Executive Retreat Golf Tournament? Why?"

Drago and Houston answered in a similar vein: satisfaction, visibility, the chance to play with Farris, better options for career advancement, et cetera, et cetera. Put on the spot, they lacked conviction. Knight listened, his head tilted to one side as a sign of earnest interest and a need to atone for his behavior, while secretly laughing at their unconvincing waffle. *Gotcha.*

"OK, I get it." He stood up and waved Dreiser over. "Julie? I need your help. Apparently, I'm the only thing between you and everlasting glory."

"Because of the tee shots? Christina has been bending my ear about that. Don't worry about it, George. It's not like this tournament means anything. It's not for real golfers. Texas Scrambles are just meant to be fun." Dreiser shrugged and headed back to her cart.

"No, no, Julie. It seems that this is important—no, *critical* to our teammates." Sarcasm hung on every word. "And I need to buck up to make it happen. So, as the outstanding player here, would you mind giving me some tips?" He couldn't resist reminding Drago that she wasn't the star player. "Perhaps I can ride in your cart? Christina can take my place with NASA."

"Yeah, sure, OK, George," Dreiser replied placidly.

"If he thinks it will help. Anything. Get him to focus on the tee shots. He has to play all three well. After that, he can do whatever the fuck he wants," Drago snapped.

Drago climbed into the cart with Houston. "That guy is such a fucking condescending jerk. He asks why we want to win. What sort of question is that? Because if you don't win, you lose. Does he want to be a loser? Jesus, what does anyone see in him, NASA?"

"I think you might be surprised, Christina. It takes all sorts. You've given him a kick up the pants. I think he'll respond. Don't underestimate him. Hang in there."

■

Knight joined Dreiser in her cart.

"Thanks for taking me in, Julie. I was taking a lot of flak back there."

"My pleasure, George. I was glad you suggested it. It suits me—I was tired of riding with Christina. She gets so intense. It's OK in small doses."

"That's funny, NASA said the same about me a few holes back. I'm OK in small doses. I think he was tired of me joking about. I guess a dose of me and a dose of her would be about right." Knight laughed philosophically. "That's too funny. What was she banging on about? Work, work, and more work, no doubt."

"No, not at all. Golf. Her swing, her alignment. What did I recommend for this shot, that shot? Which club to use? What make of club should she buy next? What make of ball should she use?" Dreiser rocked her head from side to side to indicate the nonstop inquiries. "It's been like playing with my six-year-old niece."

"Brilliant. This gets funnier. I should have swapped carts earlier."

"So I'm happy to have you aboard. Although don't assume I disagree with her completely, George. You have been a pain in the ass at times."

"Fair, Julie, very fair. I haven't exactly made a big contribution, have I? Honestly, I'm not much of a golfer. I don't play very often, and usually it's just a bit of fun."

"And you've been trying to cover that up by being all larger than life?'

"No, not consciously anyway. That's just my usual happy-go-lucky self. Although I was suffocating with NASA. He's a lovely bloke, but all those clichés . . ."

"Enough said, George. I've known him for years. I've watched that paint dry too."

Knight paused for a moment, choosing his words carefully. "I don't want to get into Christina's needy territory, but do you have any suggestions for me? Now that I've been slapped, I'd better make an effort."

"Nope, nothing to tell you. Your practice swings have looked fine to me all afternoon. You've chosen the right club too. Maybe not when you went in the ditch. You were just screwing around for the cameras then."

"So I shouldn't change anything?"

"Nothing physical, George. Nothing physical. I'll tell you my approach. On the course, I just forget about the golf shot. Forget about the ball, the club, the score. My swing. I let it just be unconscious. What I do think about is the picture, the scene, how it will look as the ball flies away. I conjure up the feeling I'll have when I hit it perfectly. My pride, the smiles, the high fives and atta-girls."

"That's it, Julie? It's all about the power of positive thinking?" Knight smirked.

"Don't start that sarcastic, patronizing shit with me, sunshine. You asked for my advice. If you can't picture yourself hitting a good shot, you won't. And there's no reason why anyone else will believe you will either."

Knight looked down. He steepled his fingers around his nose and blew out his cheeks. He was embarrassed with himself.

"Yeah, I apologize, Julie. Thank you for the advice. I'll try to put it into practice."

"Hey, you're welcome, George. Just do yourself justice on this next hole and I'm sure it will come together."

And do himself justice he certainly did. When they got to the tee, he said, without any sign of cockiness, "As mine is the only shot that can count here, I think we can skip protocol and I'll go right ahead. OK, folks?"

"Yep, have at it, George. Let her rip," Houston answered, sitting impassively in the cart with Drago. Dreiser joined Knight on the tee box to offer a little moral encouragement.

Knight took his time and stroked a good-looking shot, straight down the middle. It didn't go a huge distance, but it would give them a chance to make the green in two. He wouldn't be the cause of any dropped shots.

"Phew, thank goodness for that," he said out loud, really just to reassure himself.

"Well done, George. See? I told you it's not so hard." Julie gave him a playful punch on the arm.

"One down, two to go, George," Houston added grudgingly.

All Drago could manage was a spiteful "About fucking time" under her breath as they headed off in the cart. Houston scowled at her.

"What? He's Tiger fuckin' Woods now? Come on, NASA."

They closed out the hole, with Knight sinking an easy putt to seal a par that kept them seven shots ahead of their nearest challengers.

Knight rose to the challenge on the next tee too and found the fairway without drama. He let out a celebratory "Yeah!"

Dreiser gave him another punch. Houston seemed to be coming back around too and stepped out of his cart to shake Knight's hand. "Good job, George, you're on a roll."

Only Drago remained unmoved.

"If he can play like this, why didn't he do so earlier in the round, hey? Was he just fucking with us, NASA?" She wasn't letting go. "I'm not celebrating yet. He could still screw it up for us, NASA. A bunch of swings and misses, a shank into the woods."

"Relax, Christina. He's doing fine now, turned over a new leaf. You should be pleased. You gave him a wake-up call. It was your little talk that turned things around. Besides, it's a par three. Even if he hits a bad shot, we should be able to rescue it. We might drop a few shots, but we've got plenty to spare. All's well that ends well." They headed to their last hole.

■

Later, as he held sway in the bar, Knight would tell everyone that he'd pictured the flight of the ball in his mind. He claimed he knew it was good from the moment it left his club. He also gave Dreiser plenty of the credit, thanking her brilliant coaching.

He wasn't totally sure, but he thought that he'd actually hit the shot with his eyes closed. He gave it a healthy whack with a smooth swing, and it headed in an arc toward the green.

"Looks good, George," Dreiser was the first to see the potential. "Very good." The ball landed a few feet in front of the flag. "Go on, go on, go onnnnn . . ." And then rolled into the center of the hole.

Knight held his arms aloft. He'd got a hole in one. "Well, look at that. Brilliant." Knight had a huge smile. Dreiser and Houston rushed up to hug him, erupting in spontaneous delight.

Drago couldn't bring herself to join the celebration. Some part of her wanted to recognize his achievement—a hole in one was a rare feat, one that she had yet to accomplish—yet the prospect of his gloating made any praise stick in her throat. As Knight and Dreiser rode off to the green to collect his ball, a beaming Houston came back to join her.

"Jesus fucking wept. We're not going to hear the last of this, are we?"

"Don't get your knickers in a twist, Christina. I told you you'd get a response, didn't I? You should be careful what you wish for."

■

The awards banquet was the grand finale of the event. Suits and cocktail dresses replaced resort casual as the executives and their partners dressed to impress in the hotel's grand ballroom. The meal itself, although delicious and accompanied by some notable wines, wasn't the focus of attention. In a tradition dating back to the early years of the company, the final act of the evening was the recognition of the business units that had made their numbers in the previous year. The recognition was marked with the presentation of a large golden letter *L*, set on a black marble base, to the head of each successful business unit. Each member of the team got a smaller version. "Getting the *L*," as it was known, was the most sought-after achievement at Lassiter. It signified success, foresight, teamwork, and competence. On the other hand, not getting your *L* repeatedly suggested failure, inattention, and dysfunction.

The *L*s were set out on the stage at the start of the evening. As the guests took their seats, much of the conversation was made up of speculation as to the number of *L*s and which business units were the recipients. The seating arrangements were the other main topic. Most of the executives took a good look around to see who was sitting with whom. A place at a table with Farris or members of his senior team was seen as an indication of a degree of favor or a loyalty repaid. Sitting at a Board member's table was a sure sign of being either close to an honorable retirement or a rising star, one for the future.

So it was that Knight and Drago found themselves sitting next to each other at a table with Kathryn Gerrard, the only female on Lassiter's Board. Formerly a top marketing executive with several multinational corporations, she brought a media-friendly perspective, as well as much-needed diversity, to the otherwise staid, misogynist group.

She had assumed the role of host, introducing herself, making sure everyone at the table knew one another. In her sixties, she was clearly accustomed to these opulent surroundings, and her hospitality was welcomed by everyone without question. Her dress sense also asserted her authority. She was wearing a black jacket over a white dress. Black heels, a ruby necklace and bracelet, and a rose-gold Rolex complemented the outfit. Style and substance.

The other guests at her table were both longtime Lassiter employees who were retiring later in the year. Their wives were with them too, enjoying their last retreat. They all knew one another well and were soon chatting away with Gerrard, leaving Knight and Drago with only each other for company.

They sat brooding for a while, looking around the room, studying the menu—anything to avoid making eye contact. As the others went off to get a group photograph, Gerrard engaged the odd couple.

"So, George, I heard about your hole in one. Well done."

Drago stiffened, rolling her eyes.

Sensing an opportunity for self-effacement to defuse the tension, Knight replied, "Oh, thanks, Kathryn. It was just a fluke. Like that saying about a blind squirrel eventually finding a nut. I played terribly all the round, as Christina will undoubtedly tell you . . ." He invited her to be cruel or kind.

She paused, weighing up her options, before answering, "No, I have to hand it to him, Kathryn. It was a great shot and a great way for us to finish the round."

"And you guys won the whole thing, right?"

"Yes, we did, Kathryn. No real thanks to me. Yes, I chipped in at the end . . ." Knight paused to see if they'd picked up on his pun. Seeing no reaction, he continued, "It was Christina, NASA Houston, and Julie who deserve the credit."

"Well, well done to you both anyway. It's always good to see our hi-pos winning things," Gerrard continued. "Neither of you have a guest this week?"

Drago replied first. "No, I'm solo these days. Lassiter keeps me too busy for much else, Kathryn. I thought about bringing my mom, but she'd have been bored while I was at all of the working sessions."

"That's a shame, Christina. I guess it gave you a chance to focus on things. What about you, George?"

"It's a bit different for me, Kathryn. My wife couldn't make it as she had to take care of the kids. We don't have family here. It was all a bit too difficult. It would be better if they arranged this event once school is out. Then we could bring them with us, maybe arrange some things for them to do. It would —"

Gerrard cut him off, "I see, George. Novel idea." Evidently, she wasn't interested in continuing a conversation about Knight's children's retreat proposal. Instead, she returned to Drago. "Which session did you find the best, Christina?"

"Oh, definitely the one where we discussed the new operating model. That was so energizing."

"I snuck into that one. I thought that was excellent too." Gerrard continued to address Drago.

Knight's mind began to wander. *God, that session was so boring. Who gives a toss about the operating model? The customers certainly don't.*

"You made some really great points in that session, Christina. Showed your deep understanding of the way the industry is evolving."

Yeah, right, I remember now. She was one of the people that were all serious, making loads of notes and asking questions, most of which she'd already known the answer to.

Drago and Gerrard eulogized about the conference until the others returned from their slot with the photographer. They resumed their conversation with Gerrard, leaving Knight and Drago to each other again.

"Look, Knight, this is the last thing I wanted, sitting with you, but I guess we can't ignore each other all night."

"Yeah, does seem a bit childish, doesn't it? I'm sorry I pissed you off. Hey, at least we won the thing." Knight smiled weakly, hoping she'd accept the olive branch. "Truce?"

"Truce."

"And please call me George. Everyone else does."

"Nope, that's taking it a bit far. I'll stick with Knight."

"OK, OK, fair enough. It is our first date after all." He grinned. "You've enjoyed the conference?"

"Yes, it's been excellent. What about you? It's your first one, correct?"

"To be honest, I've found it a strange old affair, Christina. I didn't really know what to expect. This place is really nice, a beautiful setting with the mountains, nice weather, not too hot. Although I couldn't figure out the right mood. It's been like there are two different events."

"Oh, I haven't noticed that. What was going on?"

"Well, there's definitely two types of people here. There's the serious bunch. They're always smart; the men look like they are auditioning for a job at Brooks Brothers, and the women on one of the cosmetics counters in Nordstrom, mascara at breakfast. Then there are the others who just seem to be here to enjoy themselves come what may. They play golf; they white-water raft; they're always the first into the bar and the last out; they seem to miss most of the working sessions and don't give a rat's about the latest business issues and external speakers."

"That's very astute, George. I guess I was in the first group . . . without the mascara. No prizes for guessing which one you were you in."

"As it was my first time, I should've joined the serious crew. I know that would have been the wise career choice. I tried on the first morning. It was so lame. Then, with the golf and that hole in one, I decided life's not a rehearsal, as they say. I had some serious fun instead." He finished with a broad grin.

"So, what did that entail?" she asked, keeping the conversation going, but without any real interest.

"I enjoyed meeting some new folks, especially those Aussies. Boy, they like a drink. We had a great night singing along to the piano player in the pub. We had another night when we sat up till dawn drinking and smoking cigars outside by a big fire pit."

"Fascinating. Like you said, Knight, a whole different event."

The half-hearted conversation petered out again. Drago shifted in her seat toward Gerrard. She rejoined the discussion with the others, leaving Knight feeling flat and isolated.

After a few minutes eating his salad and a bread roll, he tapped her on the arm.

"Hey, Christina. There were some odd moments you should know about too."

"Like what?"

He leaned in conspiratorially. "There seemed to be a lot going on behind the scenes. Maybe it was because I was a new guy. I couldn't really tell what it was all about."

"Interesting. I didn't notice. Tell me more."

"There have been a lot of small private meetings. Didn't you notice that several of the sessions started late as Gene Farris was 'attending to urgent business'?" Knight was excited to have her attention. He also wanted to see if she knew anything about it.

"Oh, I was too busy preparing material for the sessions. I welcomed the delays. I didn't think anything of it," she replied.

"You must have heard the rumor that went around that Farris is looking to sell the company and is negotiating the terms?"

"What?" She was suddenly very interested in what Knight had to say. "Oh, I must have missed that too. I'm not real good at spotting those things. I'm more of a data-driven person."

The business intrigue provided them with a common ground, and they continued a respectful, intelligent conversation about the company's prospects and long-term strategy for the rest of the meal. Knight's earnest concentration was only briefly interrupted as the huge video screen showed the footage of him splashing around in the drainage ditch. At the time, he'd found it hilarious. Now it seemed stupid. He crouched low in his chair as the room echoed with laughter.

"I noticed another strange thing, Christina," Knight returned to his conspiracy theory as they finished dessert. "We drove past Farris's group as they were finishing their last hole. Did you see one of the other guys—I think it was Daniel Grauermann—seemed to go crazy on the green, hooting and hollering, running around like he'd won the lottery?"

"Yes, now you mention it, I did see that. God knows what that was all about as it wasn't as if they won anything in the tournament."

Then it was time for the *L*s. Knight's business unit was one of the winners. He went up onstage while Mariani received the big *L*, then returned to the table proudly cradling his miniature.

"Congratulations, George. Quite a week for you. You win the golf, get a hole in one, and now the *L* too." Gerrard shook his hand while the others at the table applauding him politely.

"I was pleased that we made our numbers. It's awesome to get the award. Makes it all feel worthwhile. It's been an *L* of a year."

"Yes, you're right, George. That was good. But what was up with your boss, Lou? I expected that he'd be all bubbly and proud. He seemed really down. He gave a very short thank-you speech. Couldn't get off-stage quickly enough."

"Yes, I noticed that, Kathryn."

"It's not like him. Normally he buys his team a drink to celebrate. He disappeared straight after his speech, didn't he?"

"Maybe he's just exhausted. It has been a busy week." Knight was also puzzled and disappointed with Mariani's abrupt departure.

The event drew to a close as Farris wished them all well and told them that he looked forward to seeing them in another year. As the table broke up, Drago, who to her great disappointment was not part of an *L*-winning team, said to Knight, "Knight . . . George . . . maybe I was a bit harsh to you on the golf course. Houston told me that I shouldn't underestimate you, and he was right. I won't again. You seem to screw around, not take anything seriously, but you walk away with all the prizes and you spot the big moves. You must be one lucky son of a gun." It was neither intended nor taken as an insult or a compliment.

"Well, thank you, kind Christina," Knight replied with faux formality. "See you next year?"

"Oh yes. Most definitely. You can count on it."

They went their separate ways.

CHAPTER FIVE

Business as Usual

October 2004

Initially Hastings's plan had gone like clockwork. Honoring the golf bet, Farris had duly appointed Grauermann to the new Chief Operating Officer position and given him a place on the Board. At the next Board meeting, a vote was taken on a proposal that Hastings be made Chairman, removing the title from Farris. Grauermann sided with Hastings, tipping the result in his favor. Hastings and Grauermann were very pleased with themselves. Their little scheme had worked out nicely. But Farris threw a spanner in the works. He resigned. With immediate effect. While the announcement said it was for "health reasons," he simply wasn't willing to become the lame duck meat in the Hastings-Grauermann sandwich. In the days that followed, Hastings moved quickly to convince the rest of the Board and some important institutional investors that Grauermann was ready to be the CEO. Hastings argued that a protracted period of uncertainty while other candidates were considered would be damaging to the share price. More importantly for Hastings, he would be dragged into a hands-on role, exposing his vaunted knowledge of business as, in reality, rather flimsy.

By early August, Grauermann found himself installed as the Lassiter CEO. He was completely unprepared for the transition from Chief Technology Officer to Chief Executive. By every measure, it was so different from his previous position: he had to make decisions without the luxury of time to analyze all the data; he had to deal with customers and all their unpredictable demands; and he now had to lead the business unit Presidents, his former peers, several of whom had greater experience and business acumen. They resented his rapid promotion and did not respect his authority. The most obvious rebel was Lou Mariani, who had made no secret of his contempt for G-man and his "limey butt buddy" Hastings.

Unlike most incoming CEOs, Grauermann didn't make any immediate changes to the team he'd inherited from Farris. He kept Tammy McDonald as his assistant, even though she had little enthusiasm for her new boss. Stewart Pearson remained head of HR. While Farris would wander unannounced down the hall to Pearson's office for an impromptu chat, Grauermann's more scientific approach substituted a monthly "B & P"—the acronym apparently stood for Business and Personal—meeting to get an update on HR matters.

Their first B & P took place in Grauermann's outer office conference room. They settled into the upright leather chairs.

"First things first, Stewart, thanks for meeting with me. I know you were close with Farris. Do you think you can work with me? Are you OK with all this?"

"You know, Daniel, I kinda am and I kinda aren't. I don't like what happened to Gene. He's a good friend. I know he brought some of it on himself. He lost focus. I've been through the changing of the guard before and survived, so if you want me to stick around, I'm happy to."

"I do, Stewart. I really do. Though only if you want to. I've got things under control. Hastings has made some useful suggestions."

Both men knew that the other was not being entirely candid. Grauermann knew that Pearson had contemplated resigning over the unseemly transition, only his loyalty to Lassiter had kept him from doing so. Grauermann spoke calmly about being in control, but Pearson knew of the looming challenges and sensed Grauermann's fragility.

"I'll work with you, Daniel. I'll give you my best advice and support you in the same way I did Farris. I ask only one thing in return."

"Name it, Stewart."

"You let me make sure we don't end up in this predicament again. CEO succession can't be a shambles. Next time, we plan ahead, we develop some serious long-term candidates, and when you're done, we choose one of them, properly."

He wanted control of an orderly succession-planning process, the holy grail of senior HR professionals.

"That's good with me, Stewart. You do whatever you need. Let's hope we don't have to use it for a while." Grauermann offered a weak, less-than-reassuring smile.

They spent the next thirty minutes discussing the challenges Grauermann faced. It was clear he was overwhelmed and taking too much on himself. Pearson, inadvertently becoming the architect of the grown-ups' table, recommended that Grauermann build his own trusted team, with a new administrative assistant, a Chief of Staff, and a troubleshooter.

"Great idea, Stewart. And I know who two of them should be. I'll get Patsy Myer to come in as my admin again. What will happen to Tammy?"

"I'm sure we can put a nice retirement package together for her."

"Great. So, what about my Chief of Staff. Did you have anyone in mind for the role?"

"You should ask the business unit Presidents to put forward some names. That way they'll see you're open to their ideas, and they'll have a vested interest in making the person successful."

"Wow, that's also a great idea, Stewart. You really are good at this stuff."

"Yeah, I've been around the buoy, Daniel."

"This has been a great meeting, Stewart. Anything else we should cover today?"

"There's a couple of things, Daniel." He reached inside his briefcase. "I want to lend you this book. It's called *30, 60, 90 Days: New Job,*

New Leader, New Life. It's a good read and will help you get things in order."

"Oh, thanks, Stewart. I'll take a close look at it."

"And the other thing is to remind you of a tradition that you have to keep."

"Tradition?"

"The winners of the retreat golf tournament get to play with the CEO. That's always been the tradition. I hope that you'll want to keep it up."

"Yes, of course. How does it work? I can't play with all four of them at once."

"You pick the dates and a partner—maybe it could be Hastings if he's available, or someone else you like to play with. Then you play a round with two of the winners one day, and the other two the next. You can get Patsy to arrange it all."

Later that evening, Grauermann recounted the meeting to his wife, Isobel. He was still raving about Pearson and his invaluable advice. Isobel wasn't convinced. She'd seen her husband struggle to assert his authority before.

"You shouldn't trust any of these Farris people. Get some new blood in there. All the top jobs. Finance, Legal, Sales. Turn the place over before they turn on you."

"That's unfair, Isobel. They aren't all bad guys. Stewart's given me this great book about how to get them on board."

"Stewart this and Stewart that. You've got to think for yourself now, Daniel. Or better yet, I'll do it for you. Who's the biggest problem right now?"

"Lou Mariani. He's really taken it badly. He was very close with Farris. He's angry because he thinks he should have the job. I can understand that. He does have a lot more claim on it than me. I'm going to have a B & P with him to see if we can work something out. I think he's a—"

"Fire him," Isobel snapped.

"Why should I fire him? He's a really experienced guy and he knows how the business works."

"Start by firing him. Make your mark. You can't keep your rivals around, Daniel," she insisted.

"It's just not how we do thi—"

"FIRE HIM!" Isobel ordered.

"Well, maybe you are right, Isobel. He is being very unprofessional. I've heard that he tells his staff not to take any notice of me as I won't last long."

"Perfect. That gives you a valid reason too. Get your new buddy Stewart to take care of it. It'll be a good test of his loyalty too."

"I'll think about it, Isobel," Grauermann responded, stroking his mustache, his lack of enthusiasm evident.

"Daniel." She spoke his name slowly and emphatically, as a mother would to a child when insisting that they ate their greens or tidied their room. She did not expect to hear any more argument on the topic.

"Now, let's change the subject to something more pleasant, shall we?" she continued. "Have you confirmed the arrangements for our trip to Germany yet?"

■

The next afternoon, Mariani bowled up to Pearson's office full of his usual bonhomie, chugging a can of Coke. Pearson had asked him to stop by to discuss a few things. Mariani expected it would be about how they could work together to get rid of Grauermann. Instead of giving him the usual warm greeting at the door, Pearson remained behind his desk, nervously shuffling some papers.

"So it's not a fireside chat today then, Stewart? What's up? You look like you're shitting yourself, pal." Mariani sensed the different atmosphere, but remained blithely unaware of the real reason for the meeting.

"Please take a seat, Lou," Pearson replied calmly. Only his pallid look and avoidance of eye contact betrayed his emotions. "You're right, it's not a chat today, Lou. I'm afraid it's more serious than that. Daniel's decided on some changes to the team."

"Oh, fuck, Stewart. He's not gone and fired you, has he? Coz you were too close to Gene? That cocksucking fucker. What can I do to help?" Mariani was ready to fight for his longtime colleague.

"No, Lou, it's not me. I'm sticking around to help Daniel. You . . ." Pearson wasn't able to finish his death sentence as Mariani finally cottoned on.

"It's me? He wants to fire me? He can't fucking do that. Who's going to run this fucking place? He sure as hell won't. He's a joke. We'll see about this."

"Lou, it's a done deal. He's cleared it all with Hastings this morning. You can take retirement. Spend time with the family, play some more golf. The package is very generous. I've got some paperwork here for you to look over."

"Bullshit! I don't want to spend time with the family. And I don't need more money. I've got work to do here."

"Lou, you're fighting a losing battle. Daniel's mind is made up."

"We'll see about that. The cowardly fucker has to have you do his dirty work. We'll see if he changes his tune when he has to tell me himself." He jolted out of the chair, slammed Pearson's door shut behind him, and strode aggressively down the corridor toward Grauermann's office, still cursing and giving off sparks. He scrunched up his Coke can and pitched it hard into a decorative plant arrangement.

Tammy McDonald saw him coming. She'd seen Mariani in a temper before, but never one quite this intense. She tried to intercept him.

"Hang on, Lou. Daniel's got someone in there with—"

"Sorry, Tammy. Can't wait."

He didn't break stride as he continued his march into Grauermann's inner office.

Inside he found Grauermann and Dalton Hastings at a small conference table poring over organization charts. He stormed toward them loaded for bear, further enraged upon seeing the new Chairman. Hastings reacted first, standing to block Mariani, as Grauermann remained glued to his chair.

"Now, Lou, let's keep calm here. It's nothing pers—"

"Shut the fuck up, Hastings. Prick. You know NOTHING about this company. Anyway, I want to hear it from your boy here." He stood over Grauermann. "You want me to leave? You want me to fucking retire, eh? Do ya, G-man?" He jabbed his finger into Grauermann's face.

Pearson came running into the office behind him. He grabbed Mariani by the shoulder. "Lou, please, calm down. There's nothing to be gained by all this."

"Too late, Stewart. I just want to hear it from Dan the fucking man. Then I'm outta here." Mariani stood, arms crossed, eyes fixed on Grauermann.

"Oh, just get on with it, then. Daniel. Tell him," Hastings commanded.

Grauermann looked up toward Mariani. "Yes." He coughed nervously. "I . . . er . . . have been thinking about it, Lou, and really, I'm sorry . . . I don't think there's room for both of us here. And it can't be me that goes because . . . well, because I got the job and . . ."

"And you have Hasting's dick up your ass? Or what?" Mariani pounced on Grauermann's pause.

Hastings started to respond, but Mariani's insult gave Grauermann more confidence. He stood up, using his significant height advantage to impose himself on Mariani.

"Look, there's no need for that sort of cheap stuff, Lou. I understand that you are disappointed. And you don't think I'm a worthy successor to

Gene. There's plenty would agree with you. But that's the way it is. You can blame Gene, blame Dalton, blame me. You know things could have turned out very differently. You had a chance and you blew it."

Grauermann was right of course. Mariani's flawed temperament and lack of self-control had led to this situation. He'd known the game and its outcome since the retreat. His bravado ever since had just been his way of denying the consequences. Grauermann's dispassionate facts dissipated Lou's furor. He was suddenly a beaten man.

"Peace. That's fair. I can respect that, Daniel. Look, I'll take my medicine and go quietly. Good luck." He offered a handshake, which Grauermann accepted.

"One thing, though, Daniel. Take care of my people. There's some great folks on my team. The life blood of the company. Treat them well."

"Definitely, Lou, I'll do that." Grauermann smiled with apparent sincerity.

Mariani turned around and jauntily headed out of the office with Pearson. He winked to Tammy—"Sorry about that, was kinda urgent"—and they returned to Pearson's office to look over the paperwork.

Mariani's retirement from Lassiter was announced a week later. There was plenty of speculation about the circumstances of his departure. The rumor about the events in Grauermann's office was embellished, probably by Mariani himself, into a full-on fistfight between him and Hastings, which of course Mariani had been winning before he was overpowered by the combined force of Pearson and a security guard. Despite—or perhaps because of—the folklore that surrounded him, many of his colleagues were saddened by his departure and subsequent slide into obscurity. He wasn't perfect. Leaders rarely were. The company arranged a small leaving event for him. Grauermann said a few kind words and gave him a clock. After a loud, brash, and sometimes tempestuous career, Mariani's end came quietly.

■

Successfully handling the volatile Mariani proved a turning point in Grauermann's adjustment to the CEO role. He bolstered his team with some external recruits and promoted longtime Lassiter stalwarts like Ralph Varella and Harold Griffith. Griffith became Grauermann's Chief of Staff, an appointment that honored the commitment to Mariani to treat his folks well. Fortified by Patsy Myer's robust presence, Pearson's constructive coaching, and his wife's occasional decisive intervention, Grauermann gained confidence and began to assert his own style. The freewheeling seat-of-the-pants approach of Farris was replaced with much more structure and authorization and many more formal reviews. *Governance* was Grauermann's operative word: a company that was well governed would perform well, make money, and please the customers.

Indeed, Grauermann felt that he was making such good progress with his internal tinkering that he was very surprised with the harsh tone of his next meeting with Hastings. This time it was via a phone call as Grauermann completed his tour of Lassiter's European operations. He took the call from his hotel in Berlin as Isobel toured the city. Hastings listened to Grauermann's report of the major activities and events of the past month. Grauermann expected a pat on the back, instead he got short shrift.

"Daniel, we can't sit still and wait for all this internal stuff to pay off. This is a dynamic market, old boy. We need some growth, some new deals, and some big acquisitions. I think we need a catalyst on this, so I've decided to get some outside help. I've reached out to my chums at the Phillip Strand Group—PSG. They're management consultants. The best in the business."

"Oh, that's interesting, Dalton. What . . . um . . . what have you asked them to do, precisely?" Grauermann had been doodling on the small hotel notepad by the phone. He realized he'd unconsciously drawn a large penis. He cringed and screwed it up in embarrassment.

"Oh, you know, this and that. They'll take a look at the company— where we are in the market, the competitors, and all that sort of thing—

and then make some recommendations about how we get everything firing on all cylinders. The head guy is called Jake Wiles-Sheridan. Smart fellow. He's worked for me before. It'll be him and probably about fifty or sixty young MBA types doing the legwork. The only one you need to take any notice of is Jake. I suggest that you connect him with your Chief of Staff chappy to make sure they get all the right information."

"That's fine, Dalton. I'll take care of it." Grauermann was annoyed that his methodical approach had been disrupted so soon, an alternative path established without his consultation. He drew another penis. This time quite deliberately.

■

The PSG masses descended on Lassiter like a plague of locusts, devouring every scrap of information about the company's performance that they could lay their hands on. Griffith was nominated as their go-to guy for data and "assumption verification" as they began to assemble their initial report. They prepared the ground for the presentation of their recommendations with an eight-hundred-page prereading deck on the company and its performance relative to its peers. Every facet was assessed by decile, quartile, leading indicator, and lagging indicator. It was truly mind-boggling. Only Grauermann read all of it. Only a few read any of it at all.

Jake Wiles-Sheridan, the PSG partner responsible for the project, didn't endear himself to anyone, continually name-dropping other clients and their senior executives and stressing his direct connection to Mr. Hastings. Grauermann and his team gathered in the boardroom for the final PSG presentation. It began conventionally with one of their midlevel associates giving twenty minutes of information on the market and competitors. Then Wiles-Sheridan jumped in to cover the meat of the recommendations.

"We see two critical areas where Lassiter must double down: first, you must reap the inorganic adjacency benefits from the potential of rapid globalization; and second, you must aggressively position your secular services to exploit the economies of scale in the large-volume transactions now coming to the market."

"So, we buy companies overseas and drop the prices for big deals then?" Varella paraphrased for the benefit of the bemused audience.

"Yes, Ralph. If you want to put it like that, that's right. But, as I'm sure you know when you think about it, it's not quite that simple. If you remain patient, I'll cover the where and the how for you." Wiles-Sheridan settled the heckler with a hint of condescension.

He carried on to explain the countries that offered "the strongest correlation of the net present value of ROIC upside with the fixed parameters in Lassiter's investment thesis model."

"Those are the best bets we can afford then," Varella again summarized with a grin.

Wiles-Sheridan ignored him and continued with his classification of strategic targets, opportunistic accounts, and generic coverage, and the different approaches that Lassiter should employ for each group. Grauermann listened to the whole presentation attentively without comment or question. It was impossible for the group to tell if he welcomed the PSG recommendations or found them worthless. Wiles-Sheridan's final slide concerned the current clients. He explained that Lassiter's share of wallet was well below their competitors'.

"You clearly do not do enough to up-sell and cross-sell. You have to land and expand with wedge offerings, then penetrate and radiate with component solutions in today's market. Your clients are satisfied, yet they aren't advocates. More has to be done to secure their loyalty and fire up the virtuous cross-sell paradigm."

His specific first-step recommendation was to create a Strategic Advisory Council consisting of senior executives from Lassiter's clients. Once assembled, this group would help guide Lassiter's investments in new services and provide constructive feedback on the overall customer experience.

Wiles-Sheridan advised that the major initiatives had to be managed together as a comprehensive integrated change program, or CICP. He had a team of consultants from PSG ready to lead the activity. He even recommended a name for the program: "Project Break Out."

"With this program, and PSG's insight and expertise, we predict that Lassiter will break out from its current constraints and establish a new market-leading position," he ended on a high note. The room was quiet as the team waited for Grauermann's reaction.

"Thank you, Jake. You have certainly given us a lot to think about. We will need some time to discuss it all. We will get back to you. If we have any questions, I will be in touch." Grauermann continued not to give anything away.

■

Once Wiles-Sheridan and his PSG colleagues had left, Grauermann asked his team their views. He wanted to give them the opportunity to debate whether they should proceed. He was walking a tightrope, though, as he knew that Hastings was a strong supporter of PSG, the CICP, and Project Break Out. Wiles-Sheridan had briefed Grauermann and Hastings separately, and this whole presentation and subsequent debate of the merits was just for show, a convenient corporate charade. Grauermann's team, perhaps sensing the foregone conclusion, all readily supported the Break Out plan. The emperor's new clothes were indeed mighty fine.

"I'd like to take on that user group idea that he mentioned, Daniel." Varella saw an opportunity to do something fun for a change.

"Great, Ralph. You can lead the project then. You'll need to pick a client to head it up."

"Yep, I have just the person in mind."

"Excellent, Ralph, glad to see you jumping into this with both feet. Now what about the other aspects, who wants to take those on?"

They spent another thirty minutes discussing the assignments. The meeting ended in high spirits. The team was beginning to gel and was fired up by the possibilities of Project Break Out.

Returning to his office, Grauermann called Hastings to let him know the outcome and the enthusiastic response of his team.

"That's bloody good, Daniel. I really think you're getting a handle on this lark, my boy. Well done."

Grauermann sat back and took in the feeling, a brief moment of self-satisfaction. *Yes, maybe, just maybe, I am cut out for this after all.*

The Grauermanns had been members of the Presidential Country Club for several years. The golf course was known for its long, tough layout. It had hosted professional tournaments, including the US Open. Still, many of the members didn't golf—the club was also popular for its tennis, spa, fine dining, and lively social scene. Membership—purchased with a joining fee of one hundred thousand dollars, plus monthly dues of one thousand dollars and up—conveyed a certain status among the region's abundant nouveau riche. Despite their financial investment, the Grauermanns didn't have a great affection for the club. Daniel golfed occasionally, but he found the course took such concentration, he couldn't relax and just enjoy his round. Isobel was not interested in the facilities and disliked the events—unsophisticated, trivial, overcrowded, vulgarly commercialized gatherings that she saw as fitting for her sister, definitely not her "scene," if indeed she had a "scene" at all.

However, the Presidential did prove useful as the venue to host the winning group from the retreat tournament. Grauermann, demonstrating his growing confidence and managerial savvy, summarily rejected Pearson's suggestion to invite Hastings. He figured Hastings would monopolize proceedings and bore them all with his self-congratulatory anecdotes, his abundant verbiage a barrier to any other more modest interchange. When he asked Isobel who else he should take in his cart, to his surprise, she suggested that she would come. She said she wouldn't golf. She would ride along and get to know the winners. Later, she'd give him her assessment of each of them, their potential, and how he should use them in the future.

Myer, newly appointed as Grauermann's Executive Assistant, arranged the schedule: round one with Houston and Dreiser on Saturday afternoon, then a casual dinner for the Grauermanns and all four winners on Saturday evening, followed by round two with Knight and Drago on Sunday morning.

Round one was largely uneventful. In both of the key activities, golf and conversation, Houston was much as expected. He played the percentages, nothing risky, nothing risqué. He golfed moderately well without any signature moments, and talked with his hosts modestly, revealing very little about himself that wasn't already common knowledge. Isobel later wrote him up as a "trustworthy journeyman, no potential."

Dreiser golfed sublimely, as ever. And, without any sense of ingratiation, she took every opportunity to engage in conversation with the Grauermanns. She answered Isobel's probing questions on a wide range of society's problems. She stuck to her principles despite Isobel's evident disagreement. Her inquisitor's summary: "Very professional and confident and dangerously LIBERAL!"

They finished the round and, following a quick shower to freshen up, met in the clubhouse bar for a well-earned drink before dinner. The three golfers settled for an undemanding Miller Lite while Isobel rehydrated with a mineral water. As planned, Christina Drago joined them. She was soon interrogating Dreiser about the golf round, the course, and the secrets of success.

Dreiser, showing a rare flash of annoyance, whispered emphatically, "Just give it a rest, Christina. I'll give you a full debrief when we're done with dinner." And then, addressing the whole group, Dreiser said, "I wonder where Knight has gotten to."

"Yes, he should be here by now." Grauermann looked around the room, as yet unconcerned by Knight's nonarrival.

"We should eat, Daniel. We don't want a late night. We have to get home and then we're back again tomorrow." Isobel sounded weary and bored. She was annoyed with herself for getting involved.

Grauermann agreed and led them into the dining room. They ordered high-end comfort food—gourmet burgers, wood-fired pizza, lobster mac 'n' cheese—and began to eat with still no sign of Knight.

Drago tried extremely hard to stay clear of the subject, applying every ounce of generosity she could muster, every sinew of tongue-biting self-restraint stretched to the full, but to no avail. As the waiter cleared their plates, she couldn't resist any longer.

"Maybe Knight has got a conscience after all, Daniel."

Grauermann looked at her quizzically. "Why's that, Christina?"

"Well, he didn't exactly contribute anything to us winning, so maybe he's just too embarrassed to show up. I would be."

"That's a bit harsh, Christina," Dreiser countered, looking angrily at Drago.

"Yes, I thought he got a hole in one?" Grauermann said.

"That was just a fluke. And it was irrelevant. It was the last hole and we'd already won. He was totally pathetic for the rest of the round," Drago insisted.

"I see. I see." Grauermann stroked his mustache, uncomfortable at being dragged into this discussion. Isobel had totally lost interest and was ready to leave, which provided him with a convenient way out.

"Well, folks, we're going to head out. Thanks to you guys for today. And we'll see you tomorrow, Christina. Tee time is nine o'clock. I'm sure Knight will turn up." At that, Isobel slithered away immediately without a word. Grauermann settled the check, made handshakes all round, and then left. He joined his wife in the back of the SUV. Their driver had collected the clubs, and they were soon on the road home.

"Thank goodness that's over," Isobel complained.

"You volunteered. I didn't ask you to come," Grauermann replied defensively.

"I know, but you didn't tell me these people were so tawdry, with their pathetic little grudges and constant sniping." Isobel was evidently above such things. "I won't bother with tomorrow. You can go by yourself."

Once he was sure that the Grauermanns had left, Houston coughed up a fur ball that he'd been struggling with for a while. "That really wasn't nice, Christina," he chastised Drago. "Stirring the pot like that. You've no idea why Knight isn't here. He could be sick or have a problem with one of his kids. Anything."

Dreiser piled on. "I'm with you, NASA. Christina, you really should cut out the spite. You may think you're really sharp, taking every chance to shit on people. It'll catch up with you. One day you'll need people to help you, to want to work with you. And you'll come up short."

"Thanks for the advice, Julie. I'll take my chances, especially when it comes to our friend Mr. Knight," Drago replied dismissively.

"Your call. It's your life." Dreiser nodded. Instinctively she wanted to support another female executive on her climb up the ladder. But she refused to see everything through Drago's "I win, you lose" lens. She hoped that the message of the risk of isolation would affect Drago and get her to reconsider.

"Yep, it sure is." Drago immediately set this topic to one side and sought Dreiser's advice without any hint of reflection or hesitation.

"Now you've done sermonizing, tell me about the golf. What should I expect from Daniel tomorrow?"

"I think you'll just have to take your chances with that too, Christina. I'm calling it a night now. See ya later." She left the table calmly. She wasn't angry, just disappointed. *Some people are just beyond help,* she thought to herself as she collected her clubs.

"What about you, NASA? Can you give me any tips?" Drago switched her affection quickly.

"No, 'fraid not, Christina. You'll just have to figure it out for yourself. Good night." Houston trudged off gloomily. He too felt sad about Drago's shameless careerism. *I don't like her. That nastiness is not necessary. Just unseemly . . . Or maybe that's what it takes these days? Should I be more aggressive? I'm not going anywhere. Perhaps I'll try to—*

BEEEEEEP. Houston came to his senses as Dreiser's car swerved to avoid him. He'd walked straight out of the clubhouse without looking, lost in his own thoughts. Dreiser's reactions spared Houston any personal injury, but she did give his golf bag a resounding wallop. There was a loud pop as the side pockets burst and his stock of balls went bouncing across the drive. Dreiser pulled over, and together they collected the debris. As well as the damaged bag, the shafts of several of his clubs were bent beyond repair. Dreiser was very apologetic, yet Houston still accepted it was his fault. "It serves me right for thinking about things too much, Julie," he observed cryptically as Drago shot past, oblivious to his predicament.

■

The next morning, Drago left her downtown apartment bright and early. On a quiet, traffic-free Sunday morning, her Porsche made short work of the journey and she pulled into the clubhouse at 7:30 a.m. It was a little chilly, and an early-morning mist shrouded the course. Failing to get any advice from Houston or Dreiser, she was pleased that she'd had foresight to book a lesson with one of the club pros before her round with Grauermann. They met on the driving range at 8 a.m. for a tune-up. The pro gave her some advice about where to play her tee shots, which holes to play safe or aggressively, the green sizes and slopes. She wasn't going to leave anything to chance in this round. Oh no. Once the lesson was done, she sat in the locker room quietly and went over her notes of the things she wanted to bring up in conversation during the round. She had two goals: play better than Knight—no contest there— and spend more time talking to Grauermann than Knight did—possibly a challenge if Knight were to use his charm on Isobel and thereby earn Grauermann's interest and approval. As she rehearsed her lines nervously, little did she expect that she would succeed on both counts, before even striking a ball.

At 8:50 a.m., she put her clubs on a cart and took a seat impatiently waiting for the others. She'd acquired a new Lassiter logoed polo shirt and cap for the occasion. A few minutes later, Grauermann appeared, accompanied by a young assistant carrying his bag. She climbed out to meet him.

"Good morning, Daniel. Looks like a great morning for golf."

"Yes, I guess so, Christina. I'm sorry. My wife isn't able to join us today. She's not feeling well," Grauermann replied.

"Oh, I'm so sorry to hear that, Daniel. Nothing serious I hope?'

"No, no, nothing serious." He didn't offer any further explanation. "I'm sure she'll be fine. Now have you seen Knight this morning?"

"No. I've been here a while. He's not shown up."

"It's very strange. Do you have a number for him? Cell phone?"

"No, I don't. He's not a regular contact of mine. Sorry."

"We'll give him until a few minutes past nine, then we'll have to get going as there'll be others behind us wanting the tee."

"Yes, I agree completely, Daniel. There's a lot of etiquette to these things. I'd expect Knight would know that, but I understand he's a bit of a law unto himself."

"Oh, what makes you say that, Christina? I don't know him well. I'm told he's a great guy."

"Yes, I'm sure he is, Daniel. In the right circumstances. Lou Mariani must have thought a lot of him as it was him who brought Knight over from the UK, I believe."

"Oh, is that so?"

"Yes, as you know, Daniel, I'm not in that business unit, although I heard he was really close to Lou when he ran things at FRSC."

As they continued the conversation, Drago changed the focus from

Knight's connection to Mariani to her own career and personal background. The time crept along to 9:10 with Knight still missing.

"If he has a problem, I would have thought he would have been in
touch to let us know." Drago made a show of checking her Blackberry
for messages. "Has he been in touch with you at all?"

Grauermann checked his device also. "No, nothing."

"Seems rather rude to me. I wouldn't dream of standing up the
CEO, not once, but twice, without making an attempt to explain myself. Then again, I'm not George Knight."

"We have to get going. We'll just take the one cart and ride
together, OK?"

"Yes, that's fine, Daniel," Drago replied eagerly, inwardly delighted
at the opportunity Knight had given her. She intended to take full advantage of the situation.

The next couple of hours went as well as she could possibly have
imagined. She golfed well enough to be in contention with Grauermann on each hole, but, unlike Dreiser the day before, not so well as
to leave him feeling inadequate. She decided that she'd done enough
Knight-bashing, yet she still kept the conversation flowing freely, never
an easy feat with Grauermann. The only lapses were when each of them
was about to play a shot. They played out the ninth hole and pulled up
to the clubhouse for a midround break.

"You know, Christina, if you don't mind, I think we'll call it a day
here. Twenty-seven holes in a weekend is enough for me."

She was disappointed. She wanted the other two hours with him.
She was about to ask that they play on. But, with a rare touch of empathy, she noticed that he did look drained. Mentally, she ran through
the topics on her list: her education—undergrad, MBA—check; background—lower middle class, hardworking, just like him—check; her he-
roes—Jack Nicklaus, Jack Welch, all about results, being number one—
check; Lassiter's strategy, Project Break Out, PSG, great move—check;
female senior executive underrepresentation—check. She had covered

the waterfront and found Grauermann interested and receptive to her ideas. So probably best not to push it today. Go out on a high.

"That's a good idea, Daniel. I'm fine with finishing now. I've actually got a lot of work to do this afternoon. Preparation. I'm heading out to Europe tonight." She removed her cap and offered a handshake. "Thank you, Daniel, it's been a pleasure and honor to play with you. Maybe we can take the other nine holes sometime? Next spring, perhaps?"

"That would be a pleasure, Christina. I'll get Patsy to arrange it. Good luck on your trip tonight. Europe? Anywhere nice?"

"Paris initially, then straight to India, then Singapore, then back via Japan."

"That's quite something. Keep in touch." He was genuinely impressed with her dedication and commitment. "Christina, you're a great asset to our company. Keep it up."

They left the cart and went their separate ways. Drago's excitement was overwhelming as she headed back into town. Her 911 could have been a magic carpet as she sped back to the city in triumph.

Grauermann was relieved to find the comfort and quiet of his car. He'd driven himself for a change. As he cruised along the interstate, he reflected on the morning. He still saw things in mathematical terms, so he was 90 percent convinced that Drago was a superstar in the making, a long-term potential successor, a meticulous technocrat, a symbol of the new Lassiter. The other 10 percent was skeptical. She was just too . . . too . . . He couldn't quite put his finger on it. He had a complete assessment of Knight though, no gaps there: a 100 percent dud, flash and unreliable, rude and incompetent, overpromoted by Mariani, and an offensive reminder of the prior regime.

On the Friday before the Grauermanns' golf outings, Patsy Myer had taken a day off, heading for a long weekend away at a tattoo convention with her new man. She'd had an agency temp stand in for her. As temps always left things in a mess, Myer intended to get in early on Monday to clear any backlog. The gods conspired against her and, quite by chance, the unfortunate George Knight. A bad car accident held up traffic for miles, making her commute a nightmare. When she did make it to the office, she was two hours late and it was chaos. Grauermann's schedule of meetings had already started without agendas, chart decks, or dial-in numbers; there was no coffee on; the phone was ringing; and there were dozens of emails to be answered. In her scramble, she didn't notice a phone message slip that had been left by the temp on Friday. The message read "Mr. George Knight called several times for Mr. Grauermann. Apologies. Urgent family issue and cannot golf at the weekend. Please call him for details." As Myer scrambled to straighten out her desk, the small piece of paper found its way into a pile of documents, and then into her pending tray, where it remained for several weeks. When she eventually came across it, she decided it was too late to do anything about it. So, she casually tossed the message into her trash can, a slip of no consequence.

■

Later that same fateful Monday morning, Isobel Grauermann had an important lunch meeting. It was a warm fall day, so she opted for a table outside in the courtyard at the Old Fisherman's Inn, one of her favorite spots. Tall and thin, and as always very elegantly dressed in a cream and beige suit, cream blouse, and brown court shoes, she had that imperious air about her that seemed to demand special treatment from the staff, an obsequiousness they were well trained to provide. Isobel was in a cheery mood as she waited for her guest. At least initially she was. She sipped her Perrier water as she surveyed the scene. The courtyard was busy, with most of its thirty or so round wrought-iron tables occupied. Several of the tables had been brought together to accommodate a group of hikers who had stopped off on their trip along the Chesapeake and Ohio Canal. They were a jolly bunch, noisy, although by no means offensive. They were chatting away animatedly and occasionally bursting into laughter as they told stories of hikes gone by. Isobel watched them closely. She wore a fixed smile, a slight demure one, a civilized one. She was happy with them.

Her mood began to sour when twelve noon became twelve fifteen. She ordered a second Perrier and continued to people-watch. The hikers' joviality began to grate on her. She envied their camaraderie. What could be so much fun about slogging along a canal, getting hot and sweaty and bitten by mosquitoes? To sate her growing temper, she began to mentally characterize them in their workplaces. Middle manager. Go-getter. Loser. Has-been.

When twelve fifteen became twelve thirty, she was very irritated, her fuse well and truly blown. She wasn't in the habit of being kept waiting by anyone, least of all her nincompoop of a nephew. And the hikers' chumminess had become oppressive. She detested them now, this band of nonentities, her contempt fanned by the sight of them in their stupid clothes—that ridiculous uniform of baggy shorts, long socks and big ugly boots, reminiscent of her unhappy time as a Girl Scout; her sensibilities offended by the smell of them—a toxic combination of sweat, sunscreen, and insect repellant—which, like a collective halitosis, seemed to intensify as they grew more excited; and, worst of all, her consciousness overwhelmed by the sound of them, a cacophony of laughing and joking, back-slapping, high-fiving bonhomie, a brash, boastful performance, but shallow, a disguise, a charade of reckless indifference to responsibility, an avoidance of reality—which, in her mind, poisoned as it was by bitter experience, labeled them as fools, simpletons unable to ever make a meaningful contribution to society, unworthy, parasitical scum who had no right to intrude on her world. She screamed at herself for not getting the private room upstairs. Mixing with people who did not respect her status was a mistake. She would get them thrown out by the maître d'. Or find out their employers and make a few calls to get them fired. She was consumed by her rage.

"Hello, Aunt Isobel . . . Aunt Isobel?"

Her nephew Jebby had loped up behind her. When she appeared not to notice him, he touched her shoulder and she came back to the moment.

"Oh, hello, Jebby. Nice of you to show up finally."

His arrival had broken the trance of her fury with the hikers, although she retained a little bile for him.

"I'm so sorry, Aunt Isobel. Things dragged on a bit at school and I couldn't get away."

"And I assume that you don't have a cell phone?" Her mood mellowing somewhat, her dial was now on its biting sarcasm setting.

"Well, now that you mention it, no, I don't. We've had a lot of problems with those at school. The boys lose them and then their parents make a lot of fuss about it. As the head of the middle school, I decided to ban them. I didn't want to seem a hypocrite, so I don't have one myself either. I'm on a bit of an anti-electronics campaign generally."

Jebby blurted all this out without stopping for breath. Dressed in khakis, a tweed jacket—with elbow pads—a button-down shirt and crested tie, he looked every inch the private school teacher he was.

"I can't think that makes you popular with the SUV brigade and their precious darlings, Jebby. They'll think you're Amish. Are you going to grow a beard?"

Isobel's temper abating as quickly as it had risen, she was now at her generous and engaging best, the dial at its default setting of condescending mockery.

"There's nothing wrong with the Amish. Those people have a lot going for them. They learn the value of real things, like family, love, and trust, not all the make-believe of the consumer generation. I'm thinking—"

"Oh, Jebby, please shut up. Still the same misguided hippy nonsense I heard from your mother back in the sixties. How is she by the way?"

"Well, I think she's doing OK. I haven't heard from her for a few weeks. She went to Greece last October, and she's pretty much gone off the radar."

"Oh, how nice for her. A Greek tragedy," Isobel replied.

Her sister Sabina—Sabbi—was the black sheep of the family, dropping out of college when she'd fallen pregnant and given birth to Jebby. His birth certificate read "Father unknown." Of course, the family had hushed it up and he'd been raised by Isobel and Sabina's parents, attending boarding schools and receiving occasional bouts of attention from his mother, and consistent and very generous financial support from Grauermann and Isobel.

Meanwhile, three husbands and countless lovers later, Sabbi was still enjoying her carefree lifestyle.

"Why do you have this feud with my mother, Aunt Isobel?"

"Oh, Jebby. We don't have a feud. I don't really care what she does, how she chooses to live her life. That's her decision."

"But you don't approve, do you?"

"She doesn't need my approval, Jebby. But no, I don't care for her lifestyle—so many changes, the marriages and the lovers. She's totally unreliable. No responsibilities. No commitments. Look how she just abandoned you."

"She thinks that you're jealous of her."

"JEALOUS? What has she told you?"

"Oh, nothing really. Just said you were envious of her, that's all."

"Oh good. Nothing specific then? Jebby, why would I be jealous? I have everything I could possibly want. I have my home, my businesses. My husband is a hugely successful executive. What could I possibly want that she has?"

"Yes, I'm sure she has it all wrong. And you're right, we can't rely on her. It's a good thing I have you to look out for me, Aunt Isobel." Jebby steered the conversation away from the cul-de-sac of sibling hatred. "Talking of which . . . do you have any news for me on the headmaster job?"

"That's better, Jebby. A little ambition. A little self-interest. A back-bone. We will order some lunch and then get to business."

They placed their order, a Caesar salad and another Perrier for Iso-bel and crab cakes and an iced tea for Jebby.

"So, Jebby, you've outgrown your middle school headmaster job and want to move to the head of the whole school?"

"Yes, that's right, Aunt Isobel. I want the headship of the whole school. I know that the current headmaster is due to retire and they'll be looking for a new one soon. It would be a great fit for me. I'd love to get a chance to interview for it. I've prepared some ideas around how to modernize the curriculum, bringing more attention to character build-ing, ethics, and honesty, that sort of thing. I think if I got the chance to interview I'd—"

Isobel raised her hand to interrupt his breathless manifesto. "My dear Jebby." She paused and took a sip of her Perrier. "I have it on good authority that the D'Ayncourt School Nominating Committee has al-ready decided"—she fixed her gaze on him and took another sip of Per-rier—"that they will offer you the job of headmaster starting in the next school year."

Jebby froze. He stared at her for a moment, apparently emotionless, his head in a spin. He so wanted to believe what he thought he had heard, but had he heard her correctly? He *had* the job. Did she really say that? Maybe this was another one of her cruel character-building jokes? Like eight weeks of sleep-away camp in eighth grade? Or that prostitute she'd arranged on his twenty-first birthday?

"You don't seem very pleased, Jebby. I expected that you would be delighted. I can always have the offer withdrawn if you don't want the job."

"No, no, Aunt Isobel. I want the job. I was just taking in what you said. I have the job? No interview? No other candidates?"

"Don't be naive, Jebby. Of course you will have an interview. Of course there will be other candidates. Everything will be done properly according to their rules. I have simply told you of the outcome. Your outcome."

"I'm . . . I'm still stunned. And I have so many questions. How did—"

"Jebby, you can ask me about the details. The when and where. That sort of thing," Isobel told him pleasantly. Then her face hardened as she continued more emphatically, "But not the how. You are never to ask me how. Are we clear on that?"

"Yes, yes. Certainly. I'm sorry."

"And, Jebby."

"Yes, Aunt Isobel?"

"I'm still waiting for the magic words."

"Oh, oh yes, of course. Thank you, Aunt Isobel. Thank you."

"Ahh, good, here's our food. Let's eat and we can discuss those details." The sweet smile had returned. "I think I'm going to have a glass of wine to celebrate. Care to join me?"

They both enjoyed their lunch. The crab cakes were a particular specialty of the inn. Isobel had a glass of Chardonnay. Despite his euphoria, Jebby stuck to iced tea. He would need to be fully focused for a dangerous and demanding after-school task. Isobel passed on the details of the interview process, the timetable, the people involved. She told him what to expect in his job offer and how he could negotiate to improve it. By the end of lunch, he was completely convinced that it was not a ruse.

"I'd better be heading back to D'Ayncourt, Aunt Isobel. I've got to direct the middle school car line at three. It's always a challenge slowing down the impatient parents, speeding up their dawdling kids. I'm so grateful to you for this."

Isobel picked up the check.

"You're welcome, Jebby. Just before you rush off, I've a favor to ask you."

"Right, good. Anything."

"You're still responsible for the admissions decisions at D'Ayncourt, aren't you?"

"Yes, I am. I have the final say on who gets admitted to the middle school. I'm also on the review panel for the lower and upper schools. Why do you ask?"

"One of my business ventures, the relocation company, is working with an executive moving to the area at short notice. She would like her children to go to your school. In January."

"Oh, that's not a problem, Aunt Isobel. We have a midyear admissions process for people in that position. If they apply, we'll bring the children in for an interview, look at their academic records and so on. If we think they'll fit in well, we can offer them a place."

"That's good, Jebby. Here are their application forms." She handed him a folder. "They can follow your process. However, I'm sure that you will ensure that the school comes to the right conclusion on their admission, won't you, Jebby?"

"I see. Yes. I'll take a look and see what I can do. Usually if it's borderline, a generous check to the annual fund can swing the decision."

"Jebby, think again. In the circumstances, you really don't think that will be necessary. Do you?"

"Oh, no, of course not. I get it. Wow. Yes. I'll take care of it."

Jeb had finally cottoned on to the bargain to which he was now party.

"Good boy. Enjoy your stressful carpool duty."

He strode off with a satisfied smirk behind his deadpan innocence. Only his watery brown eyes gave away that he'd expected all along that there would be a price to pay for her help with his promotion. After all, there really was no such thing as a free lunch with Aunt Isobel. He'd rather enjoyed acting the ingenue to her scheming and had exactly what he wanted out of the Faustian bargain. Who was controlling whom? In a family like theirs, nothing was quite as it seemed.

■

An hour later, Isobel was in her office at Excel Concierge, a firm that provided assistance to people moving into the area—the typical engagement beginning with a search for suitable houses, then possibly securing places at private schools, and subsequently arranging utility connections, and tradesmen to complete refurbishment and redecoration. Excel worked with several of the foreign embassies and large corporations, so had a steady stream of cash-rich yet time-poor clients. Isobel had a stake in several companies, although she was not involved in their management. She had bought Excel Concierge outright a few years back when they had helped with her move into the area. She took an active role in the sales side of the business, often entertaining the embassy people and HR execs at the big companies to lobby for their business.

She left the operational side to the staff and rarely interacted with those relocating. She didn't have the patience to listen to their pathetic whining about everything. She felt that when someone signed up for the foreign service or a large corporation, they knew what they were letting themselves in for. She had coped with the frequent moves, the lack of friends, the isolation and loneliness. Why shouldn't they?

However, that afternoon she was breaking a habit: she was actually meeting a client. In fact, she'd see two clients. Ms. Cynthia Patten and her father, Mr. Edmund Patten III.

"Edmund, so nice to see you again. Thank you for coming over to the office at short notice," Isobel greeted him warmly, as an old friend. He was dressed formally in a navy-blue suit, white shirt, and navy-and-white paisley tie. Navy and gold cufflinks, a striking Panerai watch, and a relaxed, confident air completed the impeccable ensemble.

"Isobel, my dear, it is my pleasure. May I introduce you to my daughter? This is my pride and joy, Cynthia. Cindy, meet Mrs. Isobel Grauermann."

Cindy was also well presented in a pale gray pleated skirt and jacket and burgundy blouse and shoes. While not outwardly nervous, she was wary, like an overprepared candidate at a job interview. She was very consciously competent as she began the discussion.

"Isobel, I'm delighted to meet you. I'm glad that you will be able to work with me and the boys."

Isobel smiled curtly and, turning to Patten, asked, "So, Edmund, can I summarize what we have here and where Excel will be able to help?"

"Go ahead, Isobel," Patten replied.

"Ms. Patten has recently separated from her husband. She wishes to move into the area to provide some space for herself and her boys from her estranged husband," Isobel read from her notebook.

"Yes, that's right, Isobel. And please call me Cindy."

"Initially, Cynthia is looking to rent a house, with a view to purchase when her divorce is finalized," Isobel continued to address Patten.

"Yes, it may take a while until the divorce and the money is all settled, so I thought renting might be the best option," Cindy again responded, determined to assert her place in the conversation as Isobel continued to read her notes.

"Cynthia does not intend to take a job. She will focus upon getting 'settled in.'"

"Well, I guess that's how I put it to your person who I talked to on the phone. I know that I sound like a lazy, overentitled bitch when you read it back like that, though. I will be looking to get a job pretty soon. I'll resume my legal career, but I do want the boys settled first. They've been through a lot in the past year or so."

Isobel carried on reading the notes clinically. "She has some close friends—from college I believe?—in the area, and they have recommended the D'Ayncourt School for her boys. She has looked at the school's brochure and new website and is very anxious to get them admitted."

"Yes, my roommate at college. Her sons go to D'Ayncourt. It seems the perfect environment. It has great academics and sports. And there's lots of focus on their character and values. Some good role models to provide a real antidote to their father," Cindy explained.

"Thank you for completing our initial requirements survey and for your additional comments, Ms. Patten." Isobel closed her notebook. "Edmund, I think that we will be able to help your daughter with each of these factors—a home, possibly a job, and the schooling. The first two will be quite straightforward. There is a good selection of properties to rent in the area, and many offer rent-to-purchase agreements. It's competitive, though, with all of the embassies, the World Bank, and the corporations in the area. We will need to move quickly and be prepared to pay seven to ten thousand a month for something suitable."

"Yes, I know the market's tight, Isobel. It's the same where I am in New York," Patten replied. His daughter had slumped back in her chair sulkily as she remained the third party in the conversation.

"As regards a job as an attorney, they really are a dime a dozen here, so that will not be a problem at all. She should just let us know when she feels suitably 'settled in' and we'll fix up some appointments."

"I figured that too, Isobel. DC's knee-deep in lawyers and lobbyists." He smiled encouragingly at Cynthia. "See, sweetie? I told you this was going out to work out."

"The only tough part is the schools. D'Ayncourt is extremely difficult to get into even if you submit the applications on time. They rarely admit boys midyear. I really don't see much chance of them giving out two additional places. Not at this late stage. I'd encourage your daughter to look at some of the other excellent private schools in the area. Or even consider the local public schools. Some of them are really good."

"No, my boys are not going to a public school, Dad. We need to get them into D'Ayncourt."

"Is there nothing you can do, Isobel?"

"Do the boys have any special talents? Already aced the SAT? Are they sports players, lacrosse perhaps? Musicians?"

"They are bright, but no, they haven't aced the SATs yet. They're in fourth grade for God's sake. They like sport, soccer and baseball, but no, they're not exceptional. They're just normal, good kids."

"Unfortunately good and normal are not what a place like D'Ayncourt is looking for. Perhaps we might strike it lucky if someone who has a place drops out. It's a long shot. You'd better give me their names, dates of birth, and so on so we can submit applications for them."

"Oh, I gave all of that to the lady on the phone last week. Don't you have it?"

"Yes, just to make sure we have it correct, repeat it please."

"The boys are Eric and Jason Katz. Katz is my mar—their father's name."

Isobel confirmed the details of the boy's birth dates and current school. She turned on the charm as she brought the meeting to a conclusion.

"I think we have everything. I'll get back to you, Cynthia, in the next few days with a plan on the housing and an update on the schooling. I'm sorry if my candor upset you. I believe in telling my clients the truth. You should look at those other schools. They are much easier to get into. And the public schools too."

Patten stood up to end the conversation and head off any feisty reaction from his daughter.

"That's fine, Isobel. We both appreciate what you're doing for us. We know you'll try your best. Cindy, could you wait for me out in the car? I have another matter to discuss with Isobel."

Cindy stood up abruptly and stormed out, evidently very disgruntled about being excluded from the conversation.

"She'll calm down. She's just a little emotional right now."

Patten stood up and watched from the windows as his daughter strode angrily toward the waiting town car, the driver scrambling to open the door for her.

Once he saw that she was safely in the car, he eased himself gracefully back into his seat. From his suit he pulled out his checkbook, bound in a tan leather cover, his initials embossed in gold letters on the front.

"So, how much?" His tone was matter-of-fact yet tinged with a mild irritation.

"What do you mean 'how much?' Edmund. For what?" Isobel replied calmly.

He rose to his feet, his temper continuing to rise.

"Why don't you cut the crap, Isobel? We're all men of the world here. The BS might work for your other clients and was a nice little circus for Cindy. However, I know as well as you do that the way into these private schools is with a hefty gift to their annual fund. How much is the going rate for this D'Ayncourt place? Name the price and I'll write the check here and now."

Isobel remained impassively in her chair, a study in composure. "While I might choose to quibble with being called a man, Edmund, I thank you for the compliment of being regarded as your equal."

Her sarcasm immediately disarmed him. He was amused, even pleased. He smiled. "Touché. Touché."

"You may be right about some private schools, Edmund. However, you are wrong about D'Ayncourt. That place is so well endowed that even your riches can't corrupt them. It takes a little more . . . let's call it finesse. The sort of finesse that you can only get from me. I will get your grandsons places at D'Ayncourt."

"I write this check to you then? How much are we talking?"

"No, Edmund, I don't want your money. I want your time and influence."

"My time and influence? What the hell for? Please, not another charity affair? I'm really busy running the fund right now and I can't take another silent auction."

"No, not a charity event, Edmund. And this concerns your fund."

Patten put his checkbook away and relaxed back into his chair. "Go ahead. Tell me what you want."

"As you know, my husband is now the CEO at Lassiter."

"Yes, I know. We approved all that."

"Yes. I understand that your fund is now the largest Lassiter shareholder."

"True. Where's this going, Isobel?"

"Daniel's settling in well to his new role. It's given him a lot more insight into the company. He's very frustrated with the Chairman, Dalton Hastings. Daniel feels that the company could really accelerate if he could shake off Hastings's conservative influence. Too slow, too indecisive. He says the share price should be twice what it is today. Think what that would do for your fund."

"Yes, that would be great. I've no love for Hastings either. Pompous Brit ass. But what do you want from me?"

"I want you to meet with Daniel and listen to his plans. If you like what you hear, work with him to develop his ideas. Improve them, be ready to implement them. When the time comes, you support him to make them happen by getting rid of Hastings. Daniel serves as Chairman and CEO. Not as any favor to me or to Daniel of course, but because you believe he offers the best value to the shareholders. Of course, you'll share your assessment with the other large institutions to make sure they buy in too."

"That's it? You want me to be Daniel's coach? A mentor? And then support him to oust Hastings and have the freedom to implement a plan that probably makes me several billion dollars?"

"Yes, that's it. Two happy boys, one delighted daughter, and lots of wealth creation. The American Dream."

"Yes, you do have it all figured out, don't you, Isobel? It's a little bizarre, but the ends do seem to justify the means. You have a deal. I'm in."

"Excellent, Edmund. And we'll keep this between us. There's no need to let anyone else know of our arrangement, including my dear husband."

"Of course, Isobel. Of course."

They shook hands conspiratorially and said their goodbyes. He made his way out to join his daughter in the car and directed the driver to take them back to the private aviation facility. His daughter was still fuming.

"What a fucking condescending bitch. She couldn't bring herself to talk to me. Oh no. Had to deal with Mr. Patten. Well, screw her, Dad. I'm sure there are lots of other firms in this relocation business. Let's stay down here overnight and find another one."

"No, we won't be doing that, Cindy. It's all sorted out. Don't be angry with her. Isobel was just negotiating, that's all. She knows no better. I took care of it. We don't live in your ideal world of integrity and honor. Sometimes"—he paused midsentence as a memory eclipsed his train of thought—"often in fact, you just have to deal with people you don't like. People that make your flesh creep. That's the real world, Cindy."

Cindy rolled her eyes moodily. He'd given her the "real world" lecture a thousand times before. Although he had been right once with his warnings about her scumbag musician soon-to-be ex-husband, she intended to keep making her own calls. *And if a few of them turn out bad, I'll always have my dear billionaire recluse father to straighten things out, won't I?* she thought to herself. *The real world is very overrated.*

She refused to speak to him, silently screaming her schoolgirl sulk until their G6 was airborne. Then, as he passed her a glass of her favorite champagne, she apparently came to her senses. She smiled and kissed him on the check.

"Thanks, Daddy. You're still the best."

■

Meanwhile, Isobel had left her office for the short drive home. The Grauermanns' house was a traditional limestone Colonial manor house dating back to the 1700s; it had a stream, several acres of land, and a stable. Under Isobel's watchful eye, it had been carefully restored and tastefully modernized, an elegant contrast to the area's new colonists—"those places" as Isobel referred to them, the gaudy McMansions that had overrun the area in the past decade.

She arrived at 6 p.m., noting that her husband was not yet home.

She assumed that he'd leave the office around 6:30 p.m., so she had an hour or so to herself. She felt quite tired and had a persistent mild headache. It had been an intense day, but one full of success. She smiled to herself as she imagined those hikers still trudging mindlessly along some trail to nowhere.

She listened to a couple of messages on the answer machine. She'd deal with them both later. For now she'd take a soak in the bath and relax ahead of her next important meeting. She sank into the warm water. She had one thing on her mind. Daniel. He was now the CEO. Yet it wasn't enough for her. She took no pleasure in his current status. He still had to take orders from Hastings. She didn't like that. And he capitulated too easily. He was too willing to compromise. This ridiculous PSG Break Out program was the latest example. No, to fulfill his destiny, he had to rise further, he had to have complete control. He had to be the Chairman and Chief Executive. He just HAD TO BE.

Of course, she'd seen his potential right away. When they first met, he was fresh out of grad school and was working at her father's engineering business in Madison. He had great technical abilities though dating one of the owner's daughters hadn't harmed his early career either. He'd quickly moved up a couple of rungs on the ladder. They had soon married and could have stayed there, settling down to take over the reins of the family business. But she hadn't wanted to be stuck in a place where everyone knew her and all her family. She'd needed to escape, so she'd persuaded him to look elsewhere. He'd moved to a larger regional company, and then on to a nationwide firm, leading their distinguished engineering team. The whole world had become their stage as this company was acquired by Lassiter. From then on, she'd steered him to grasp the many chances for promotion that had presented themselves. And now she had taken things just a little farther. She had carefully crafted this special opportunity for him. Would he have the courage to break free of Hastings? How would she persuade him to take it? She knew the way. He really had no choice, no voice at all.

CHAPTER SIX

The Wall Street Shuffle

May 2006

It was a fitting start to the celebrations: an excellent lunch in the plush surroundings of the Stuyvesant Room at the Black Swan Hotel in Lower Manhattan. Some indulged in a gin and tonic or a glass of Pinot Grigio to accompany their horseradish-crusted beef tenderloin. After lunch, the guests enjoyed magnificent panoramic views out over New York Harbor. Many would have preferred to linger out on the deck, admiring the Statue of Liberty standing proudly in the distance. However, in the Land of the Free, they all felt the obligation to watch the next show on the Business Channel. The group gathered around the large-screen TV in anticipation.

As the credits rolled, George Knight and Vadim Barthez stood together on the fringe of the group. Knight, like most of the other execs, was in full sail: a black suit, white shirt, and red tie—the company colors. Barthez had just arrived from Paris and had not yet changed out of his casual jeans. The two men had known each other for many years and always enjoyed each other's company. They shared a common irreverence for corporate HQ.

"Here we go, should be good for a laugh, Vadim," Knight said quietly.

"Shh. Let's just watch it. We might learn something," the Frenchman replied earnestly. They regularly shared a joke at their colleagues' expense, but usually in private, not in full view of many of those they parodied. So Barthez was a little reluctant to pick up the theme.

"Yeah, right. Dream on, partner," Knight continued.

The show's host, Alana Day, began: "Welcome to *Ticker Tales*, our weekly look at a company that's making the headlines. Today we feature Lassiter Corporation, a company that for most of its history was a quiet achiever. While many companies in its sector have come and gone, Lassiter has carried on grinding out steady results—nothing spectacular, yet never going backward either. A tortoise among the hares, you might say. Well, not any longer. In the past year, Lassiter has been making some bold moves and attracting a lot of attention here on the Street. With me in the studio today are three esteemed financial analysts who have followed Lassiter's progress for many years, Moira Kenney, Kirk Moyes, and Caitlin Ramsey. Let's start with you, Moira. How do you assess Lassiter's recent progress?"

Moira Kenney: "It's been a spectacular change, Alana. It began back when Daniel Grauermann took up the role as CEO, and long-term Board member Dalton Hastings became Chairman. They brought a new style. Gone were the days of low-profile, steady progress. Grauermann's strategic plan is called Project Break Out. We have seen immediate changes in the operations, and a more aggressive approach to new deals. Several big acquisitions have added new services and extended Lassiter's global network."

"She's good, this host. Hardworking." Knight seemed unusually serious.

"What are you talking about now, George?" Barthez asked.

"She puts it 'Alana Day's work.' Get it? All in a day's work . . ."

"Oh, *mon dieu*, do you ever stop?"

Kenney: "As the company celebrates its fiftieth year by ringing the closing bell today, its valuation is roughly 50 percent higher than when Grauermann took over as CEO. Quite a performance."

"Oh, my young friend, they make it seem like the G-man is the only one that works here, no?"

"They're analysts, Vadim. They always fall for the obvious. They have to dramatize. You can't expect any depth, or even accuracy."

Day: "Yes, it seems everyone at Lassiter has done well. Chairman Hastings—who like Moira is from Britain—was recently knighted by the Queen to honor his services to industry. He's now Sir Dalton, folks. Now let's turn to Kirk. What do you see in Lassiter's future? Can they maintain their progress?"

Moyes: "Well, the short answer to that is yes, Alana. I expect that Lassiter will go from strength to strength. I think they have room for some more acquisitions—they've shown that they can integrate them successfully. I expect them to add to their global reach with operations in several new countries."

On the other side of the room, Houston and Varella were watching the show. They also enjoyed a private conversation.

"There you go, NASA, the smart analyst says we're going to new countries. Maybe we can get out of our corporate straitjackets and do something useful out in the brave new world."

"Oh, that's right, Ralph. The brave new world. You? You wouldn't last five minutes out there. No way, José. Stick with what you do best, buddy. Meetings, metrics, PowerPoint templates. That's where you add value," Houston whispered back.

Day: "What about the people side of things, Moira? What do you see happening behind the scenes?"

Kenney: "I expect Grauermann to consolidate and strengthen his position at the helm. The board initially gave him a two-year contract. I expect they'll extend that, and there's a possibility that now that he's proven himself they'll give him the Chairman title too. He'll be working to secure his eventual legacy. He's been stacking the deck with his own people recently, employing several new hires like Robert Livingston. Also advancing his protégé, Ralph Varella, into a senior position—it looks like he's being groomed as the long-term successor. I'm watching some of the up-and-coming execs like George Knight and Christina Drago, who I expect will feature in the succession planning at some point if they maintain their current progress."

Houston dug his elbow into Varella's ribs. "'Groomed as the long-term successor,'" he mocked the analyst's statement. "Woo hoo. See, didn't I just tell you all those meetings with PSG were working for you, Ralph? Promotion by PowerPoint. Stick to HQ and your future is bright. Can I get you a chair, oh great anointed one?" He was teasing although his voice carried a taste of bitterness.

"Very funny. Just some dopey analyst who knows diddly-squat. I hate all those fucking meetings just as much as you. Daniel wants this, Daniel wants that, Daniel wants the other. We've got another one tomorrow. Board presentation. A royal pain in the ass. I wanted to go watch the Yankees. I've got two tickets. Because of this it looks like I'll have to miss it."

"Tough break, buddy. You'll just have to accept that grooming and enjoyment are mutually exclusive. I'm not into baseball, but I'll take one of those tickets and go to the game just to piss you off," Houston replied chirpily.

It was well known that Varella was frustrated with the futility of his HQ box-checking job, only his ambition prevented him from doing anything about it. Houston himself was not on anyone's radar as a contender for promotion, although as one of Varella's closest associates, he would probably benefit from Varella's success. Deep down, Houston would have preferred things to be the other way around, yet he contented himself by needling his friend.

Day: "Finally, we'll bring in Caitlin. Now, you have a very different view of things, don't you?"

Ramsey: "Yes, I do, Alana. I really do. I see some big risks looming for Lassiter. These seem to be in three areas. One, they have not yet shown that they can integrate and get value from their acquisitions. They paid some big premiums for those companies, and their business case will only hold up if they get a lot of cross-sell from them. Two, they've taken on a lot of large new deals, some with very high-profile customers. There's a feeling in the industry that they might have overstretched themselves and may struggle to meet their commitments and deliver respectable profit margins. Three, I worry about the ability of the executive team to perform if the going gets tough. Yes, they have looked good lately, but it's easy when you're spending borrowed money on acquisitions and buying business. They also seem to have relied heavily on outside consultants to drive their Project Break Out. I'm not sure that they have a strong team or that CEO Grauermann has the leadership skills to keep things together if they hit problems."

Day: "Strong opinions there, Caitlin. Care to quantify them? Lassiter's stock is trading today at twenty-eight dollars a share. Where would you see it in, say, a couple of years' time?"

Ramsey: "I'll say in the ten-to-fourteen-dollar range, Alana."

There were audible groans around the TV as the third analyst made this gloomy prediction.

Day: "How do the others react to that? Kirk?"

Moyes: "I can understand Caitlin's position, Alana. She's right to point out that there are some risks out there. There is for any company that's pursuing a bold new strategy, taking market share. There's even greater risk in standing still, though, and letting the market change around you. Lassiter was for a long time a fast follower. Now it's trying to be innovative and lead change. I'd rather take a bet on that than it slow down again and risk becoming irrelevant."

Day: "So your share price prediction in a couple of years . . . ?"

Moyes: "It will keep appreciating. I'd say perhaps fifty dollars a share by then, Alana."

"That's more like it!! YO, Kirk!" Knight vocalized all their thoughts, drawing applause, grins, and a high five.

Day: "And finally, Moira. How do you see things?"

Kenney: "I'm totally with Kirk on this. Business success these days is about momentum, speed, and dynamism. Lassiter has all of those and then some right now. Gone are the days when the focus was on operations and execution. It's about branding too. I'm really impressed with Lassiter's new branding initiatives. They make a real statement—more aggressive, more confident. With Grauermann continuing to drive it forward, I think this company has a lot of upside potential."

Day: "So your prediction on the share price, Moira?"

Kenney: "It's a broad band—I'd say somewhere in the seventy-five-to-one-hundred-dollar range, Alana."

Day: "So there were have it for this week's show. Lassiter—on the crest of a wave? Or headed for the rocks? Thanks to our analysts, Moira, Kirk, and Caitlin. I'm Alana Day. We'll see you next time on *Ticker Tales*."

As the credits rolled, Varella burst into song:
"We love you, Moira, oh yes, we do."
Knight and Barthez took up the next line:
"We love you, Moira, oh yes, we do."
Then most of the group joined in as Varella climbed up on the table to conduct them:
"We love you, Moira, we do."
And even the normally stoic Houston threw caution to the wind to join in the last line.
"OH, MOIRA, WE LOVE YOU."

■

Less than a half hour later, the management group reassembled in the hotel lobby. Some had continued to relax in the Stuyvesant Room, fortifying themselves for the afternoon's event. Others had retreated to their rooms to write emails, make calls, or in Barthez's case to change out of his jeans into a business suit. It was Wall Street after all.

There were two other groups in the lobby. The Lassiter Board members were waiting patiently with Daniel and Isobel Grauermann. They had enjoyed a private lunch away from the madding crowd. Another group stood apart, looking nervous. They were regular employees selected by the business units to come to the event. They had flown in from all over the globe—Australia, Singapore, Italy, Argentina, and of course other operations in the US. Following a few awkward moments of respectful class separation, the groups began to mingle. Knight recognized Li-Hua, a young Singaporean engineer, from her days with the FRSC account, and he led the way to integrate the management and employee groups. Pearson also brought Sir Dalton Hastings over from the Board group to meet Grete, the strikingly beautiful Argentinian Marketing manager. Hastings was soon spinning his yarns trying to put her under his spell.

As the groups became one and the hubbub from the conversation grew, only the Grauermanns remained apart, watching from the corner of the lobby. They were in an animated conversation. Isobel was making some forceful points to her husband as he tried in vain to make eye contact with someone who would give him the opportunity to get away. Even his security detail, the three burly ex-cops in cheap suits and obligatory curly ear pieces, seemed unwilling to rescue him. Isobel signaled for Varella and Elliot, who was in charge of the day's arrangements, to join them. Her husband appeared to give them some last-minute instructions.

Then as the time approached 3 p.m., Elliot stood on the steps leading to the main doors to take control of proceedings. "Ladies and gentlemen. Thank you all for being here on time. As we told you in the documentation, that was important as this event is on a strict timetable. Let's go over that now. You should all have it with you. If you don't, please share with someone."

He brandished the brochure that all of the guests had received.

"So, we'll leave here at 3:05 p.m. and *walk* to the Stock Exchange building. That should take approximately fifteen minutes. It is essential that we stick together as a group, so please just follow along in the order that you leave the hotel. For those who cannot manage the walk, of course there is a shuttle, which will also leave at 3:05 p.m. You'll have twenty minutes to tour the floor of the exchange, talk to the traders, and take some photos. Remember the warning from the Investor Relations team printed in the brochure: you can't talk to anyone about Lassiter's performance, future results, new deals, anything that might be interpreted as significant information."

"Except to Moira Kenney. We can talk to her," Ralph Varella piped up cheerfully, provoking laughter.

"No, Ralph, not even to Moira, much as we love her," Elliot replied with a smile.

Houston quietly responded to Varella with a more pointed rebuke. "Ralph, get a grip. Keep your mouth shut. Need to know—it's just common sense. Where does that rank in your grooming?"

"Yeah, you're right. Ignorance is bliss. If we see her my answer will be 'I Kenney tell ya anything, Moira.'" Varella attempted a Scottish accent with mixed results.

Elliot frowned at them and put his fingers to his lips. "Ladies, please keep it down. At 3:50 p.m., Mr. and Mrs. Grauermann and the employees will make their way up to the balcony. Mr. Grauermann, you'll take your place at the podium with the team arranged either side of you. At 3:55 p.m., the Board members and management team will congregate beneath the balcony. At 4 p.m., Mr. Grauermann will ring the closing bell and the Lassiter logo will appear on all of the TV screens around the floor. The group below should applaud. Afterwards we will adjourn to the meeting room for a champagne toast and further photographs. Oh, one last thing. Please make sure that you're wearing your Lassiter NYSE bell-ringing pins. They'll be collectors' items soon."

The majority headed outside and waited on the sidewalk. Before joining them, Hastings wanted a word with Elliot.

"Elliot, a moment. I'm meant to be up there on the balcony for the bell ringing too. That was what we agreed. I am the bloody Chairman."

"I'm terribly sorry, Sir Dalton. I'm only following orders from Ralph Varella, my boss. It will be just the Grauermanns and the employees up there. Sorry."

"Well, we'll see about that. I'll talk to Daniel." He wheeled around angrily, but too late to catch Grauermann, who had been ushered into a limo by the security team.

"Bugger. I'll catch him at the stock exchange and we'll sort this out."

He strode toward the shuttle. His temper receded instantly when he saw that Grete, the Argentinian beauty, had waited in the lobby for him. She expected him to join the walkers. Yes, he would enjoy a stroll. Why the hell not? They walked out together arm in arm as he returned to his tales of corporate derring-do.

Led by members of Elliot's staff carrying small flags with the Lassiter logo, the group was too unwieldy to make progress together on the busy sidewalks, so they naturally fell into pairs, walking side by side.

Varella and Houston trundled truculently along.

"This feels like a kindergarten trip to the zoo," Varella said, showing his irritation. "We should have a rope with knots on it to stop any of us getting lost. I shouldn't joke, NASA. I think Mr. Elliot might need a rope to get Sir Dalton Scumface back there off that poor Argentinian girl. What a douchebag."

He paused to watch Houston's reaction, but got nothing more than a breathless grimace. Varella glanced behind him, then continued his monologue.

"Thinking about it, I'm sure she can take care of herself, NASA. She's no fool. Anyway, it looks like he's out of gas already, I doubt he'd be able to keep up if she quickened the pace much."

In contrast to the first pair, Knight and Barthez ambled along amiably.

"So, George, you are 'ere with the big boys now. And the TV lady says you are an up-and-coming. Bravo!"

"You know, Vadim, I think I know her—that TV woman, Moira. I've been racking my brains since that show. I think I was at university with her. Short, Scottish, quite cute. She dated one of my mates."

"Well, with that kind of luck, you have it all perfect, don't you? Please do not forget your friends in France when you rule the world."

"Friends? France? Me? You know I hate the French, Vadim. I think I'd sell your business off, probably to a German or an English firm if I get the chance," Knight replied with a deadpan face, then cracked a broad smile.

"Ah, George, always quick with the banter. Like Ralph Varella, only you are actually funny. Keep that up. Don't lose it among those corporate types."

"I'll try not to, Vadim. Some days, though, I think being true to yourself isn't really compatible with being successful here. G-man and his cronies want conformance to some boring standard model. Ninety-nine percent effort, one percent inspiration."

"Nonsense, George. They love me and I don't conform. Look at Pearson too. He's seen CEOs go and come, and he's still his own person. It's not about not conforming to a standard Lassiter model. It is about them knowing you, understanding you, you knowing and understanding them. Remember that and you'll be fine, George."

"Yes, good advice, Vadim. I'll try. But it's hard. I like Stewart. I trust and respect him. None of the others, though. I can't be bothered getting to know them. I don't want to share myself with them."

"Well, that is your choice, George. You may limit your career, that's all. There's plenty of others who will play the game."

Pearson had come up alongside them.

"Hi, George, how are you? What's your game plan for tonight? Any soccer games we can go see?"

"Not tonight. Well, there might be some MLS game on. Nothing from Europe, though—not live anyway. Besides, we have another Lassiter dinner to go to."

"Oh yes, that. We'll probably have to endure another one of Grauermann's appalling speeches too. Well, let me know if you decide to do anything after that. Maybe there's another club room around here, eh, George? Catch you later." Pearson quickened his pace to catch up with the next twosome.

"What is this 'club room,' George? You been taking Pearson to the red lights, no?"

"No, nothing like that, Vadim. Just an old memory—a good memory, but an old one." Knight smirked to himself. He may not have any time for Grauermann and his stooges, but he was getting to know the right people. "I'll chat more later, Vadim. I need to ask Pearson about something."

Knight strode ahead.

"Stewart, can I chat with you as we walk along?"

"Yes, of course, George. What's up?"

"Did you hear what that woman said on the TV? About me being on the long-term succession plan? That can't be right, can it?"

"Yes, it's right, George. Well done."

"It feels like Grauermann doesn't like me much though. He doesn't give me the time of day. Seems like I've offended him at some point."

"There may be something there, George. But he's never mentioned anything to me. I'll try to find out for you. He has been really busy. You have to hand it to him. The company's been on a hot streak since he took over as CEO."

"Yeah, I agree. Project Break Out really seems to be going well. It's good for all of us."

Knight certainly couldn't deny the results, although he wasn't convinced about Project Break Out. The PSG people generated lots of wonderful presentations. As the centerpiece of the employee communications sessions, they'd produced a video series—short, snappy pieces full of new business models, road maps of innovative services, plans for accretive acquisitions, really compelling stuff. Farris had actually said most of it before, but now Grauermann said the company actually meant it.

"My only concern with all that, Stewart, is there's a lot more bureaucracy these days. All these darn metrics reviews. At times it feels like that nursery rhyme "The Grand Old Duke of York." Up the hill, gather this data, fill out this template. Down the hill, that's not the priority, dial into this call, attend this workshop. Most of it's internal too, not doing much for the clients."

"Just go with the flow, George. You're in the plan because of your great results. We can't ignore them. Plus, the customers seem to love you, and people like really like working for you."

"OK, got it, Stewart." They were approaching the Stock Exchange Building. "One last thing. Christina Drago? Is she really my main competition? She seems so uptight. Kinda one-dimensional."

"Seems so, George, seems so. You shouldn't be scared of a little competition. Remember the advice I gave you back in Japan? That's the way to beat her. Enjoy the event."

■

Once inside, the party broke out into small groups and entered the trading floor. For most, it was their first visit, and they wandered around wide eyed, marveling at the intense energy of the place. They felt the heat and bright lights. There were several small TV studio sets on the floor. Some of the groups watched while the young reporters gave their viewers updates on the latest financial news and stock movements. Some listened to traders explaining their roles and demonstrating the array of tools that their abundance of technology offered them. It had been a down day for the Dow. It was heading for a fall of over one hundred, so the traders' mood was rather gloomy. Lassiter was also down twenty-five cents or so. Still, the party was determined to enjoy the experience. A photographer moved among the groups capturing the sense of excitement and wonder.

Kathryn Gerrard was talking quietly with Christina Drago. Since sharing the table at the awards banquet, they'd been in regular contact. Gerrard had become Drago's unofficial mentor.

"Kathryn, I'm so grateful for all of the coaching over the past few months. It's been really helpful."

"You're very welcome, Christina. Us girls have got to stick together."

"Too right. Talking of which, did you hear that analyst on the TV show earlier? Suggesting that I could be in line to be CEO one day?"

"We didn't see it as we were having a separate lunch. The Marketing people gave us a transcript. So, are you pleased?"

"Yes, of course, very." The words didn't fit Drago's frowned expression. "Just, I was very surprised with the other name they mentioned. Surely they got that wrong?"

"George Knight? No, he's a contender. He has a few things going for him. He gets good results. But relax. You're in a better position, especially because Daniel doesn't seem to rate George highly. It's Pearson who keeps talking him up."

"Why? What does Pearson see in him?"

"What do older guys like about their younger colleagues, Christina?"

"I don't know. As you said, I guess he gets good results, makes his numbers. His client advocacy scores are outstanding too."

"Nope, that's not it. Nobody is liked for their stats, Christina. Be a little more emotional."

"Emotional?" Drago was flummoxed. "Sorry, Kathryn, I just don't get it."

"So here's the deal, Christina. Pearson likes Knight because he somehow reminds him of himself. The 'chip off the old block' thing. I heard that they even went off to see some soccer tournament together a while back."

"Holy shit, how do I compete with that? I'm not a good ol' boy. And I don't know anything about soccer. Is there a course I can take somewhere?"

"No, but you don't need to compete with that either. Just keep doing your thing. Just try to work on your . . . approachability. Find things in common with people, share your interests. That will round you out and make it easy to see off Knight—and anyone else for that matter."

"Right, I'll put a draft approachability plan together. Maybe can we review it on our next call?" Drago replied appreciatively. "Look out, my competition is headed our way now."

Knight breezed over to join them with a confident smile. "Isn't this just terrific, Kathryn?"

"Yes, what a privilege to be here, George," she replied.

"Excellent, Kathryn, excellent." Then turning to Drago, "Christina, nice to see you. We missed you at our lunch earlier."

"Yes, some of us had work to do, George," Drago replied pointedly.

"Oh well. You missed the fun. You were mentioned on the TV program. I'll catch up with you later and give you the scoop at the dinner maybe?"

"Yes, maybe. We'll see, George." Of course, she had seen the show in her room and didn't need his input, thank you very much.

"I hope this turns out to be as good as the awards banquet, don't you, Christina?" he said casually.

"Oh yes, George, but this is about all of us. You won't be getting an *L* today." Drago wore an apparently sincere smile. Inwardly she cursed his boasting.

"Touché." He grinned. "Ladies, a pleasure as always. I'll catch you both later then."

Knight wandered away to join another group, nonchalantly working the room.

The Grauermanns didn't partake in the floorshow. Instead, they were escorted from their limo through a private entrance. From there, the NYSE staff whisked them to an anteroom that looked out onto the floor. Iced tea and water were available. Grauermann asked if they could get him something a little stronger. A large scotch was quickly served. They surreptitiously observed the group below.

"Hastings is going to be really mad, Isobel. He wanted to be up here for the bell."

"Daniel, I've told you. Relax. Just tell him you knew nothing about it. Let Varella or one of his minions take the blame."

"Yes, I've got it. Plausible deniability. Sorry, just a little wobbly about tomorrow. I can't believe it. By the end of the Board meeting, I won't need to worry about Hastings anymore. He'll be gone and I'll have it all. Chairman, CEO, President."

His eyes glazed over as he muttered to himself, "Yes, this whole business could be over with the one vote at the meeting. That can settle it once and for all and we can move on. But I'm worried that stabbing him in the back like this will come back to haunt us. He is the Chairman and I'm still an employee. He's here at this event at my invitation. And that third analyst predicted all kinds of doom and gloom. There's no reason to go ahead with this . . . this ambition, greed, and vanity."

Then he addressed his wife directly, "We're not going ahead with this, Isobel. Hastings has been really good to me. It was his scheme that got me to be CEO. I don't want to dismiss his support."

"Are you afraid, Daniel? Afraid to actually do what we both dream of? Are you going to always see yourself as a coward, letting your pathetic excuses get in the way? Take Hastings out. Be a man. Keep your promise. You owe it to me."

"What if the vote fails?"

"If the vote fails? Get your act together and it won't fail. It's all arranged. When they get to the agenda item on the extension of your contract, Lyons will read the letter from Patten. Patten is available to call in, or worst case, he'll come over to the hotel. When Hastings doesn't accept Patten's request, then you call for a vote. You'll hold sway, trust me."

"OK, Isobel. I'm calm again. I'll do it. Let me get my game face back on. Can't give up now, can we?"

He drained the last of his scotch, stroked his mustache, and snatched another quick look at his briefing notes. Pearson had provided a short profile on each of the employees. Courage and composure restored, he welcomed the group, engaging in some superficial chitchat. He delighted them with his apparently sincere interest in their work with particular clients, and the progress of their projects. He made the Lassiter Italy representative's day by asking about the health of his spouse and their newborn baby.

At 3:55 p.m., the doors opened with a flourish and there they were on the balcony overlooking the trading floor of the New York Stock

Exchange, a defining moment for Lassiter. The team below waved and cheered enthusiastically, carried along by the occasion. Hastings—"Oh, my friends call me Dalty, my dear"—appeared to have forgotten about his unfulfilled date on the balcony and was more intent on fulfilling something else as he continued to monopolize the Argentinian beauty. Then the electronic clock ticked over to 4 p.m. Grauermann proudly pulled the cord to ring the closing bell, the tickers flashed "LASSITER LASSITER LASSITER," the flash bulbs popped, and for a brief moment everything was harmonious in the world. The Board members, the C-suite, executive management, and employees were all as one. Corporate nirvana.

While the closing bell ceremony was taking place, the NYSE staff set up the anteroom for the champagne reception. The Grauermanns and the employees filed in from the balcony and were soon joined by the bigger group from the trading floor. The staff handed out glasses of champagne, and after a short speech from the small stage, Daniel Grauermann proposed the toast to Lassiter. The group returned the toast and took a draft of the bubbly before breaking out into applause. Then it was time for more photos: three group pictures—one for the Board Members, one for the executives, and one for the employees. In each photograph, the Grauermanns took center stage as the others filled in excitedly around them. Then, as they left the stage, each shook hands with Grauermann as Isobel hung a special commemorative medal around their necks.

The group meandered back to the hotel, where there was time for a few quick emails, a nap, or a shower to freshen up. Hastings continued his wooing of Grete on the walk back and suggested a drink in the bar. Alas, it wasn't to be. He realized that he had run his course when his prey told him she'd be changing and going for a jog around Battery Park before dinner. He declined her invitation to join her, citing an urgent phone call he had to make.

The food at the dinner was again excellent, and there were entertaining speeches from an honored guest, the popular analyst Moira Kenney, and Hastings. Grauermann gave a short vote of thanks to the staff who had organized the event. After that, the evening flagged, the mood became subdued. Perhaps it was tiredness; perhaps it was the realization that this all meant nothing in the broad scheme of things—no medals had really been earned as the race never ended. The dinner petered out around 9:30 p.m., and most headed immediately for their rooms, stifling their yawns. The party was definitely over.

For most people. Knight sought out Moira Kenney as she left the room.

"Excuse me, Moira. I have to ask you. Are you, er . . . ? Hmm, this is awkward. I think I know you. Didn't you date . . . ?"

"George Knight! Well, my, my, I had no idea that was you. Yes, of course you know me."

"It is you. Thank goodness, I thought I was going barmy. You dated my roommate at college. I hadn't heard that you were over here. Always thought you and him were set for life. I thought you'd have settled down and had lots of babies by now. You did enough practicing back then. You were always at it."

"Long story, George. We split up years ago. No babies, I'm afraid."

"Hey, do you fancy a drink? I'm putting together an escape committee to go down to the hotel bar," Knight asked.

"Sorry, I can't tonight, George. I've got another TV slot tomorrow and I need to be on good form. My bohemian days are all in the past. Here." She gave him a card. "Call me next time you're in New York. I can tell you about my new life. And you can give me lots of juicy gossip on Lassiter."

"That's a deal, just so long as you keep telling your viewers how great I am." He grinned.

"I gave you all those compliments before I knew it was you. If I had done, I'd have said what a lazy good-for-nothing drunken layabout you are," she said with great seriousness and headed toward the elevator. He assumed she was teasing.

"Cruel. You have me all wrong." He cracked up laughing. "Bye, Moira, it was great to see you again. I'll definitely call you."

He joined his little band in the hotel bar, although they found it rather quiet and boring there. Knight, not wanting to end the night on a low note, suggested they venture out to a nearby pub called Ulysses. He convinced several of his more adventurous colleagues to come along, insisting that it was only a short walk away.

He led the way, like the pied piper, arm in arm with Li-Hua and Grete. Pearson also decided to tag along, hoping for the chance to watch some soccer. And to Knight's and Pearson's great surprise, Christina Drago went along too. She'd been watching Knight closely all evening and, when she noticed that he'd added Pearson to his entourage, decided that she had to join them. She had really no interest in the Lower Manhattan bar scene, but was worried she might miss something.

A live band was lined up, so there was a ten-dollar cover charge to get in. Knight took care of it for all of them, and they were soon shown to a large round booth. As they returned from the bar with their drinks, Drago skillfully placed herself between Pearson and Knight, without it appearing deliberate.

"Thanks for arranging this, Knight," she said, between sips from her glass of wine.

"I didn't really arrange anything, Christina. Just googled 'Irish bars' and here we are," Knight replied, and quaffed his Guinness.

"Well done, anyway, George. Great idea." Pearson was scanning the bar for a television. "I'll be back in a few minutes, guys. You two play nice," he added mischievously as he left to watch a rerun of a soccer game from the previous weekend.

"What did he mean by that?" Drago asked.

"I guess he meant not to let the silly TV talk about us being rivals spoil the fun," Knight replied with a shrug. "It doesn't bother me. Though I was curious why you blanked me earlier when I tried to chat with you and Gerrard. Did I interrupt some secret plot?"

"No, no, of course not. No. Just Kathryn being Kathryn. You know how she is."

No, I don't actually, Knight thought to himself, *but no matter.*

"Did you enjoy the Wall Street visit?" Drago asked, changing the subject artfully.

"No, not really. That bell ringing was such an anticlimax. Standing around on the trading floor trying to look interested until Grauermann appeared on the balcony with his wife to ring the bell. The little band up there with him, applauding and waving Lassiter flags. The whole thing put me in mind of a South American dictator celebrating his latest election victory. Don't cry for me, Argentina."

"Oh, that's just too cynical, Knight. People made a lot of effort to make all that happen."

"Yeah, I guess. Fair enough. Elliot and his folks did work hard. But you have to agree that was a really boring dinner. Talk about after the Lord Mayor's show, it was totally flat. It felt more like a wake than a celebration."

"I thought it was quite good actually. The speeches were enlightening at least."

"On that, Christina, we'll have to agree to disagree." He finished his beer. "Another drink?"

"No, thanks, I'm OK with this one for now."

He took the order from the rest of the group and wove his way over to the bar to get the next round. As the formal events were over, they could all let loose. The live band came on to play, and the group had quite the craic with some of the other folks in there, mainly tourists and a group of nursing students on a big night out. Toward the end, Knight insisted on strutting around the dance floor. Fortunately, his memory of this spectacle would be a little faded.

The next morning, the crumpled bar tab on his hotel room floor told him two things. One, that they'd left around 3 a.m. And two, that he'd paid for everything, for everyone, all night. Would he ever learn?

He certainly wasn't in great shape. Relieved that he'd had the presence of mind to go to New York on the train and didn't have to face driving home, he slept in, taking advantage of the late checkout the company had arranged. He'd just about collected himself together sufficiently to head for the station by the 3 p.m. checkout deadline. He had hoped to sneak out without anyone seeing him—a plan that failed miserably with not one, not two, but three close encounters.

He was headed down in the elevator when another man stepped aboard. *Oh shit. It's only Daniel freaking Grauermann!* Knight looked like death warmed up, jeans, unshaven. He wanted desperately to disappear into the background. His concern was unnecessary. Grauermann didn't notice him at all, totally lost in his own thoughts, mumbling something to himself over and over. Knight didn't catch it properly. He thought it sounded like "Be strong, be strong, be strong." Grauermann dashed straight out of the elevator and into the bar. If Knight had been fully functioning, he might have thought Grauermann's behavior a little odd, but instead he was just relieved to get away without barfing on his CEO's shoes.

Knight still wasn't in the clear, though. As he checked out, Varella came bouncing by, wearing a blue New York Yankees cap and one of their pinstriped white shirts. Knight remembered that behind his back, Varella was known as "Benny the Ball," after Top Cat's blue-furred friend. In his Yankee uniform, he looked so like the cartoon character, Knight struggled not to laugh out loud. Varella waved very cheerfully. "Can't stop, George, I'm off to watch the Yankees." Benny was going to the ballpark. Knight felt a strange affection for Varella. Like Benny, Ralph wasn't the sharpest cat in the alley, yet you always believed his heart was in the right place.

Knight's pulse settled and he thought he was finally going to escape without actually having to speak to anyone. Then Drago came up behind him at the checkout desk. She was smartly dressed in a business suit, looking very self-possessed with her matching metallic carry-on and briefcase.

"Hey, Knight. Thanks for organizing the trip to Ulysses last night." She smiled. Then with a sparkle in her eyes, she added, "I never knew that Joyce could be so much *fun.*"

She had the distinct advantage: it seemed she could remember everything that had happened, whereas Knight clearly could not. He wasn't thinking straight and assumed the worst. *Who the hell is Joyce? Was she one of the nurses? Oh shit, what have I done?* He suddenly felt very sick.

"OK, thanks, Christina, see you next week," he mumbled.

Then he bolted outside, dragging his case. He made it just in time to throw up in a dumpster in a service alley. Of course, later he realized Drago was making a literary reference to James Joyce and had not intended to upset him. He'd started that book twice and never gotten beyond fifty pages. There was nothing remotely fun in that.

◼

Hours earlier, while Knight had been blissfully sleeping off his hangover, the Board meeting had started with a breakfast buffet. The venue was not the dramatic sun-flooded Stuyvesant Room, but the wood paneled, windowless Morgan Room on the second floor. After the Board members had helped themselves to the fruit, pastries, juice, and coffee, chatting amiably across the room, Hastings called the meeting to order and went over the day's agenda. The morning would be taken up with the usual reports from the various Board committees and completion of formal Board business, such as authorizing the next dividend payment and other financial transactions that required their approval. The afternoon promised to be livelier. There would be a strategic plan presentation to the Board by one of the senior executives. Then the last agenda item was the extension to the CEO's contract. Hastings expected it to be a straightforward rubber stamp exercise, led by the head of the compensation committee, Howard Lyons. They'd be done by 4 p.m. and able to head out early to get their cars to the airport or railway station for their journey home.

With Hastings moving things along briskly, they worked through the morning's business to the prescribed timetable. The Chief Accounting Officer was wheeled in. Pearson reported on HR matters.

In the stuffy confines of the Morgan Room, several of the Board members struggled to remain fully focused through the minutiae toward the end of the morning. There were gaping mouths and even a few snores as they considered the details and then gave approval for three new multibillion-dollar contracts and the one-hundred-million-dollar acquisition of a Hungarian company.

Hastings chaired the meeting, moderating the discussions. Normally Grauermann would be actively involved, explaining his actions, supporting his guys as they presented, occasionally probing them with questions to test their mettle. That morning, he was strangely withdrawn, sullen, preoccupied, so distracted that he scarcely said a word. Hastings had to prompt him to make his formal Chief Executive representations on the new deals.

As the others left to take lunch, Lyons remained in the room and beckoned to Grauermann to do likewise.

"Are you OK, Daniel? You don't seem yourself."

"I'm fine, Howard. Just tired from yesterday."

"Good, good. I thought that must be it. You're not worrying about the, hmm, about the plan, are you?"

"Worried? Why should I be worried? Isobel has assured me that you have it all under control." Grauermann's tone was harsh, contemptuous even.

Lyons, one of the several members added to the Board since Grauermann became CEO, was intimidated by the sharp response. He immediately regretted his show of compassion and could only stutter out, "Oh, sorry, sorry, Daniel. Yes, it's all arranged," as he left the boardroom.

Grauermann did not join the others for lunch. Instead, excusing himself to make an important call, he headed back to his hotel suite, where Isobel was waiting for him. She had ordered some food for them from room service. She took his suit jacket. He slumped into a chair at their round smoked glass dining table, his head in his spidery hands. He looked on the verge of tears.

In contrast, Isobel was overly sunny. She had a guidebook about Budapest and a collection of brochures about cruises on the River Danube. She read brightly from their pages: "Explore four of Europe's most enchanting countries—Hungary, Austria, Germany, and Slovakia— along the storied Danube River. See the range of architectural wonders in Budapest and Bratislava. Sail through the spectacular Wachau Valley and take a tour of the nine-hundred-year-old baroque Benedictine abbey at Melk on this amazing eight-day itinerary."

Her brooding husband lifted his head from his hands and gave her a weak smile.

"They did approve it, didn't they? The Hungarian firm?" she asked, reverting to her normal harsh tone.

"Yes, they approved it. We'll be able to go over there next month. I know you've always wanted to see Budapest," he replied submissively.

"And Vienna, Daniel. And Vienna. Make sure you block off the whole eight days. I don't want any tedious customer or employee events to interrupt us."

"Yes, OK, Isobel. Did you get me a drink?"

"Daniel, are you sure you should? You have a big moment ahead of you."

"Yes, I should. I need a drink. Just one. Take the edge off."

She had anticipated this and had a glass of his favorite scotch ready. Although at some level she perhaps had noticed her husband's growing need to "take the edge off," today was not the day for that to concern her. Needs must when the devil drives.

He drained the scotch in one. His faced flushed as he stabbed dismissively at his Caesar salad. Neither spoke for several minutes. It was an unpleasant, gloomy silence. As the time for him to return to the meeting approached, Isobel attempted to lift the mood.

"How does the early part of the afternoon look? Do you have some interesting sessions to look forward to?"

He sighed. "Yes, we're getting a Latin America update. From Ralph Varella."

"Ralph, I'm glad that he gets his chance to shine. He is one of your favorites. I like him. He helped keep Hastings out of that bell ringing yesterday. Make sure you take care of him."

"Yes, I will. I'll make sure Ralph gets what he deserves. I'll see you later. Say one of your prayers for me."

■

Grauermann returned to the meeting, slipping quietly into his seat, as Hasting brought the session to order. Varella had arrived for his presentation. Hastings greeted him warmly.

"Mr. Ralph Varella, welcome."

"Thank you, Sir Dalton. Hello, everyone."

Despite having the so-called graveyard slot after lunch, Varella was relaxed. He'd presented to the Board several times and felt comfortable. With his mentor, Grauermann, to guide him, he expected a walk in the park. He could not have been more wrong.

"Before I get into the main presentation, I'd just like to give you an update on the Strategic Advisory Council, or L-SAC as we're going to call it. As you know, PSG recommended that we set this up. The first task was to identify the right clients to become members and to select a Chairperson. I'm pleased to tell you that we've secured eight senior clients to join L-SAC. And even better, Jacquelyn Crawford from FRSC has agreed to serve as the first Chair." He paused for effect.

"Oh, that's great news, Ralph. She'll be terrific in L-SAC, I'm sure. Well done," Gerrard enthused. She thought Crawford would be a great ally in pushing some changes at Lassiter.

Varella had briefed Grauermann on Crawford's involvement at his most recent B & P meeting, so Grauermann greeted this news impassively. He was ambivalent to the whole L-SAC idea, but had gone along with it. It was an easy box to tick on the Project Break Out scorecard. Then Varella surprised him with some additional news.

"Thank you, Kathryn. I agree completely. In fact, I had an initial meeting with her last week. She's a big fan of ours. She told me that we had been critical to her success at FRSC. She would like to see us getting more business, strengthening our brand."

"That's interesting, Ralph. Did she have any suggestions for us?" Gerrard was enjoying this unexpected bright spot to the day.

"Yes, she did as a matter fact. Do you want me to cover them now?" he asked no one in particular, but looked to Grauermann for approval.

"Ralph, I think it would be better if you put together a—" Grauermann wasn't prepared to allow Ralph to continue without his prior review.

"Oh yes, please, go ahead, Ralph. That would be very interesting." Gerrard wasn't going to let this be sloughed off to some endlessly unproductive subcommittee.

Varella was trapped. Continue and upset Grauermann, or bail out and alienate Gerrard? His enthusiasm—and perhaps, subconsciously, his new protégé status—got the better of him.

"One of her main recommendations is that we get our name associated with some big events or maybe a sports team. FRSC are big sponsors of the soccer World Cup." Varella avoided eye contact with Grauermann as he answered Gerrard.

"Oh God, not bloody soccer. Or football as I would call it. That's not our cup of tea at all. Wrong sort of people," Hastings interjected. "What about golf? Now that's more our style."

"If I may, Sir Dalton, I'm quite knowledgeable about this. The problem with golf is that it's extremely expensive, and many of our competitors are already involved. We need something different," Gerrard stated authoritatively.

"Well, Ralph, you really have opened up a hornet's nest here, haven't you?" Grauermann said patronizingly. "I think you'd better get on with your scheduled presentation now. We can discuss this another time."

"A professional cycling team," Varella replied to Gerrard, ignoring Grauermann's rebuke. "That's Crawford's recommendation. FRSC has been sponsoring a team for a few years. They've been really successful, and FRSC has gotten great publicity from it. Their contract is up soon and they've decided to do something different. It'd be perfect for us— global, teamwork, high-tech. And cheap too."

"Ralph . . ." Grauermann was getting annoyed with Varella and his premature, ill-considered proposal.

"Oh, I like that idea, Ralph. Lots of potential. Can she put us in touch with them?" Gerrard was on a roll.

"Yes, definitely, Kathryn. She knows them well," Varella enthused.

"I think that's settled, then. We should let Ralph put it all together and brief us at the next meeting. What do you say, Daniel? Are you happy with it?" Gerrard asked.

Grauermann wasn't happy at all. He'd been railroaded. He contemplated shooting the whole idea down in flames there and then. He decided not to make an issue of it. There were other battles to be fought later.

"Yes, I guess I can live with it. Go ahead, Ralph. Just don't expect to see me in spandex anytime soon." He added a touch of humor, sensing it might sweeten the obvious sour taste in his mouth.

He actually didn't object to the cycling team idea. It hit the right note for Lassiter's brand. He also liked Varella, who, as Isobel had pointed out over lunch, was loyal and competent. Yet when he'd heard that the TV pundit had described Varella as his protégé, his long-term successor, it had unnerved him. Varella was blameless for that, but Grauermann didn't want the responsibility of a protégé: someone he would need to nurture, coach, and encourage, a dependent whose success or failure would reflect upon him. Oh no. That game was for fools. Now, Varella had indulged in this show of independence, some might call it insubordination. That was just too much. It was time to put Varella back in his place.

Varella began the planned presentation. He had just moved to his third chart, which portrayed the market share of Lassiter and its major competitors in various regions of the world, when Grauermann interrupted, removing his glasses for added emphasis.

"Ralph?"

Varella was in full flow and didn't immediately hear Grauermann.

"And here we have 16 percent, here we are steady at 12—"

"Ralph, Ralph, RALPH, STOP!!" Grauermann shouted to get his attention.

Varella paused. "Yes, Daniel?"

"This isn't the template you were given."

"Oh, hmm . . . no, it's not, Daniel. I just thought that this was a better format to get this information over."

"It's not your job to choose the template, Ralph."

There was an awkward silence in the room as Varella stood impassively.

"Move on," Grauermann directed, replacing his glasses.

Varella pushed the remote, and the projector moved to his next chart which fortunately for him was to the prescribed corporate template. He was about to move on when Grauermann interrupted him again.

"This chart is too busy. I can't read it. You guys really need to learn how to make charts. Perhaps we need to get you some help. A specialist."

Varella was a little flustered. He'd expected a few softballs from Grauermann to make him look good, not this nitpicking hostility.

"Well, Daniel, this is the standard template. And a specialist graphics guy prepared it. It's just tough to get all this information on a single chart." He gave a shrug, a weak smile, and a sigh, hoping he'd be allowed to move on.

"Ralph, half of your information is wrong anyway. Have you actually checked any of these statistics?" Grauermann continued snidely.

"Yes, of course I've checked it, Daniel."

Varella was trying to remain on track, hoping to settle his boss down, but Grauermann was raging now. The others avoided eye contact with Grauermann. They shuffled their papers and glanced at one another anxiously, embarrassed at the unseemly hectoring.

"Why did you waste our time with this sloppy work?"

Grauermann was flushed, the veins standing out on his neck as he asserted his superiority.

Varella stood quietly at the front of the room and took stock of the situation. He assessed his three options. He could retreat. Wave the white flag. A demeaning *Yes, Daniel, you're right, my bad. I'll fix it for next time* might have rescued the situation and allowed Varella to get through the rest of the presentation unscathed. Or perhaps he could risk pushing back just one more time. Maybe Grauermann was just testing him. It could be a factual retort, calmly explaining the stats. He might even impress the Board members with his foresight. His third option was the boldest, the bravest, the most compelling, a way to free himself from this demeaning charade. Fatally, he took it. He turned the mirror.

"So, Daniel, I need your guidance here as I seem to be making so many mistakes. Are we looking to grow in Latin America or not? You tell me. Do we want to make an acquisition there or not? Where do we stand on LATAM, Daniel?"

Grauermann was taken aback by the response and took a large draw from his mineral water, wishing it were something stronger. He took off his glasses and started to respond.

"Ralph, you know as well as I do. That's something we need to consider—"

"Yes, Daniel, I get it. So these charts, Daniel, do you want to use the standard template or produce something useful?"

"You need to work that out, Ralph. I know how I would present it. I can't tell you how to do everything. You're meant to be a leader here." It was Grauermann who retreated to his safe province of narcissistic sarcasm.

"Fair enough. I'll work it out. Just so I'm absolutely clear, in your definition, can a weakness or a threat apply to the whole industry? Or do they only apply to an individual company?"

By now this interchange was seriously embarrassing the other Board members. Hastings sensed their discomfort and intervened.

"Gentlemen, we are running out of time for this item. Clearly there's some work to do. Why don't we reschedule Ralph for another meeting?"

"Yes, that is a good idea, Sir Dalton," Gerrard concurred and then added sympathetically, "Sorry, Ralph, tough crowd today. At least we got the cycling team sorted out."

"Right, OK, well, thanks. Sir Dalton, Kathryn. I'll work on this and catch you next time."

Varella departed, doing his best to maintain his normal cheery demeanor. Inwardly he was feeling hurt by Grauermann's betrayal and proud of his own resistance. His consolation was that he could get away early enough to catch the last five innings of that Yankees game with his pal Houston. He told Houston that it had all gone well and that he would be invited back. Varella did not yet know, but he would never get the opportunity to present to the Board again, a casualty of his premature status as a protégé, and of a putative ward of a guardian unable to accept that onerous responsibility.

■

With the abrupt curtailment of the presentation, they were ten minutes ahead of schedule. Hastings proposed a brief comfort break before the final agenda item. As the Board members rose to use the restrooms or replenish their drinks, some asked, "What was that all about?" They were perplexed by Grauermann's assault on someone they had previously considered one of his favored sons. Grauermann himself said nothing and left the room brusquely. He made as if to go to the restroom, but instead stepped into the elevator, oblivious of Knight cowering in the corner. He headed down to the ground floor.

"A scotch. Double. No ice," he snapped to the barman.

"Any particular one, sir?"

"No, just make it quick. I've only got a few minutes."

His nerves were fraying. He needed a drink and could not allow Isobel to find out. He downed the whiskey and headed back to the second floor.

He was the last to reenter the boardroom after the break. He took a Dr Pepper from the credenza, sat down, and helped himself to one of the Life Saver mints that were in glass bowls around the tables. Hastings called the meeting to order.

"So, ladies and gentlemen, we come to the final item of the day, the renewal of Daniel's contract as CEO. Howard, you're on point for this."

"Yes, thank you, Dalton." Lyons took a drink from his water very deliberately, glanced at Grauermann, and opened his manila folder. The briefest of eye contact had confirmed that the coup was still on. So close to his defining moment, Grauermann felt his pulse racing beneath his dark suit, and the perspiration rings under his arms soaking his shirt.

"As you know, almost two years ago, Gene Farris resigned and the Board offered Daniel a contract as President and Chief Executive Officer. Dalton Hastings, Sir Dalton now, became our Chairman. It was always our intention that Daniel's contract would be renewed and extended, assuming that the company's results—according to the financial and other operational metrics set by the Board—were satisfactory. I'm pleased to report that those targets have all been met and, in many cases, exceeded. Therefore, in my capacity as head of the compensation committee, I am proposing that Daniel's contract is renewed and extended for an additional five years. You have details of his proposed compensation package in your briefing documents."

Lyons paused as they took a cursory glance through the provisions. It was a typical CEO package: salary, stock options, restricted stock, retirement benefits, use of the corporate jet, dry-cleaning allowance, et cetera, et cetera. All in all, its value was around 350 times the salary of the average Lassiter employee, nothing extravagant.

Hastings asked for any questions. They all shook their heads, appeared content. Hastings expected to close the action with a quick vote of approval. To Hastings' surprise Lyons added, "There is, however, another element to the proposal."

Lyons paused and took a deep breath.

"A group of our major shareholders have requested that in Daniel's new contract we add the Chairman position as well as the President and CEO. Edmund Patten, who as you all know runs Collateral General, our largest shareholder, represented the group. They believe that Daniel's performance has lifted any probationary period concerns and that unifying the roles will lead to quicker decision-making, greater cohesion, and even stronger performance."

Lyons had started strongly, although his voice tailed off toward the end of his speech, betraying his nervousness. He cleared his throat and continued.

"Edmund Patten is available by telephone or, if necessary, will join the meeting if we want to hear more about this request."

There was a stony silence as they processed Lyons's proposal. Several had known it was coming and looked uncomfortably at their briefing packs. For the others, it slowly sank in. If the major institutional shareholders asked for something, the Board had to agree or face a major sell-off of the stock. And if Grauermann was to be the Chairman, what was to become of Hastings? Would he revert to being a regular Board member? By the time they had gotten this far, Lyons was ready with the answer. He passed to each of them copies of a three-page document.

"I'm distributing three things. A revised version of the proposed contract for Daniel, incorporating the Chairman role; the basic terms of an agreement with Sir Dalton to retire from the Board with immediate effect; and a press release announcing the change. Sir Dalton, Robert Livingston and Stewart Pearson are waiting outside to finalize this with you. They'll need to take your Blackberry and your Lassiter laptop, I'm afraid."

Hastings chuckled heartily and masked his shock with a broad grin. He'd not seen this coming. Not for the first time in his career, he was being fired. He read the documents quickly.

"My god. You've fucking thought of everything, you bastards. I'm astonished. Are you all in on this, the whole fucking lot of you?" He learned enough from their averted eyes and body language to know the answer. He was done. He wouldn't have the votes to resist.

"And you, Daniel? I didn't think you had it in you. Congratulations. I guess my work is done here." Hastings gathered his belongings and left the room without protest.

The next morning, the following press release was moved before the opening bell:

LASSITER APPOINTS DANIEL GRAUERMANN TO BE CHAIRMAN, IN ADDITION TO PRESIDENT AND CEO. SIR DALTON HASTINGS TO RETIRE.

Lassiter (NYSE: LAST) today announced that the Board of Directors has appointed Daniel Grauermann to be the Chairman of the Board in addition to his positions as President and CEO. Sir Dalton Hastings will retire from the Board with immediate effect.

"I am honored to be appointed as Chairman," said Grauermann. "After our exceptional performance last year, I am confident that we will continue to build upon the great heritage of our company. With our Project Break Out strategy, we are moving ahead with new products and into new markets." He continued, "I would like to thank Sir Dalton Hastings for his service to the company as a Board member and, for the past two years, as Chairman. I have learned a great deal from him."

"It has been a privilege to work with the Board, the executives, the employees, and the clients at Lassiter," Sir Dalton Hastings commented. "I'm pleased to pass on the chairmanship to Daniel Grauermann and feel sure that, under his leadership, exciting times lie ahead."

CHAPTER SEVEN

Wheels within Wheels

June 2008

Knight saw some of the nicer parts of the City of Brotherly Love on a Sunday in early June: the Benjamin Franklin Parkway, Fairmount Park, Lemon Hill, and Manayunk. They were all on the route of the Philadelphia International Cycling Championship. As it was one of the biggest cycling events held in the US, all the top cycling teams were there.

He was puzzled how Lassiter had gotten involved in the sport. Out of the blue, they had become the main sponsors of a cycling team for the new season. The team was based in Germany, although the riders were from many countries—Belgium, Spain, America, France. The top rider was an Australian. The team was in the US for a spell of training that would culminate in this race. Lassiter had arranged some serious hospitality at the event. Several of Knight's customers from the area decided they wanted to go, so he had to be present. Beforehand, he hadn't fancied it at all. He wasn't into cycling and thought the race would be boring as hell, like a NASCAR event he'd attended. In his mind, NASCAR was nothing but cars driving round and round in a concrete bowl, round and round, crash, stop, catch up, round and round. Talk about BORING. This cycling event proved to be infinitely better. He had quite an adventure, to say the least.

It was a beautiful day, hot and sunny, which brought out a huge crowd. The TV news crews were reporting that there were over one hundred thousand spectators around the course. Some of the areas were jam-packed, especially the steep half-mile climb in Manayunk that had been dubbed "the Manayunk Wall." While it wasn't quite the Alps or the Pyrenees of the Tour de France, the riders had to get out of the saddle to get up this stretch. The spirited crowd helped, roaring the athletes on. As the day drew on, many of the spectators on that stretch became the worse for wear. All the bars were open, some street vendors were selling cans of beer out of big coolers, and one group of fans had kegs out on the sidewalk. One TV reporter put it euphemistically, "There's a spirited and passionate crowd on the Manayunk Wall."

Knight got to experience it all firsthand. As he arrived at the Lassiter marquee, which occupied much of a small park on the side of the Benjamin Franklin Parkway, Zach Elliot grabbed him.

"Hey, George, glad you could make it. I hope you don't mind. I've put you down to ride in the team director's car."

"Oh, OK, Zach. How does that work then?" Knight replied.

"Next time it comes back round, you just hop in the back as quick as you can. The car follows the guys round the course."

"Right, count me in. I'm game. In for a penny, in for a—"

"Great. Hansi Olsen, the team director, will tell you what's going on. It should be exciting. Enjoy."

Ten minutes later the car, a station wagon decked out in Lassiter colors, came screeching to a halt by the marquee. Knight's attention was drawn to how crowded the car looked. There were spare bikes on the roof and spare wheels in the back. How on earth was he going to get in there? He was so focused on examining the car that he forgot to jump in.

"COME ON! COME ON! We can't wait all fucking day!" a voice barked out of the car.

Knight scrambled in, and the car shot off before he'd had chance to sit down and get a seat belt on.

"I'm sorr—" Knight started to speak to the guy who had shouted at him. Knight guessed that it was the team director, Olsen.

"Zip it. Your job is keep out of the fucking way. Don't touch anything, and don't say anything," he ordered.

Knight wasn't going to argue. He'd heard that Olsen had been in the Danish army. Special Forces. He could tell. He looked as hard as nails. Knight made himself as comfortable as he could. The car was hot, cramped with all the spare gear, and had a strong smell of oil and rubber. Knight felt sick in his claustrophobic little cell, zipping through the streets, weaving in and out of the tail-enders.

Olsen didn't speak to him again while the race was on. He appeared to resent Knight's presence. Knight guessed that sharing the car with the sponsor's guests was just something the team had to do, part of the deal.

And anyway, Olsen was focused on the race, barking out instructions on his walkie-talkie or screaming at the car driver, "Keep up! Catch up! Slow the fuck down!"

Knight found it exciting on the big wide stretches. But in those narrow streets around the Wall it was scary. He was flustered, shaky, sweating like a pig. He felt sure they were going to hit someone in the crowd or knock one of the TV cameramen off his motorbike. He started to appreciate the security of his little cell after a while, glad to be in the back seat.

He got almost thirty minutes in the car, once round the circuit. Then he was unceremoniously hauled out, and the next passenger was quickly bundled in and off they charged again. He was happy it was over. It was fun like a roller coaster is fun . . . Fun like he didn't want to try it ever again. How anyone stood that for three or four hours he would never know.

■

After that, things took another bizarre twist. Knight needed some peace and quiet to wear off his adrenaline rush. He was sitting by himself in the corner of the marquee, in the shade, minding his own business.

He'd even turned down a beer in favor of water—most unlike him. He picked at his food, the typical cold meats and different salads served at these events. He still wasn't feeling too good and allowed himself to doze off for a while. As Knight slumbered, one of the waiters quietly took his plate.

Meanwhile there was a bit of a commotion near the entrance to the marquee. It appeared that someone had collapsed. A small crowd had gathered round. Elliot was waving frantically to try to attract the attention of the paramedics out on the course. The medics revived the patient. He was soon sitting up and drinking some water. They helped him up and brought him over to Knight's table.

"George, would you mind if we took this chair?"

Knight woke up with a start. "Yes, of course. Go ahead, Zach. What's the problem?"

"Oh, I don't think it's anything serious. He's just fainted from the heat."

Knight came to his senses, a rude awakening. *Shit, it's G-man.*

He rushed over to the commotion, and his mind flashed back to his earlier encounter with the CEO in the New York hotel's elevator. This time, though, it was Grauermann who was in a dreadful state. He was red-faced, flustered, and perspiring profusely, his thick thatch decidedly ruffled. Part of his problem was that he was way overdressed. He was wearing a black suit with a white shirt. His red tie had been loosened by the medics and now hung around his neck. He had certainly prepared more for an air-conditioned box than this baking tent.

Knight handed him some iced water. "Here you are, Mr. Grauermann. How are you feeling now?"

"Thanks. I still feel terrible. It was that car ride. Made me a sick as a dog."

Knight's realization broadened. Of course, it was Grauermann who had been bundled into the director's car next. That trip had made Knight woozy, and he was wearing shorts and a Lassiter polo shirt. No wonder Grauermann had fainted in his heavy suit.

"Mr. Grauermann, it might be a good idea to take your jacket off. It'll help you to cool down. We don't want you to faint again."

"No, that wouldn't be good. Thanks," Grauermann replied painfully.

"Hey, Zach, Mr. Grauermann's still overheated. Do you think we could get him a Lassiter polo shirt or something a bit cooler?"

"Oh yes, great idea, George. I'll get right on it."

Elliot was back quickly with a shirt.

"Mr. Grauermann, you can use the RV out the back to change. It has air-conditioning there, so you'll be able to cool off."

Grauermann didn't say anything, but followed Elliott out of the marquee.

Ten minutes later, Grauermann returned looking a lot more composed. Knight stood up to introduce himself.

"That looks better. I'm George. George Knight. I guess you knew that."

"Of course I know who you are," Grauermann replied, in a tone that was both dismissive and embarrassed. "I'll be OK now. Thank you." He paused. "The race seems to be going well." Clearly he wanted to put the fainting episode behind him.

They talked briefly about the race and, as Grauermann seemed settled, Knight offered to get him some food from the buffet. Grauermann accepted gratefully, and Knight brought him over a healthy full plate. As Grauermann ate, Elliott came over and took a seat.

"Excuse me, Daniel, do you think that you'll still be able to do the TV slot?"

He shrugged his shoulders.

Elliott continued, "I hope you can still do it. You know that the race is being covered live on national TV. As one of the main race sponsors, we get to give an interview to promote the team and the company to one of the ABC reporters during the race. It's a great opportunity and—"

Grauermann interrupted him, "Yes, Zach, I know all that. And let there be no misunderstanding. I'm only here to give this goddamn interview."

"I know. We're all excited. You'll be a great spokesperson to represent the company."

"That's all well and good, Zach, but this has been one issue after another. You weren't clear about where the interview would take place. I was under the impression that it would be recorded at the local ABC studios. That's why I was in my business suit, not dressed casually like Knight here." He smiled mockingly at Knight, emphasizing his discomfort, his unhappiness with Elliot, and his general disenchantment with the whole thing.

"Then you spring on me that it's set to take place trackside—and live, as the race goes on in the background. Outside and live was not what I bargained for, believe you me."

"I'm so terribly sorry for that, Daniel. Things were changing with the TV company and we didn't get the full story until this morning. I hope you can be flexible."

"I could just about get over all that. But that ride in the car? Another one of your spur-of-the-moment things?"

"Yes, I thought it would help you get into the feel of things. George did it too. You enjoyed it, didn't you, George?"

Knight didn't want to throw Elliot under the bus so replied with typical British understatement, "Yes, Zach. It was certainly interesting."

"Well, I absolutely hated it, Zach. It was too fast, too cramped, too hot, too smelly, too scary . . . and two laps. Why did Olsen make me do two laps for Chrissake?"

He was still upset with his shabby treatment. Despite appearing to have cooled off in his new polo shirt, his temperature started to rise again. He decided that he would not do the interview. He told Elliot to find Mrs. Grauermann and then get the driver to take them home, *immediately*.

"Oh, no. It's due in twenty minutes, Daniel. Please reconsider," Elliot pleaded.

"No, my mind is made up. You'll just have to find someone

else, preferably the most senior Lassiter exec around," Grauermann replied emphatically.

"Well, I think that's Christina Drago. She's a VP, and she's here somewhere with some of her clients. I'll try to find her. I hope we have time," Elliot replied with relief.

In a split second, Knight processed a whole bunch of thoughts.

Drago was a real career woman—very focused, sharp. But she could be a little uptight and intimidating. Not made for TV like him! Would she stand back and let him do this if the situation were reversed? Nope, definitely not. Besides, this was the perfect opportunity, just like Pearson had said back in Japan, for him to network with the senior execs and do some media events. He'd be killing two birds with one stone.

So he interjected confidently, "No need, Zach. Don't interrupt Christina if she has guests with her. I'll do it. I'm a VP now too. I can handle it. I did something similar at the Soccer World Cup a few years back." He embellished his Tokyo experience with the BBC a little.

Grauermann's anger evaporated. Although he held very different views of his two potential understudies—admiration for Drago, contempt for Knight—Grauermann really didn't care who gave the interview, so long as it wasn't him. Knight was right there, in the right place at the right time; and besides, if he screwed it up, as he most likely would, then his flaws would be there for all to see.

"OK, fair enough. Knight can do it. Zach, make sure you tell him how to handle it. I'm sure they'll love his *British accent*." He made a sneering attempt at a British accent himself as he said this, failing miserably.

Elliot had to go with what he had. He started pouring into Knight's ear all the points they wanted him to make in the interview, along with a few pointed comments about how important it was, how seriously he should take it, that it wasn't time for any fooling around. A few minutes later, Knight was escorted by a couple of ABC production assistants from the marquee to the spot on the track where they were filming the interviews.

The handlers were young and very fussy. They asked him if he needed a cold drink, anything. He was thinking more about the important
things, chief among them his appearance. He was glad he'd shaved that
morning, which was unusual for a Sunday. Elliot had found him a fresh
polo shirt. Should he wear his cap? Sunglasses? He hoped he hadn't gotten sunburned. He called home and told them he was going to be on
TV and to set the DVR. Surprisingly, he was completely relaxed about
the interview, despite Elliot's lecture. The reporter was the local ABC station weather correspondent, so Knight didn't expect the in-depth grilling
you'd find on *Panorama* or *60 Minutes*. It also helped that he had scarcely
any time to think about it.

With a quick "Testing, one, two, three" sound check, he was live
on national TV. The interviewer made it easy. She served up the Dor-
othy Dix questions, and he smashed home the Lassiter "brand value"
answers. He got all the buzz words in at least once in the three-minute
slot. "International team," "individual riders," "team success," "hi-tech,"
"Lassiter brand," "innovation," "pragmatic" . . . blah, blah, bloody blah.
The timing was great too, as the leading group, featuring several of the
Lassiter riders, sped by as they filmed. The only mild disappointment
was that the interviewer was immediately off to her next piece, so he
missed sharing his "How was that for you, darling?" analysis with her.

He walked back to the Lassiter marquee by himself. The pre-in-
terview attendants had disappeared. For a brief moment, he felt rather
deflated, his Andy Warhol moment evidently over. As he replayed the
interview in his head, he was very pleased with himself. He thought he'd
done a half-decent job. When he got back to the marquee, the reaction
confirmed his assessment. Quite a crowd had gathered to watch the interview on the TVs set up for people to follow the race. He got a round
of applause and a lot of "Great job, George" comments from the Lassiter
folks and their guests.

"Fantastic, George. You got all the right plugs in for the Lassiter
brand." Elliott was giddy with excitement. "I've got to hand it you, you

really surprised me. That's the best PR piece I've ever seen a Lassiter exec deliver."

"Never in doubt, Zach."

"Can I get you a beer to celebrate?"

"Yes, why not? Thanks, Zach."

Knight sat down to relax in his new exalted status. To his surprise, Grauermann and his wife were still in the marquee. They had a table in the corner to themselves. They didn't join the celebration.

"Who is that, Daniel?" Isobel asked her husband.

"That's George Knight," Grauermann said coldly.

"I recognize that name. Have I met him before?"

"No. You were meant to. He didn't show up for that dinner at the golf course, remember?"

"I do remember now. Such an insult. Now he's the center of attention here. My goodness, you need to get a grip on these people, Daniel," she carped. "Where's our driver? I want to leave."

"I just need a word with him. Knight. He did do the TV interview for me. I should thank him."

"Thank him?" She scowled. "It's him who should be thanking you for giving him the opportunity."

Grauermann crossed the floor to join Knight and his fan club.

"George, I had a change of heart and stayed to watch your interview. You did well. I couldn't have done it much better myself. And it's good for the company's image that it was an up-and-coming employee. Thank you again for stepping in at short notice."

"Oh, that's OK, Mr. Grauermann. I quite enjoyed it," Knight replied modestly.

He was flattered with all the attention, yet he wasn't enjoying the moment; his mind was elsewhere. Something wasn't right. Perhaps he sensed that Grauermann's kind words were just a facade of politeness, disguising irritation and envy; perhaps he sensed that Grauermann could have done the interview just fine, and that his earlier meltdown was totally unnecessary; perhaps he sensed that he had inadvertently broken a golden rule—a maxim from Sun Tzu for the ambitious and career-minded, to never, ever, outshine the master; probably he knew it was all of the above. Meanwhile, Grauermann rejoined his wife and they slipped away quietly with their driver, their departure either unnoticed or ignored.

■

Ninety minutes later, Lassiter won the team event, with number-one rider Dusty Rhodes taking the individual first place. The team got up on the podium to receive their trophies and winners' checks from the governor of Pennsylvania. Then they did the typical big champagne-spraying routine. It was only a small crowd, without the same pizzazz as a Formula 1 event, yet it was exciting for Knight to be part of it.

After the presentations the team went over to the marquee. It had gotten very crowded. The Lassiter folks, who had only turned out because they had to, and their guests, who were here just to enjoy the day in the sun, had become die-hard Team Lassiter fans. Knight smiled to himself. *What's that phrase? Success has many fathers, failure is an orphan child.* Everyone wanted a piece of the glory. The Marketing team had set up a long trestle table draped with a big Lassiter banner. All of the riders and the director, Hansi Olsen, were seated behind the table in a row. Their new fans queued up politely and moved down the line as the riders signed autographs on caps and shirts and posed for photos.

As Knight joined the hero worshippers, the Dane introduced himself graciously, "Hi, George. I'm Hansi. Thanks for riding with us today. You brought us luck."

Knight was a little wary. He didn't want another earful. Olsen had been downright nasty before.

"Yes, thanks. Congratulations."

"Did you enjoy the ride? We had a great day."

Olsen was a completely different guy. Quite charming. Knight assumed his mood had changed for the better because his team had won all of the top prizes in the race. He was obviously really proud of them.

"Was it a good event for you and your guests?" Olsen continued with a huge smile.

"Yes, I enjoyed it. It's been quite an eye-opener for me, Hansi."

"Well, we certainly appreciate you being here. Lassiter is a great sponsor for us."

They chatted for a while. Olsen explained the history of the team, the different roles of the riders, the race tactics, their training regimen. Best of all, he gave Knight a set of their race gear—the spandex shirt, shorts, and socks, and a smart jacket. Knight put the jacket on right away. He didn't see himself getting a lot of use out of the cycling gear. Maybe he'd give it to a deserving charity as a silent auction prize.

The Aussie rider, Dusty Rhodes, was the star of the show. He'd won the race, so he deserved to be the center of attention. Yet there was something else about him too. All eyes were glued to him. Knight sensed that he'd still be the star if he'd come last, or fallen off. Hansi introduced them and they had a short conversation and had a photo taken together— Rhodes toned, tanned, and triumphant, and Knight happily basking in reflected glory. With that, Knight decided he'd better head home. It was back to the grindstone on Monday. Once in his car, he called Ball and recounted every detail of his exciting day.

"That's the news from Philadelphia tonight, Dunc. I'll definitely do these cycling events again. I had a thrill ride, acquired a cool new jacket, appeared on TV, and bailed out the G-man."

"Sounds marvelous, George. All in all, not a bad day's work for a Sunday."

CHAPTER EIGHT

A Twin Set and the Girls

February 2010

Following the success of the cycling event, Knight had settled into a nice steady rhythm at work. There had been a lot of changes at Lassiter. He had a new boss, Julie Dreiser. He liked her. She was very experienced and seemed to know what she was doing. She let him get on with things and didn't hassle him too much, except when she was under the gun from HQ. He continued to be successful and became a key member of Dreiser's team. She entrusted him with greater levels of freedom and responsibility. With that, she also set an expectation that he get more involved in the company's community work. He'd always liked doing that sort of thing. He'd done walks, gone go-kart racing, and even flown in a tiny little helicopter along the coast of England one weekend. That had been fun and scary at times. Now he was really busy with his job and family activities. He wasn't very enthusiastic at the idea of more time away.

Dreiser set him straight during his annual appraisal meeting.

"Look, George, this is American corporate community service, a different animal completely. None of that action man bravado. You don't actually do much. For appearances' sake, you go to a few meetings each year. Crucially, though, you sign a big fat check from the company."

"Yeah, I get it, Julie. The bigger the check, the more the company is featured in the charity's—sorry, I really must master this American language, the nonprofit's promotional literature, and the higher the class of award we get from them at the end of the year."

"Bingo. Maybe twenty-five thousand gets you a bronze plaque. Fifty thousand a silver. One hundred thousand merits a gold plaque and induction into their national hall of fame. And, George, bear in mind that you are also expected to make a sizable personal contribution."

"Yeah, and I'll probably spend a few thousand at the obligatory annual silent auction too."

"Probably. Don't be too cynical about it, George. Remember these organizations all do great work. Get out there and give the Lassiter brand a real boost."

Accepting his boss's coaching, he searched for a worthy cause to support. He attended the fundraising meetings for the local Shakespeare festival, but soon dropped out of that one. It wasn't that he was a philistine—he actually had a far greater appreciation for the Bard than most—the meetings were just too much ado about nothing. He really didn't enjoy the cloying, pretentious talk-fests for wealthy retired people, all very affected, and, more importantly, the scant networking value. The cause that he chose to support was the Childhood Economic Literacy Foundation, a group that offered training programs on economics and financial literacy for kids. Knight hit it off right away with Kenneth Stone, the president, who ran the foundation full-time. He was a real larger-than-life character. He'd been in the role for years and knew everyone in the area, and was still really enthusiastic. He loved the organization and its mission, and his passion was infectious.

Knight was soon making an impact at CELF. He did the expected things, like providing funding from Lassiter and going to all the meetings. He also volunteered to go into schools to teach some of the classes. That was great fun, teaching basic economics to third graders, or helping the high schoolers prepare for work. At an early session, he got a question from one of them: What did he do? He explained in typical business speak—he had responsibility for this, was accountable for that and so on. The kids' faces were blank. The same questioner replied, "OK, that's great. What do you actually *do*, though?" Then it dawned on him that she was looking for a physical answer. The best he could come up with was that he went to meetings, talked on the telephone a lot, and used his computer. His seven-year-old inquisitor was far from impressed.

With such a broad involvement, when it came round to looking for a new chairperson for the CELF board, Knight was the ideal fit. He didn't need asking twice. He was delighted to take it on. He made sure that Dreiser knew about it too, earning himself some more brownie points and a "maturing well" comment in his next appraisal.

It was through CELF that he experienced one of the most bizarre evenings of his whole life. Knight had been in some surreal spots and a few scrapes, but really, this was a collectors' item.

Each year, the organization held a fundraising event based around a Monopoly game. A spate of themed Monopoly sets came out one year, and they decided to try to ride that wave. The foundation designed a board around the local area and charged companies to get their logos on it to sponsor the properties. Then CELF charged the same people a fortune to book a table at the event, enjoy a little food and wine, and play CELFopoly with their guests. It worked a treat and raised a lot of money.

Of course, no event like that could go without an auction of some kind. CELF arranged both a silent one—with the usual lineup of sports tickets, spa vouchers, and baskets of goodies—and a live one with a professional auctioneer. He took a cut of the proceeds on live auction items, so he was highly motivated to drive up the bidding. He got a bonus if he collected over twenty thousand dollars.

Like the silent auction, the live auction offered the regular items—a week at the beach, rounds of golf at some prestigious course. It also featured some more unusual things, one of which was Knight—or more accurately, his services as a chef. Knight would make dinner for eight at the winner's house. He'd bring all the food and some good wine. Stone was included in the package too as a waiter, washer-upper, and general entertainer. Knight had become a pretty good cook, especially when he took the time and trouble to prepare something special for a dinner party. It was a good prize, especially as it included the wine. Knight and Stone got up on the stage in their aprons and chef's hats, hamming it up to get the bidding going. They were the last item of the night. They'd expected to get maybe four or maybe five hundred. It was more for fun than anything else.

They were very pleasantly surprised when their culinary skills proved so popular that they provoked a bidding war between two ladies who were at the same table. The bidding got really intense, as both women seemed determined to win. There was no fun in it for them. Their faces were set hard and their bidder's paddles shot up aggressively each time they made a new bid. Five hundred, five fifty, six hundred. The bidding cruised quickly up to one thousand dollars. By this point, all the other bidders had dropped out, leaving it to them.

"We need to keep up the interest. Work it, guys, work it," the auctioneer prompted. Knight and Stone did another little prance around the stage and then the bidding was off again.

"Eleven hundred."

"Twelve hundred."

"Who will give me thirteen hundred? Thirteen hundred for this fantastic evening of entertainment from these gorgeous young men?"

The paddles were going up a little slower now, and the auctioneer had to wring the bids out of them. Eventually he coaxed $1,500 from one of them at the "going three times" count. The auctioneer did some mental arithmetic and realized that he was still a little short of his twenty-thousand-dollar bonus target.

"Will you guys do a doubleheader?" he whispered to his two chefs.

Neither of them understood what he meant, but bowled along by the excitement, they agreed enthusiastically.

"So, folks, as this item has proved so attractive, we've decided to make it twice as good. The package will now include two dinners.

George here"—Knight did a little twirl—"will be the chef at the first. And Ken"—Stone bowed—"at the second. They'll bring all the food and the wine. You get to entertain your friends twice. Who will start the bidding at three thousand dollars?"

If the auctioneer expected the two ladies to go back at it, he had made a bad call. They kept their paddles down and looked less than pleased at the turn of events. The auctioneer kept working it for a while.

"Come on, folks. Where have you big spenders gone? This is a once-in-a-lifetime opportunity to enjoy restaurant-quality food in the comfort of your home . . . not just once, but twice."

Unfortunately, it seemed that his ploy wasn't going to work; there were no takers for the doubleheader. He made one last appeal, seemingly rather resigned to failure.

"Right, folks. This is the last call. Someone bid me the three thousand for the two or we'll close the auction on the fifteen hundred with the lady at table six."

He pointed to the lady holding the $1,500 bid. She perked up with a triumphant smile while her rival looked even more annoyed. Then, just at the last second before he banged his gavel, the guy who was sitting between the two ladies stood up, raised his paddle, and shouted, "I'm in. We'll take the two. Hit me up for the three grand."

Knight belatedly recognized him. It was Conrad Konetski. He was on the CELF board. He was senior partner with Doolittle Associates, a leading firm of headhunters, or "executive search consultants" as they preferred to be known. Each year, Konetski wrote a nice big check on behalf of his company, but didn't do much else for the organization. When Knight had first met him, he'd thought, *Great guy, full of energy.* More recently, Knight had written Konetski off as a bit of a jerk because he never responded to invitations and would go months without attending a meeting. Then Konetski would turn up to one, full of ideas, suggesting he would do this and that, set up something with these people and those people. And then they'd not hear from him again for months. With no follow-up, he was an awful communicator, a common characteristic of his profession.

The auctioneer quickly brought things to an end and, to a big round of applause, announced with great satisfaction that with that last bid, they had raised over twenty-one thousand dollars from the live auction and around forty-five thousand from the whole evening. It was a great return. Knight and Stone thanked the delighted fast talker and then had a quick chat with Konetski. They learned that the two ladies in the bidding war were his wife, Elise, and her almost identical twin sister, Kara. It was Kara who had been about to win the single dinner. Konetski had decided to buy the doubleheader in an effort to keep the peace between the two of them. Three grand seemed a heavy price to pay, although it was going to a good cause. They arranged the first dinner at Konetski's house in a couple of weeks.

Perhaps Knight should have realized that it was going to be a strange evening when about a week before, Konetski called him to say that they hadn't been able to get all of the other guests they'd expected for the dinner. He invited Knight to bring his wife along and said that he was also going to ask Stone to do the same. Knight offered to postpone and rearrange for a better weekend. Konetski wasn't having any of it and insisted they went ahead.

So on the momentous evening, the Knights headed over to Konetski's place. It was enormous, a cross between a Disney castle and a Courtyard by Marriott hotel. A long way out in the mushroom-growing country too. Knight preferred fewer square feet, a shorter ride to work, and no unpleasant smells, but wasn't fully Americanized yet. Knight and Stone and their wives met up outside the house where they'd parked their cars. They lugged the large coolers filled with the food and wine up to the door.

Knight pressed the door chime and immediately the door opened. Elise met them. She was dressed in a pair of torn black spandex leggings, a green camisole, and old tennis shoes, and had her hair tied up in a headscarf. She was flustered and sweating heavily. She flung the door open, thrust a large plastic bowl in Knight's hand, and said, "Welcome. I'm dealing with puke here."

She rushed off back inside the house. Knight was assaulted by the combined punch of disinfectant and vomit in the bowl. A child was bawling in the background somewhere. After a minute or so of standing in the hall not knowing quite what to do with themselves, Stone suggested that they head to the kitchen. They found their way there and discovered the source of the problem. A girl, maybe around two years old, was sat in a high chair screaming continuously while her mother was mopping the floor around her.

"Ahh, there you are. Are you just going to stand there? Give me that bowl," Elise ordered, as Knight looked on with a typical male aversion to such a scene. He didn't like the look of this at all. "Auctioned as a chef" had a bit of panache to it, Gordon Ramsay eat your f'ing heart out. But domestic help, particularly child puke cleaner-upper, was not something he'd signed up for, three thousand dollars or no three thousand dollars. Instead the two men busied themselves unpacking the groceries while their bemused wives helped Elise to settle her daughter down.

All the while, another girl, probably seventeen or eighteen, sat at the kitchen counter playing with her iPhone. She had lank unnaturally black hair, heavy black eye makeup, and badly chipped black fingernails and wore a My Chemical Romance T-shirt.

"Are you a goth or an emo?" Knight asked her.

She mumbled a "Duh, goth" reply, barely lifting her head from her texting, Facebooking, and instant-messaging marathon. Knight assumed that she must be the eldest kid and that the screaming two-year-old was some "drunk and we forgot the contraceptive" accident. He was reminded that even the lead singer of My Chemical Romance admitted that "Teenagers scare the living shit out of me."

He discovered later that she was actually the babysitter. The cheek of it. Knight had to admire her negotiating skills: she was getting paid ten dollars an hour to text her friends. Apparently, babysitting did not involve any form of actual childcare, and definitely no cleaning up.

Elise finally got her daughter to calm down, and the toddler soon fell fast asleep. Her relieved mother carried her off upstairs, with goth girl following ponderously behind, still texting feverishly. The amateur chefs and their wives got on with preparing the dinner, assuming that the drama was over. They'd all been embarrassed by their kids or their own overreaction to them at some point. Things seemed to be returning to normal.

Without any of them really noticing the time slipping by, it got to 8 p.m. and they were still in the kitchen. They hadn't seen anything more of Elise. Konetski hadn't made an appearance at all. They were also expecting another couple to make up the numbers. Stone went on a reconnaissance mission. He found the dining room, with the table beautifully set for eight, yet no sign of anyone else. Back in the kitchen, Knight decided to open a bottle of white wine, and they sat at the breakfast bar. Stone told one of his more entertaining anecdotes. They'd all heard it several times before, but it was worthy of another listen. Outwardly they were unconcerned, although Knight was beginning to feel uneasy, as were the others. It was quite bizarre, surreal, as if they were trespassers on the *Mary Celeste*.

They were starting to get seriously concerned when finally, around eight thirty, the circus sprang to life again. First they heard a car roar up to the house, the driver slamming on the brakes on the gravel driveway. Then Konetski came bounding inside, closely followed by his sister-in-law, Kara. They hadn't expected her to be there.

Konetski dashed into the kitchen and addressed himself to no one in particular.

"I'm so sorry for keeping you waiting, guys. We've been playing golf and things dragged on at the club."

"That's fine, Con. We'll be ready when you are."

"Great, thanks, George. We'll change quickly and be back down for dinner soon. Sorry again." He rushed off upstairs.

As they left, Elise returned. She'd changed into some low-waist designer jeans, and a very low-cut white top that displayed her ample cleavage. Fully made up, and wearing abundant jewelry, she'd had quite the transformation. She stood with them in the kitchen, grabbed a glass of wine, and joined in the conversation without making any mention of the earlier incident. They let sleeping dogs lie, steering clear of the late arrival of her husband, and asked her about the evening ahead.

"Who are the other guests, Elise?" Carole Knight asked.

"They'll only be seven of us, Carole. My sister, Kara, is the seventh. Unfortunately she'll be 'unaccompanied,'" Elise replied with an air quotes gesture.

That killed the conversation stone dead. Elise flushed and was clearly embarrassed by it all. It begged lots of questions. They were all wondering why her sister would be solo. Had Kara been stood up? Her familiarity with the house when she came in, dropping her golf bag and heading upstairs without pause, suggested someone who lived there, rather than a guest. Knight was also concerned with the practical things—should he still cook all the lamb chops? What should he do with the extra mousse and pudding? They kept their questions to themselves to maintain the awkward silence. Elise smiled a helpless, resigned smile and poured herself another glass of the Riesling.

To get things moving, Stone plated up the mousse and suggested that they head into the dining room. They took their seats and made some lame attempt to engage Elise in a conversation about the table decorations—"Such attractive chargers"—but her attention was elsewhere. The room fell silent again. Knight was about to suggest that they just call it a night and rearrange, when Konetski bounced into the dining room. His hair was still wet from the shower and he had changed into jeans and a very snazzy open-neck dress shirt with a paisley pattern in the collar and cuffs.

He was full of congeniality.

"Welcome, all of you, to my home. It's great to have you all here.

Doesn't the table look fabulous?" He walked around, greeting everyone. He shook hands eagerly with Knight and Stone, gave Carole and Amy a kiss. His abundant aftershave was a pleasant change to the disinfectant smell that still lingered in the air.

"Can I replenish everyone's glasses?" He poured from the second bottle of white wine. He did not speak to his wife, or even acknowledge her presence. She sat there impassively as he took center stage.

Kara waltzed into the room a few minutes later. She also had wet hair and had changed into a pair of white culottes and a navy-blue T-shirt. She'd put on a little subtle makeup and seemed more natural and relaxed than her sister. In fact, for near-identical twins, they couldn't have created a more different impression. Pantomime dame and ingenue. Kara took her seat and, unlike Konetski, apologized for keeping them waiting, opening the conversation with a question about the menu. They started on the food and engaged in some gentle chatter, the latest family news, and the housing market, that sort of thing. As Stone cleared the plates and Knight went to the kitchen to finish off the chops, it looked like they were now finally set to enjoy a normal, polite dinner party.

As they returned a few minutes later with the main course, Konetski was holding court on his golf round.

"Kara and I were playing together in a club tournament today. We did quite well, didn't we?" He winked at his sister-in-law. They continued to relive their afternoon.

"Yes, at one point we thought we might win, didn't we, Con?" Kara added.

"We ended up in third place. Not bad, though."

"We played some good golf. Con hit such a great drive on the tenth."

"And your chip on the thirteenth was awesome. We make such a great team, Kara."

The mutual admiration society continued as Knight served the chops and Stone poured everyone some of the red wine. Meanwhile, Elise was still silent, and started to roll her eyes and make childish sneering faces. Then, as Konetski paid Kara another compliment, out of the blue, Elise exclaimed, "Oh for God's sake, why don't you just fuck her on the table? Right here, right now? Or did you just do that in the shower?"

Knight almost choked on a lamb chop. Stone spurted red wine over his plate. After the outburst, Elise dashed from the table, tearfully clutching her napkin. Konetski and Kara fell silent, avoiding eye contact with anyone. Their body language suggested that there was some truth to the accusation. Knight couldn't take any more. He stood up.

"Con, I think it's time we were leaving. We'll come back tomorrow to pick up our things."

"No, George. I won't hear of it. Please stay. Let's finish the great food. Don't take any notice of Elise. She's not feeling well. There's been too much going on. Stay here. Please don't go. It will all be OK. She'll be back soon."

He left to find his wife. The visitors should really have ignored him and left. Yet they were too polite to cause offense, or perhaps secretly too inquisitive to find out how this drama would unfold, so they remained in the dining room. Stone threw out a question about the golf round, and now it was Kara's turn to be part of a conversation, but with all of her thoughts elsewhere.

Konetski and Elise returned a few minutes later. She had stopped crying, although her eyes were very red. Knight sensed she seemed a little spaced out.

"I think she's hit the Prozac," Knight whispered to his wife.

Elise settled back in her seat and resumed her dinner without a word, like nothing had happened. Konetski apologized for the interruption. The visitors were still in a state of shock, none of them willing to take the risk of launching a conversation that could spark another scene. They finished the course with only their host's repeated praise for the excellent food interrupting the silence.

Knight returned to the kitchen to finish the puddings. It had been a very tough job with all of the coming and goings, although they turned out well. He served them with some honey and lavender ice cream. They were, by his own modest estimation, pretty darn delicious. He was very proud of them. Much to his disappointment, none of his paying customers ate one.

He brought them in and tried to lift the mood.

"And now, I present the pièce de résistance."

He was wasting his breath. Konetski was talking on his cell phone.

"So sorry, guys. I've got to take this call. Important business. I'll be back shortly." He left the room. They did not see him again.

Kara made her excuses too.

"I'm going to call it a night too. I'm feeling very tired from the golf and I'll head to bed. Thanks for a great meal. I'm really looking forward to the second one."

That left only Elise. Dear Elise, their medicated hostess, who was now fast asleep, face down on one of those beautiful chargers. Carole tried to wake her, get her to go to bed, but she was out for the count.

Knight didn't know whether to laugh or cry. Or scream. Getting out of there quickly was the general consensus. They loaded up their cooking utensils, popped four of the puddings back into a cool box, grabbed the unopened wine—waste not, want not—and headed for the door. They did one last check on Elise. There was no waking her. No sign of Konetski or Kara either. Only goth girl, who had returned to the kitchen counter, was around.

"Excuse me, we're leaving now. Elise is asleep in the dining room. She probably could use some help when she wakes up. Can you take care of her?"

She remained glued to her phone and could only manage a comforting "Yeah, whatever."

In hindsight, they realized that not one aspect of the whole evening was normal. Yet, as it was unfolding, they'd just gone along, assuming that it would come back, that it would eventually conform to their expectations of how people behave. Instead, it was a high-class soap opera.

"Maybe Konetski *is* screwing his sister-in-law," Carole suggested as she and her husband drove home. "It sure seemed that there was something more between them than a good putting stroke."

"Blimey, he has quite a nerve. Right under her nose. And they're twins too." He took a curve a little too quickly. "Just like those two in in that Coors ad. I wonder if they . . ." Knight had found a new level of respect for Konetski.

"Don't even think about it, sunshine. Just drive the bloody car," Carole interrupted his little fantasy.

"Yes, you're right. What a strange evening that was. You know he paid for two."

"We have to hope he'll just write off the second dinner to experience. Draw a line in the sand. I don't want to go back there. Just too weird."

"Absolutely. Weirdest thing ever. I think he'll want the other one though. He was embarrassed with things, yet he seemed sort of proud of it too." Knight braved another rebuke from his wife, although she had apparently fallen asleep.

He returned to his own thoughts. *Shame on me that was fun. I was cringing at times, but I found it all strangely invigorating. I hope he'll call us to arrange the second meal. What a night. I can't wait to tell Dunc about this.*

■

As Knight expanded his community service effort, Christina Drago also enjoyed a period of personal growth and increased maturity. As part of her career development, she was asked to take on an overseas assignment. The Lassiter business unit in Scandinavia was small in the wider scheme of things, but it was in deep trouble. It was not performing well financially, the clients were unhappy, and the employee attrition level was very high. No one could remember the last time that the

Scandinavian business unit had picked up an *L* at the awards banquet. To make things worse, Lassiter was getting a lot of negative publicity from the media in the region. It was Grauermann's idea to send Drago over there. He'd fired the Regional Manager following another dreadful quarter. She didn't need asking twice. If the company needed her to lead the turnaround, she would be there. Besides, it would put her in fantastic position for further promotions. She mothballed her apartment, put her Porsche in storage, and set off for Stockholm.

It had proven a very valuable experience for her. Being the Regional Manager forced her out of her comfort zone into a more outward-looking role. She had to be the public face of the company. While she still was very attentive to the operational metrics, she had to rely on the advice of others. She simply didn't have the bandwidth to do all of the analysis herself. She worked over a hundred hours a week.

After two years, Lassiter Scandinavia had turned the corner. All the key metrics were headed in the right direction, and there was a renewed sense of optimism. The team would have a decent shot at an *L*.

Her job done, it was time for Christina to hand the reins to a newly hired local executive to build upon her great work. She got her rewards too. She was promoted to Senior Vice President and put in charge of eLite, a new business venture that promised to be the future of Lassiter.

She also received an invitation to spend Presidents' Day weekend at Kathryn Gerrard's mountain chalet, along with a select group of guests: two of the other Lassiter Board members; her fellow Lassiter executive, Julie Dreiser; the Chair of the Lassiter Strategic Advisory Council, Jacquelyn Crawford; and the influential analyst Moira Kenney. The guest list confirmed that this was a significant opportunity, an invitation that she had to accept.

The invitation had emphasized that it was a fun weekend with friends, with skiing "strictly optional." But Drago's instinct told her something different. She wasn't the best of skiers, yet her fierce competitive streak would not allow her to miss out. If she accepted the invitation, she would have to ski. It was an acceptance to participate that came with an obligation, an obligation to perform that came with a methodology, a methodology to prepare that came with a guarantee, the guarantee of success of her three *P*s: planning, profiling, and practicing.

She had already established a close relationship with Gerrard through their regular coaching sessions. She saw this as an excellent opportunity to build her reputation with the two other Board members. She pulled up all the information she could on them. Then she prepared her ideal conversations with both of them. She memorized countless statistics on relevant topics so she could be a key contributor at the right time.

She bought herself some Salomon skis and boots. Rentals, as she'd used in Sweden, weren't quite the image she needed to convey. On the advice of the ski shop, she also bought a Nintendo Wii and practiced for an hour each morning on the ski simulator. Finally, she took a trip out to the gentle terrain of West Virginia for two days of back-to-back lessons. By the end of all that, while she wouldn't be blazing down the double blacks, she was ready to tackle the long blue cruisers. And if the skiing got too much, she could always seek the refuge of the chalet and a mandatory emergency conference call. She set off for Wyoming full of confidence.

The chalet was magnificent. Actually, *chalet* didn't do it justice. Yes it was slope-side ski-in, ski-out, and had a panoramic view of Grand Teton. But most chalets didn't have ten bedrooms, a separate guest lodge, an indoor and a heated outdoor pool, a wine cellar, a twenty-seat theater, and a gym. Drago was agog. It must be worth a fortune. She was shown to her room, where a three-day lift pass was already waiting. And skiing is optional? A note from Gerrard welcomed her and advised that dinner would be in the guest lodge at 8 p.m. She fired up her laptop. A quick check on Zillow confirmed the property . . . a cool $11.5 million.

At dinner on the first evening, Gerrard drifted from guest to guest, relishing her role as host, ensuring that everything was perfect, and pointing out the many features of the lodge. The Board members had brought their wives along, and evidently were there to enjoy a relaxing weekend. Drago chatted with them all briefly. Clearly they weren't interested in being lured into the deep and meaningful conversations she had envisaged. Dreiser completely ignored Drago. Scarcely a word had passed between the two since their evening with the Grauermanns at the Presidential.

Moira Kenney hadn't arrived. They learned later that her flight from JFK, via Chicago O'Hare, had been delayed. Nothing ever left O'Hare on time. That left Jacquelyn Crawford as Drago's only companion. They had met once before, briefly, when Drago had attended an L-SAC meeting. Drago had her conversation script in her head, ready for her to press play. But by then, both of them were tired. The journey, the altitude, and two-hour time change were taking their toll. They agreed to meet for breakfast and then they'd venture onto the slopes together.

The next morning, they skied down the short way to the lift station and then took the gondola to the summit. They made two cruises down the mountain. Crawford was an effortless, experienced skier, who handled the runs with ease. Drago, with intense concentration and sheer willpower, kept up with her. She was right at the edge. She coped although was not enjoying it. Sensing her struggles, Crawford suggested that they stop for a hot chocolate. Drago was very relieved. She could uncurl her toes for the first time since breakfast. As they settled with their drinks, she saw the opportunity to open up her "Crawford Scenario" folder.

"So, I know you've been at FRSC for quite a while, Jacquelyn."

"Yes, seems like half a lifetime, Christina."

"You've definitely seen the best and the worst of Lassiter then. George Knight was there in the early days, wasn't he? I've never had much time for Knight . . ."

"Whoa. Stop right there." Crawford saw right through where Drago was heading. "If you and I are going to get along, Christina, you can forget all the petty stuff. Understand?"

"I don't know what you mean. I was only saying that—"

"Yeah, I get it. You don't like George Knight. Well, I do. I think he's a great guy. So, what's next on your agenda?"

"I don't have an agenda, Jacquelyn. I was trying to make conversation, but if you don't want to . . ."

"Don't try to BS me, Christina. I've been there, done that. Counted how many points I could score."

Drago frowned as she realized that she had met her match in conversation manipulation.

Crawford continued, "Look, I get it. It's a tough road. But this is meant to be a fun weekend. Leave off the work stuff with me, OK?"

"I'll try, Jacquelyn. I'll try." Drago paused then added. "To be completely honest, I don't have a lot else to talk about."

"What about your family? How are they?"

"I don't have any family." Drago gave her preprogrammed answer to that question.

"What, none at all?"

"I'm not married if that's what you mean. I was for a while after college. It didn't work out."

"Oh, that's too bad. What went wrong?"

"To this day, I don't know. I thought we were doing great. We'd dated all the way through college. I'd been working over a weekend on a big project, came home early, and found him in our bed with one of the neighbors. That was that."

"Oh, the total shit. Any kids, Christina?"

"Oh, no, thank God. We'd not gotten around to that. We'd only been married a year."

"What a bastard. No one since?"

"No, I'm not risking that again."

"What about other family? Brothers and sisters? Your parents still alive?"

"Yeah, they are. In the same place they've lived for forty

years. My brother and his wife live just up the street. He's always there with the grandkids. He's still the apple of their eye."

"And, let me guess, despite your success, you're a big disappointment to them. They don't understand what you do, you don't visit often enough, you haven't settled down and brought them grandkids too."

"That about sums it up, Jacquelyn. Sounds like you're familiar with my condition?"

Their conversation continued for another hour as Crawford shared aspects of her life story. They ordered another hot chocolate each and returned to business to discuss their careers and what motivated them. The only fly in their bonding ointment came when Drago brought Knight into the conversation again. Crawford was momentarily angry, then commented icily, "Christina, we will never get a level playing field with men by trying to pull them down. They've got too much going for them. But we can beat them by exploiting their weaknesses. They call women the weaker sex. Not in my book. Let's take your friend Knight for instance . . ."

■

That evening, Crawford was bored with the confines of the chalet. She suggested to her new skiing companion that they go into town and have dinner there. Maybe visit a bar or even a nightclub. Moira Kenney, who had finally arrived following a night at O'Hare, was mightily keen to join them. She immediately labeled the outing a "cougar patrol." Drago was reluctant as she still hadn't spent any time with the Board members. But Gerrard encouraged her to go. Just by being there, she'd already increased her profile with them. She should go with the girls and learn something about having fun. So off they went into town. After dinner in the Snake River Grill, they spent the rest of the evening occupying the saddle-shaped barstools of the famous Million Dollar Cowboy Bar. They sang along to the live music, did a little line dancing, and enjoyed the considerable attentions of some real cowboys. It turned into a very late night. None of the ladies surfaced for breakfast. Only Crawford made it to the slopes. She took a few short runs in the late morning after her "cowboy" had woken her as he left to go to his job as a lift attendant.

Nothing was said. All abided by the "what happens in Jackson Hole" protocol. A few knowing looks passed between the three women as they left for the airport. Drago flew back east in the strangest of moods. She hadn't met any of the milestones she'd set herself for the trip, but she'd achieved something so much more remarkable: she'd actually enjoyed herself.

CHAPTER NINE

The Critical Network

December 2010

Knight's reward for his community service was a promotion to Senior Vice President. With that, he took a new role at corporate HQ, necessitating another move for his long-suffering family. New house, new schools, new friends—all part of the corporate nomad life. Carole Knight quickly became friends with Cindy Patten, another of the parents at their kids' school, D'Ayncourt. They had plenty in common. Cindy had traveled quite widely and had a broader perspective than the average American middle school mom.

Just before Christmas, the Knights were invited over to Cindy's place for a party. Cindy introduced them to some of the other guests. Carole knew a few of them from the school. After a while, Cindy gathered everyone around the fireplace to sing Christmas carols. It was a very traditional scene: a roaring fire, a beautifully decorated tree, and twenty-five or so smartly dressed, well-to-do guests. She gave out song sheets, and they did their best to sound like a church choir. The chap next to Knight certainly could sing well. Great voice. A tenor. Knight found himself miming the words so his off-key rumble didn't detract from the other guy's singing.

They came to the end of the carols and then all toasted a "Merry Christmas" with glasses of the excellent mulled wine. Knight shook hands respectfully with his sonorous companion.

"Merry Christmas and a happy New Year to you," the other man said. "I am pleased to meet you. I'm Edmund Patten, Cindy's father."

"Merry Christmas to you too. I'm George, George Knight. My wife is a friend of Cindy's."

So this was Cindy's dad. It made Knight take a closer look. He guessed he was in his late sixties, still in great shape, trim and erect. He was impeccably dressed in a light brown plaid jacket, pale cashmere round-neck sweater, and a pair of smart, crisply pressed pants. Italian luxury. Knight felt a little cheap in the best the Joseph A. Bank at the mall had to offer. They did share the same taste in designer watches, though.

"Nice watch, George." Patten smiled.

"Yes, these Panerai are great, aren't they? There's a bit of a story behind this one. I bought a fake one on a visit to Bangkok and then got so many admiring comments. I was really embarrassed. I had to get a real one."

Patten smiled although he did not offer any comparable story about how he came by his. He oozed class and expensive taste. Knight doubted that he'd ever had to buy a fake anything. Cindy's comfortable lifestyle began to make sense.

"Who are you with, George?" he asked.

"Oh, I work for Lassiter. Do you know them?"

"Yes, of course. Great company. What do you do there?"

Knight explained his many moves and that he had finally succumbed to the lure of the company headquarters.

"How are things going there?"

Knight didn't really know the guy. He seemed trustworthy enough, but still, Knight was a little guarded at first.

"It's a mixed bag, Edmund. What's your interest in Lassiter?"

"Oh, nothing much. I play the stock market with my retirement funds and I like to keep in touch with what's happening out in the real world."

Knight felt sorry for him. Patten seemed such a smart guy. *It must be hard when you retire and don't get to be in the mix anymore.*

"Well, between you and me, Edmund, I'm starting to regret taking the HQ job. We had a few good years, achieved some great results, although it's starting to catch up with us now. The outside world hasn't realized yet. Lassiter is getting left behind. Our market is changing. Our competitors are working on new technology. And we aren't responding. We just go around in circles. Nothing gets done, nothing gets decided, and nothing gets properly funded."

"Oh, I read in the *Journal* that things are going well there. Don't you have this great strategy? Project Break Out, is it? How's that going?"

"That's a triumph of form over substance if ever there was one, Edmund. We call it Project Break Down. We have these endless meetings with the consulting people from the Phillip Strand Group. They issue orders about new roles, changes to organization, and the costs to cut to pay for them all. Then we fill out more templates to report it all to the G-man. That's what we call him, the CEO, Daniel Grauermann. I don't see the point of it. He's never there anyway. He's always headed off somewhere in his jet."

"You don't think a lot of the G-man then?"

"To be honest, I try to steer clear of him. I'm not one of his favorites. He just doesn't get it. He's only interested in the internal stuff. He doesn't seem to be able to see what's going on outside the company."

"Is this just you, George? Or do your colleagues feel the same way?"

"Oh yes, everyone. They say misery loves company. The biggest thing that annoys us is that we all have to fly everywhere in coach, while he goes everywhere in his Gulfstream. He justifies the plane on the basis of 'security' because there have been threats against him. We reckon they probably came from his wife. She's a real nasty piece of work apparently. This little group of security knuckleheads goes everywhere with him too now. They're like the Keystone Cops. It's hilarious."

"It sounds a dreadful mess, George. I'm not surprised you're having second thoughts."

"Yeah, please keep it to yourself, though." Knight realized that he might have been a little too forthcoming. "I shouldn't complain too much anyway. Julie Dreiser, my boss, is great, and I've had a good career there up until now. I'm sure things will get better."

"What makes you say that?"

"Well, I hope that sooner or later someone will realize that G-man has to go. Maybe the Board or the shareholders will step up when they realize things are going south and they're being spun a line. That might be wishful thinking. I'll keep my fingers crossed."

Cindy came over to join them.

"Oh, Dad, I hope that you haven't been boring George too much. Putting the world to rights. Let me save him and introduce you to a few other folks."

"No, we've had a great—"

Knight tried to object, but she whisked her father off to join another group.

Knight was disappointed. He would have liked to find out a little more about the senior man. What had he done for living? How had he made all of his money? Was there a Mrs. Patten? He would not have to wait long to learn more about his influential new connection.

CHAPTER TEN

A Royal Visit

February 2011

The Grauermanns' world tour began in Australia. They'd taken the company jet. Isobel was relieved that they had avoided the hassles of airports, baggage check-in, and all of those other passengers. The Gulfstream was so comfortable, and the crew was very attentive to their needs. A pillow here, a cold drink there. With the threats to Grauermann's life, it was essential for security reasons. One of the members of the detail—Isobel knew him only as Bud—had flown with them. The other two had gone on ahead to review the in-theater arrangements. They were all retired cops or secret service agents and definitely knew what they were doing.

In her unique sense of morality, Isobel considered the trip as something she had earned. This was her finder's fee from Lassiter for recruiting their new Chairman when Hastings had decided to "retire." She'd been the headhunter. She deserved their undying gratitude.

Their first stop was Sydney. Grauermann had been there before; it was her first visit. They landed at 7 p.m. It was a warm, sunny midsummer evening. After clearing immigration in the private aviation terminal, they were met by Emily Webb, the head of Marketing from the local business unit. Webb, a sweet, gentle lady in her fifties, was in a terrible state with the stress of the visit. As she nervously began her pre-pared script, Isobel cruelly interrupted her big moment.

"Spare us the speech . . . What's your name?" She read the crest-fallen Australian's name badge. "Emily. Spare us the speech, Emily. My husband and I are very tired and want to get to our hotel."

"Oh yes, sorry, Mrs. G. Let me introduce you to your driver, Jerry Moore. Jerry is our most experienced driver and I'm sure—"

"Yes, fine. Just get the bags loaded," Grauermann snarled.

Jerry Moore, another congenial Aussie, was not a Lassiter employee. He operated his own small business, Jerry's Limousines. He had been warned that the Grauermanns would have a lot of luggage, so he'd brought his large black Suburban, which would easily handle their extensive collection of matching Louis Vuitton suitcases. He'd also expected them to be prickly customers. He didn't take their brusqueness personally. Webb, on the other hand, was desperately trying to fight back the tears. She scurried to help Moore with the bags. He smiled at her and said kindly, "It's OK, Emily. They're too heavy for you. I'll take care of it. Don't let them get to you."

This gave her a little more confidence to approach the Grauermanns again.

"May I tell you a little about the arrangements?"

"Go ahead," Grauermann replied irritably.

"Jerry will take you to the hotel. As you requested you are at the Sydney Swan Hotel. The Hall Suite. The hotel manager will meet you on arrival."

"Does that have a view of the Opera House?" Isobel asked in a slightly more mellow tone.

"Oh yes. Yes, it has a fantastic view of the Opera House, Mrs. G." Webb smiled, so pleased to have pleased. "Tomorrow, Jerry will pick you up at 10 a.m. to bring you to the office, Mr. G."

"Right, I've got it." Grauermann nodded and got into the car.

Webb continued. "For Mrs. G, I will meet you at 11 a.m. to take you on a guided tour of the Opera House, followed by lunch, and then on to an afternoon of shopping in the CBD."

"What's that? The CBD? I told your people that I wanted to go to the Queen Victoria Building."

'Yes, yes, sorry, Mrs. Grauermann, we are going there. The CBD is the central business district. I think you would call it 'downtown'? The Queen Victoria Building and all of our best shopping is in the CBD."

"Good. I will see you tomorrow then. Driver!"

She waited for Moore to open the door for her and stepped in to join her husband.

With the door closed, Moore said quietly to Webb, "Good luck tomorrow. Thank goodness it's only for three days, right?" He winked at her and climbed into his driver's seat. They pulled away, followed by Bud and his colleagues in their rented Range Rover.

The next morning Moore turned up at the Swan in good time for his 10 a.m. pickup. He'd switched to his sedan for the short trip out to the newly opened Lassiter offices. He waited in the car outside the hotel until ten fifteen, and then headed into the lobby to see if he could track down his VIP passenger. There was no sign of him in the lobby. Moore took a seat and waited patiently. He ordered himself a flat white—his third of a morning that had started with a 5 a.m. pickup and trip to the airport—and settled in to read his *Sydney Morning Herald*. Wait around, rush, negotiate traffic, wait around some more. He was accustomed to the pattern.

Even his laid-back approach was being tested when 10:50 a.m. arrived and Grauermann still had not appeared. He was about to go to the reception desk and ask them to call the Grauermanns' room, when he spotted Webb arriving for her outing with Mrs. G.

"Oh, hi, Jerry. What are you doing here? I hope there hasn't been any problems?" She was immediately close to panic.

"Chill, Emily. Chill. There haven't been any problems as far as I know. He's just not shown up, that's all. Been waiting over an hour. I figured he must have either slept in late or got tied up on a phone call. No biggie."

"Well, hmm. OK, Jerry. We'll wait to see if Mrs. G comes down for her trip with me, then we can ask her about Mr. G. If she hasn't arrived by eleven fifteen, I'll get the hotel to call their room."

"Sounds like a plan, Emily. What about a coffee? My shout."

"Oh, I shouldn't really. But OK, go on then, thanks, Jerry. A flat white would be lovely."

At a few minutes after eleven, Isobel walked into the lobby from the quayside terrace, closely followed by her husband. Both were dressed casually, Isobel in khaki cargo pants and a lightweight North Face jacket, Grauermann in a sweatshirt, sweatpants, and tennis shoes. They both looked a little red faced.

Webb jumped up and headed toward them in alarm.

"Oh, good morning, Mr. and Mrs. G. I hope everything is OK?"

"Yes, it's all fine. We woke early, had breakfast, and went for a walk round the quay to the Opera House and then back through the Rocks."

"Oh, that's splendid. I'm so pleas—"

"We'll go and freshen up and then be down for you to take us on the Opera House tour. We are so looking forward to that. You have arranged a private tour, haven't you? Not a public one with all the common tourists?"

"Yes, of course, it's a private tour, Mrs. G. The Opera House marketing director will be taking us round herself. Mr. G, Jerry will wait for you and take you to the Lassiter offices as soon as you are ready."

"That won't be necessary. I've decided that I'm not going to the offices. I want to go on that Opera House tour with my wife. And this afternoon, while you take her shopping, I want to play golf. Get me a round at somewhere upmarket. You'll need to get my clubs from the jet."

"Oh, OK. Right. Hmm. Yes. I'm sure we can arrange that. I'll get right on it," Webb replied, while processing a thousand urgent thoughts. *Which course? At this short notice? How to get the clubs? What about tonight's dinner? Why me? There must be easier jobs . . .*

"Just one question, Mr. G. Have you told the folks at the office that you won't be going out there? I know that they have quite a few things lined up. A town hall meeting with the employees, presenting some long service awards, a tour of the new innovation center." Webb and her team had made down-to-the-minute plans for his visit to the office.

"No, I haven't told them yet. I'll leave that to you."

Webb went into overdrive and, with some help from Moore, took care of everything. She called the office to let them know of the change of plans. She didn't have time to dwell on the astonished reaction. Moore had contacts at the New South Wales Golf Club, and he arranged a round for Grauermann.

"It's all fixed up, Emily. Per the club rules, he'll have to play with a member. They'll line someone up. It's a beautiful course overlooking Botany Bay. He has a 3 p.m. tee time. I'll drive him over there and get his clubs from the jet on the way."

"That's terrific, Jerry. Thank you. He really can't complain about that, can he?"

She explained the new plan to the Grauermanns when they returned. Then they headed off to the Opera House for their tour.

■

That evening, the eight members of Lassiter's Australian management team and their partners gathered to await the Grauermanns' arrival at a dinner to mark their visit. The group were looking sharp: best suits, with European-style cut-away collars and brightly colored ties, for the men; stylish dresses and high heels for the ladies. They could have been at a wedding or enjoying the Melbourne Cup. The dinner was set in the private dining room at Cove, touted as Australia's finest restaurant. It certainly had one of the most spectacular views, a sweeping panorama of the two icons of Sydney—the Opera House and the Harbour Bridge. The team was reeling from having to cancel the events in the office when Grauermann had stood them up earlier. Still, they were ready to swallow their resentment and make a good impression individually and collectively with the CEO and his wife. They were enjoying a beer and chatting amiably when Webb announced, "I'm sorry, folks. I just got a call from Jerry Moore. There are a couple of changes. We have to delay dinner by an hour. Mr. G has only just got back to the hotel from his golf game and needs time to shower and change. Also Mrs. G is feeling unwell and will not be joining us this evening."

There was a loud groan of annoyance from the group.

"I'm terribly sorry to disappoint you all. I just couldn't get him back any earlier. And I really don't know what has come over Mrs. G. She seemed perfectly fine when she got back to the hotel."

Isobel wasn't unwell. She had decided to skip the dinner. The tour and lunch at the Opera House had been wonderful, and she had enjoyed a successful afternoon of shopping at the QVB in the CBD. It had been rather tiring, though, quite enough for one day. She remained in her room for a well-deserved rest.

"Don't worry, Emily. Not your fault, love," her boss, Tip Hanly, the Lassiter Australia General Manager said sympathetically. "We can't expect you to control him. Let's get some more drinks up here while we wait."

Grauermann eventually arrived around ninety minutes later. By that time, standards had slipped a little. A few of the ties were loosened, a few of the collars were undone, and several pairs of high heels kicked off in favor of bare feet. Not that Grauermann would have noticed. He fitted in well in his open-neck shirt and casual pants.

"G'day, Mr. G. Glad you could make it," Hanly greeted him, not knowing quite what to expect. "Can I get you a drink?"

"Hello, Tip, nice to see you. Yes, I'll take a beer please. I'll try one of your local ones," Grauermann replied with a very consciously friendly smile.

"I'm sure we'll be able to drag one up for you. Let me introduce you to a few folks, Mr. G."

The evening went well from there. Grauermann was relaxed and talkative. Only once did he show any flash of temper. As he was about to leave, Leah, Hanly's splendidly proficient assistant, slipped into the seat next to Grauermann.

"Excuse me, Mr. G, I've got a number of messages here from Patsy Myer back in the States. She says some of them are quite urgent. She's been trying to get you on your mobile. She can't seem to get through." She passed him an envelope and he took a cursory look at the messages. His eyes rolled and his neck veins bulged.

"Can't these people do anything without me?" he hissed. "I told Patsy before I left not to disturb me with this operational crap. That's what I pay my guys for. If I have to deal with it, why would I need them?"

Leah was from strong Kiwi stock and not easily intimidated. She replied calmly, "So what would you like me to tell Patsy, Mr. Grauermann?"

"You can tell her whatever the hell you want. You decide. Just make sure she knows not to pester me again. Clear?"

"Crystal."

Leah remained at the table, her arms folded defiantly as she locked stares with Grauermann. He was the first to flinch. He stood up and circled the room to say goodbye to each of the diners.

With that, he headed down the stairs. Hanly offered to walk the short distance back to his hotel with him, but he rejected the offer. The trusty Bud appeared from the shadows to follow discreetly, his curly earpiece conspicuously inconspicuous. At the hotel, Grauermann paused briefly to consider a drink in the deserted bar, but decided against it. Instead, back in his living room, he cracked open a bottle of Glenfiddich whiskey. If he was going to drink alone, may as well make it pleasurable and do it in private. Isobel was sound asleep. Judging by the mountain of bags in the room, she must have had a good afternoon shopping.

■

The tour continued the next day, on to Adelaide, where the main task was to officially open a new office building. In reality, the offices had been in use for over six months, but an opening ceremony was good for publicity. It also coincided with the Lassiter Cycling Team's visit to the area. The mayor gave a speech; Grauermann cut the ribbon; and the cycling team—led by their enigmatic Australian star, Dusty Rhodes—did several fast laps around the business park. Later there was a reception where the champagne, wine, and beer flowed freely. On an otherwise slow-news Friday, the media lapped it up, giving the event extensive coverage of local boy Dusty and his teammates on the TV news that night and in the following day's newspapers.

Grauermann was basking in all the attention. Hansi Olsen approached him as the event broke up quickly with the arrival of a passing thunderstorm.

"Mr. Grauermann, I was wondering if we might get a chance to discuss the renewal of our Lassiter sponsorship?"

"Haven't my guys sorted that all out yet, Hansi? I told them to get it done," Grauermann lied. There was some serious doubt as to whether they would renew the sponsorship. Grauermann had directed the Marketing team to slow down the negotiations with Olsen, play hard ball on the contract, and consider alternative sponsorship options, like a Formula 1 team or a golf event.

Olsen knew who was behind the stalling. He decided to challenge Grauermann.

"No, Daniel. We haven't made any progress for months. Your guys want a one-year deal. We want at least two, with a 20 percent increase in the fees to put the sponsorship at the same going rate as for the other top teams. I'll have to look at other potential sponsors if we can't get it done soon. It would be a shame to lose you after our success over the past few years. I've got several others looking it over already."

"My guys aren't getting it done, huh, Hansi? We'll see about that. Tell them to get paperwork to me. Two years, 20 percent raise. You have a deal. I'll take care of it when I get back to the US. Just don't expect me to ride in the car again."

"Hey, thanks, Daniel. I knew you'd be able to get it straightened out." Olsen smiled to himself. This guy was such a pushover.

"You bet, Hansi. Just get us on that podium in Paris in July. My wife and I want to be there again."

The Grauermanns had chosen to stay for the weekend in the Adelaide area. Emily Webb, an Adelaide native, had offered to help them. Alas, much to her disappointment, they did not require any assistance. Isobel had apparently made all the arrangements herself as a surprise for her husband. She had booked a tour guide, transportation, and their overnight stays in quaint bed-and-breakfasts. She was very pleased with herself. Over the weekend, they visited vineyards in each of the area's famous wine-growing regions—the Barossa Valley, the Clare Valley, and McLaren Vale. The weather was beautiful, warm and sun-blessed; the rolling South Australian country was delightful, tranquil, and serene. Without the pressure of meeting expectations, real or self-imposed, and free from the urge to dominate or disown, Daniel and Isobel dropped their guards—both literally, as they dispensed with the services of Bud and his cohorts for the low-risk weekend, and metaphorically as they relaxed and enjoyed each other's company for the first time in a while. It was a blissful time.

All too soon it was over, and they were on to Melbourne for the final stop of the Australian trip. The hold of the Gulfstream was getting crowded with the Grauermanns' luggage, the crew's bags, and twelve cases of South Australia's finest wines, a small memento of the indulgent weekend. But there was still plenty of room in the cabin. Webb saw them onto the plane. She was due to take a Qantas flight to meet up with them in Melbourne. She was flabbergasted when Isobel asked her if she would like to fly with them instead.

"Oh, oh, really? Me? Oh yes, that would be terrific. Thank you so much, Mrs. G."

"You are very welcome, my dear. We have had such a wonderful weekend here. I can't wait to tell you all about it. You come and sit by me. And please do call me Isobel."

Webb was as giddy as a schoolgirl as she took her seat on the private jet next to Isobel for the short flight. She scarcely got a word in, other than the occasional "Yes, yes, absolutely" as Isobel recounted her weekend and her enchantment with Adelaide and its vineyards. The Australian was so proud and happy and excited, she wanted to pinch herself.

Once in Melbourne, the visitors checked in at the Queens Park Hotel. Later they both headed out to the Lassiter office downtown, where Grauermann took part in a town hall meeting with the employees. Tip Hanly had flown down from Sydney to take part. He was amazed at the transformation.

"Hey, Emily. What did you do to them over the weekend? Did you slip them a Mickey Finn or somethin'?"

"I really don't know, Tip. It's as if they discovered how to be nice people."

"Well, let's not knock it, girl. Only two more days and they'll bugger off to Asia. I hope they stay like this. Fingers crossed, eh?"

Hanly's wish came true. Rejuvenated by the charms of Adelaide, the Grauermanns were the perfect visitors, gracious and committed. Their stay in Melbourne went splendidly. Their final business engagement was a customer appreciation event. The local Lassiter team had hired a suite at the famous Melbourne Cricket Ground for a Twenty20 cricket match under the floodlights. It was all run scoring and fast action, athletic fielding, and regular blasts of AC/DC, more akin to a baseball game than a traditional test match, that unique sporting event, five intense days of endeavor, the tension relieved only by overnight breaks, bad light breaks, lunch breaks, tea breaks, and of course drinks breaks, necessary to allow the players to rehydrate as they suffer in the heat under their heavy caps and thick woolen sweaters, that often culminates in a no-winner outcome. The Grauermanns enjoyed this fast-paced Americanized version for a couple of hours before leaving for the hotel. Hanly saw them to their car.

"Tip, thank you for arranging everything. This has been great. You guys are doing a fine job down here."

"Well, thanks, Mr. G. That's real kind of you. Good on ya."

"And, Tip, please say thank you from me to Emily. She's a real gem," Isobel added.

"I will. I sure will."

"G'day, Tip."

Grauermann left with a smile, a handshake, and an attempt at an Australian accent. Hanly, still not quite able to believe his luck, headed back to the cricket for another beer. The Lassiter team and several of their customers pushed on late into the night, celebrating the Grauermanns' departure by getting thoroughly shit-faced.

■

For the Grauermanns it was another long-haul flight on to Singapore and the Asian stage of their trip. The journey, broken up by a refueling stop in Alice Springs, bored and irritated them. Maybe it would have been better to have taken the Singapore Airlines flight and arrived much earlier. Perhaps, after breaking free of their cloistered, joyless world in Adelaide, they should have continued to interact with other passengers rather than returning to the isolation of the security detail and Gulfstream crew. For whatever reason, by the time they arrived at Singapore's Changi Airport, the magical spell of Australia, the beauty of Adelaide, and the spontaneity of Melbourne seemed a long way off. The real Mr. and Mrs. G cleared Singaporean immigration.

All of which would come as a big surprise to their next regional host, Lassiter's Asian General Manager, Ray McLaughlan. Earlier he'd received a typically misspelled text from his pal Hanly telling him, "NO FUCKIN' WORIES MATE. GMANS IN BONZA MOOD. U CANT GO WRONG."

McLaughlan had only met Grauermann once before, at the exec-utive retreat. He had been very concerned about the visit. The G-man's fierce temper and his wife's moodiness were well known even in these far-flung parts of the Lassiter empire. McLaughlan had called Hanly to make sure he wasn't being set up. Hanly reassured his pal that it was "fair dinkum." The Grauermanns were reportedly in great spirits. Everything should be fine. All of which was music to McLaughlan's ears. He was a very ambitious fellow, known for talking himself up a little. With the news of Grauermann's good humor, he decided he would seize every opportunity to impress his guests.

He met them personally at the private aviation terminal, and after introducing himself suggested that he drive them to their hotel. The lim-ousine service would bring their luggage and the security team. Grauer-mann exchanged a quick whisper with Bud before agreeing to McLaugh-lan's proposal. Isobel followed behind without comment.

As they drove along the expressway toward the city center, Mc-Laughlan had what he thought was a tremendous idea. Instead of taking them straight to their hotel, he would show them a little of the city's nightlife with dinner at the bustling Clarke Quay. He had just the right place in mind. The Jumbo Seafood restaurant, famous for its chili crab, popular with everyone—locals, Western expats, and tourists.

Grauermann had been dozing in the car, but he woke up as Mc-Laughlan parked the car in the quay's underground garage.

"Ray, where are we? This doesn't look like our hotel."

"That's right, Daniel. I'm going to treat you to a little special local food first. Th is is the famous Clarke Qu ay. We are going to Jumbo Seafood."

"Oh, really. I'm not sure my wife—"

"It will be great, I promise you. I bring visitors here all the time. They always love it."

"No, we're tired from the flight and want to go to the hotel, Ray," Grauermann replied.

"I know you're staying at Raffles. I'll take you back there later. We won't be long. And you'll love the food."

McLaughlan jumped out of his car and opened the door for a reluctant Isobel to step out. He enthused about the restaurant, the food, and the great view as they took the elevator to the street level. The Grauermanns remained silent, their slumping shoulders and slow pace suggesting that they were underwhelmed by this turn of events. The short walk alongside the Singapore River cheered them a little. It was an attractive sight as the colorful lights of the restaurants reflected in the dark water. The respite was short-lived. As they approached the restaurant, they could see that it was crowded with many people waiting around for tables. The young greeter at the podium told them it would be a forty-five-minute wait and cheerfully invited them to take a drink in the bar in the meantime. As Isobel's face turned to stone and Grauermann readied himself to launch a tirade, McLaughlan finally began to sense that this hadn't been his best move.

"Wait here, folks. Let me fix this."

He headed into the restaurant purposefully.

"Daniel, what are we doing here? Get me to my hotel. And then fire this cretin."

"I know. I'm very sorry. I'll tell him to get us to the hotel as soon as he gets back."

They stood awkwardly in the restaurant doorway, feeling angry, isolated, and self-conscious. All the other people who were waiting seemed so happy about it, all smiling, chatting, and taking photos with their phones as if it were all part of the experience. Grauermann envied their freedom. Isobel despised the simpletons.

Within a few minutes, McLaughlan returned looking pleased with himself.

Grauermann greased him angrily. "Ray, we are leaving. Either you take us or we'll get a—"

"It's cool, Daniel. I spoke to my friend the manager. He knows me.

I come here so often, I've got some pull. He doesn't want to lose my business. We've got a table right away. Come on."

Grauermann was torn. On the one hand, his wife wanted to leave, on the other he was hungry and needed a drink. He also had no idea where they were and how he would go about getting to the hotel without McLaughlan. Where was Bud when he needed him?

At that precise moment, Bud, who had assumed the Grauermanns would be safely tucked up in their hotel by then, was actually enjoying a little R & R with his team. They'd been a little disappointed with the quality on offer in the Kings Cross district in Sydney. So, following established Secret Service protocols while accompanying dignitaries overseas, they were intent on getting their money's worth in Orchard Towers, another one of Singapore's famous nightlife spots, more commonly known as the "Four Floors of Whores."

Back at the quay, Grauermann's helplessness swung his decision. He whispered to Isobel and then they both followed McLaughlan into the restaurant.

"Right, Raymond. I hope for your sake that this is as good as you say. You better start by getting me a drink."

"Yeah, that's the spirit, Daniel. What can I get you? And Mrs. G, what's your tipple?"

"I'll take a beer," said Grauermann. "What's the local brew? Tiger? Yes, one of those, and Isobel will have a mineral water."

"You got it. I've already taken care of the food order. The banquet. Prawns, whole steamed fish, scallops, lobster. We can go and pick the fish and the lobster from the tanks over there. And of course chili crabs—this place is famous for them. They'll bring it all out."

Grauermann chose the fish and lobster from the tank and watched eagerly as they were cooked in the noisy open-plan kitchen. And then the servers did bring the food out, wave after wave of it. Enough to feed an army, there were bowls of noodles, rice, and vegetables to go along with the platter of seafood. McLaughlan was right; it was very good.

Grauermann washed it down with several more Tigers and put his earlier irritation behind him. McLaughlan's self-promoting tour guide enthusiasm seemed appropriate for the setting.

As they headed back to the car, Grauermann and McLaughlan chatted enthusiastically about the plan for the next day. McLaughlan shared that he had arranged an outing to the Bintan Lagoon Golf Club across the Singapore Strait in Indonesia. Isobel trailed along sullenly, her thoughts elsewhere.

McLaughlan deposited them at the famous Raffles Hotel, named for the founder of Singapore, Sir Stamford Raffles. Their luggage had already been taken up to their spacious Presidential Suite. With a dining room, a lounge, two bedrooms, a private balcony, elegant period furnishings, oriental carpets, and teakwood floors, it was quite special. The two bedrooms were especially useful; Isobel was beyond furious. She despised her husband's familiarity with these people, knowing that his value was in his scarcity. She took her bag with her overnight things and headed for the larger bedroom. She turned and glared at him.

"Never do that to me again."

Grauermann was unsure why she was so angry. The food had been great, this guy McLaughlan seemed OK. What was the problem?

"What's the matter, Isobel?"

"You know very well. That was just awful. That place had everything I dislike in a restaurant—crowds, spicy food, and that oppressive demand that we enjoy the experience. A bubbling cauldron of humanity, perpetual motion, flashes of flame, the sweet smell of garlic, chili, and star anise, and the noise of cheerful toasts and laughter. I hated it."

Grauermann tried to be conciliatory. "Oh, it wasn't so bad. Gave us a bit of the local flavor. I know it wasn't planned, but there's no harm in something impromptu every now and then. You enjoyed that in Adelaide."

His attempt backfired, lighting her up into a furious temper. "Don't be naive. I spent weeks planning our 'impromptu' weekend in Adelaide.

I don't do impromptu, Daniel. That was a terrible way to spend our first night here," she blasted him.

"I'm sorry, Isobel. I quite enjoyed breaking out of the routine. I didn't realize that—"

"You sound like my sister. Perhaps if you want to turn all avant-garde, you should take up with her again!" she screamed at him.

"Oh, you always have to throw that back in my face, don't you?"

"Well, you deserve it, you fool. You slept with her. You got her pregnant."

"Oh God, Isobel. We've been over this a thousand times. I'm sorry. It was a weak moment. She seduced me—"

"Yes, I've heard the story and your pathetic excuses. It still doesn't take away my pain every time I see her. And she gloats and gives me that 'I took your husband' look."

"She doesn't do that. You're just imagining it."

"You wouldn't know. You coward. You haven't seen her in years." Isobel came back to the middle of the room and angrily stood over Grauermann, who had slumped onto the sofa.

"And your son, Jebby. When did you last see him? You brought that bastard into the world."

"I don't need to see him. I've paid for everything for him, and he must never know. That was our deal, Isobel. You promised that you would never tell him."

"Yes, I did, Daniel," Isobel spoke coldly. "And in return you promised that you would never put anyone else before me again. My happiness. No one else's. And then I have to endure a night like tonight. Let's be clear. Never again. You keep me happy or Jebby gets to learn about his father."

She gave him one final life-crushing glance—a look of hatred, spite, and revenge, powerful, yet deeply scarred—and then stormed into her room, shutting the door forcefully behind her.

Grauermann was reeling, shocked by Isobel's threat. Too agitated for sleep, he needed a drink to help him relax. He called for the twenty-four-hour butler to bring him up a bottle of good scotch and some ice. It was there on the table when he emerged from the bathroom wrapped in a towel after a long, hot shower. He poured himself just a little nightcap and settled on the sofa. He began to read the batch of urgent messages that had been waiting for him at reception, finding it easier to face up to his business issues than his personal ones.

He was still asleep on the sofa at six twenty the next morning when there was a persistent knocking at the door.

"Yes, who is it? Damn." Disoriented, he knocked over the near-empty whiskey bottle as he groped around to find his glasses.

"Daniel, it's Ray. We were meant to meet in the lobby at six to go to Bintan. Are you ready?"

"Oh yes. Right, Ray. Just had to take a call from the office. I'll be down in ten minutes."

He took another shower to help get his head in the game, and then pulled out some golf wear, trying desperately to remember what McLaughlan had told him about the trip. It came back slowly.

A high-speed ferry would take them from Singapore to the golf course. McLaughlan had booked the tickets for the seventy-five-minute trip across the Strait.

He headed down in the elevator, still rather bleary. Outside, the driver had loaded up his clubs, and they were ready to leave for the Tanah Merah Ferry Terminal as soon as he got down to the lobby.

"Here, these may help." McLaughlan handed him some tablets and a can of Coke.

Grauermann swallowed the tablets with a slurp of the soda. They perked him up.

"Do you want to get some food before we go, Daniel?"

"No, thanks, Ray. Although I could use a Bloody Mary once we're on board if they can rustle one up. Just to settle the old sea legs."

"You got it. I'll think I'll have one of those too. Great idea. Oh, and by the way, my assistant, Sally, is going to take Mrs. G on a bit of tour, then shopping later. I think we're all going have a great day out, Daniel."

■

Isobel had awoken expecting to have breakfast with her husband and give him some more guidance on Mr. McLaughlan. She was surprised to see that he had already departed—apparently in a hurry, judging by the clothes strewn around his room. He'd left his cell phone on the dining table also. She dressed and decided to decline the butler's offer to prepare something for her. She would take breakfast in the Empire Café. She was disappointed to miss her opportunity to assert her authority and getting out of the room would help to take her mind off it.

As she took a table in the old-fashioned coffee house, she saw Bud loitering close by. He looked a little helpless and was indicating that he needed to speak to her. She really could not stand the man, with his huge fat belly and his pathetic earpiece, but thought she ought to find out what was troubling him.

"I'm sorry to interrupt you, ma'am. Can I ask you where CockRobin is?"

"CockRobin? Who on earth would that be?"

"Oh yes, CockRobin, that's our code name for Mr. Grauermann."

"How strange you people are. CockRobin indeed. I have no idea where CockRobin is. I assumed he had gone off to the Lassiter offices with his new buddy Mr. McLaughlan. You haven't lost him, have you?"

"No, ma'am, not lost, just temporarily misplaced. I will try to reach him on his cellular telephone. If that doesn't work, you believe he is with Mr. McLaughlan?"

"Calling his cell phone won't do you any good. He left that in the hotel room. Silly CockRobin. And yes, I expect he is with McLaughlan. I remember now, the two of them were giggling like schoolboys about playing golf today."

"Thank you, ma'am. We'll find him," Bud replied to Isobel. Then he said into his sleeve, "CockRobin is on the wing with the LaughingMan. I say again, CockRobin is on the wing with the LaughingMan."

Isobel finished her coffee and returned to her room. She was determined to ensure that her sister knew that she was staying at the famous Raffles Hotel. Even Sabbi would not be able to top this one. She might have slept with a playboy in every capital city in the world, but the bohemian bitch had never stayed at Raffles. And she wasn't going to the Davos World Economic Forum. Isobel was busy composing a suitably acidic name-dropping email to what she believed to be her sister's email address, when Grauermann's Blackberry rang. The caller ID indicated "Patsy Myer, Office." Isobel assumed that Myer must be looking for him too.

"Hello, Patsy. No, it's Isobel. Daniel went out earlier. We think with Raymond McLaughlan. He's left his Blackberry here."

"Oh, that's difficult then, Mrs. Grauermann. I really was hoping to catch him today. It's quite urgent."

"Well, can I help at all, Patsy?"

"Do you happen to know if he managed to read the messages I left for him to collect when you checked in?"

"I know that he picked them up. I don't know if he read them. It was rather late when we finally got to the hotel, and I went straight to bed. Let me see if I can find them."

She looked around the lounge and found the pile of messages. A couple of pages were scrunched up into balls. The rest were apparently unread.

"No, it looks like he didn't get around to them, Patsy. He was really tired too."

"OK, I understand, Mrs. Grauermann. Please would you ask him to look at them and get back to me as soon as he can."

"Yes, of course, Patsy. I'll do that. By the way, while I have you, the arrangements for the weekend in Adelaide were just perfect. You do such a splendid job. I don't know where we would be without you. Thank you for your help and for keeping it all a surprise for Daniel."

"You are very welcome, Isobel. I'm glad it went well. I hope to hear from Daniel later. Tell him not to worry about the time difference. Just to call me as soon as he can. Goodbye."

Isobel wrapped up her email to her sister and saved it in the drafts folder. She didn't usually pay much attention to the operational Lassiter business—the boardroom politics were more her domain—although something in Myer's tone had sparked her curiosity. This was more than one of the usual fire drills.

She was disturbed as she read through the messages. One of Lassiter's key competitors had made a bold and well-publicized move to introduce new technology. This was significantly undermining Lassiter's market position. Some of Lassiter's customers were demanding a coordinated response. Lassiter's employees, concerned for their jobs, were looking for reassurance and leadership.

There were the usual everyday issues also demanding his attention. Stewart Pearson needed approval for several new hires and promotions. Varella needed his go-ahead on the Lassiter Cycling Team deal, which he mentioned that Grauermann had previously vetoed, but now had apparently agreed to directly with Hansi Olsen.

Isobel realized why Myer was getting frantic: Grauermann's team needed guidance and action from him. He had created an organization that could not function without him; his executives were afraid to make decisions lest they incur his disapproval, and yet he preyed upon their weakness and chided their lack of action.

Isobel put the messages back in their original pile. She would have to tackle him about them later; her tour awaited. She met Sally at 11 a.m. and they headed out for a tour of the city. Although her host did her best to talk up Singapore's attractions, Isobel found it all a little underwhelming.

It was a typically overcast, humid, and unbearably hot day as they took in the Merlions, drove by the cricket club, and through the narrow streets of Chinatown and Little India. Their tour of the botanical gardens was pleasant yet hardly memorable. Isobel realized that the Raffles Hotel was the only real icon in the whole city, and while most only entered its serene halls to pick up a souvenir in the gift shop or enjoy the hotel's signature cocktail, the Singapore Sling, no tourist's itinerary was complete without a visit there.

From the botanical gardens, they headed on to Orchard Road for some retail therapy. First they took lunch at the Crossroads Café in the Marriott Hotel. Sally had brought other visitors to this restaurant, which opened out onto the sidewalk. All had agreed that it was an awesome spot for people-watching. Sally desperately hoped for something novel to enliven Mrs. Grauermann. Sadly for her, it was just the regular stream: locals taking their lunch break and tourists from all parts of the world brandishing their cameras, maps, and guidebooks. Sally ordered herself the delicious nasi goreng. Moodily, Isobel refused to try any of the Asian dishes. The tuna Niçoise was as exotic as she was prepared to go.

Sally had heard from her Australian counterpart that Mrs. Grauermann liked to shop. She hoped that perhaps the afternoon would go better. She'd planned a trip along Orchard Road, thick with well-known expensive designer stores and multilevel malls filled with smaller shops selling clothes, jewelry, electronics, and cameras. They headed off expectantly. After an hour or so, they had been through Tangs department store, Tiffany's, Burberry, and Gucci. They'd also tried the Lucky Plaza mall. Mrs. Grauermann was still not happy. She complained that the designer stores were just selling the same things as they did everywhere else; and in the mall, the pestering hawkers trying to get her to visit their stores had irritated her. No, she did not need a camera, or a cell phone, or a fake watch. To complete Isobel's misery, it had started to rain and, despite Sally's skillful umbrella work, Isobel had gotten a little wet. As they sheltered in the doorway of the next mall, Isobel announced, "I have had about enough of this. Get the car and have them take me back to the hotel."

Sally pulled out her cell phone and said a few words in Chinese to summon the driver. He quickly drew up in his black BMW. As he came over with a large umbrella to escort Isobel to the car, Sally said quietly, "I am so sorry that you did not like our city, Mrs. Grauermann. I hope that you will come back again and I will do better."

"I very much doubt that," Isobel replied and dashed to the car.

The driver pulled away and Sally was abandoned on the sidewalk, her tears of shame and confusion mixing with the rain streaming down her face.

■

Forty hours later, the Grauermanns took breakfast in their next hotel suite. Suffering badly from jet lag, they did not yet feel ready join the throng. They were staying at the legendary Steigenberger Grandhotel Belvédère, the most stylish hotel in Davos, Switzerland. They had a deluxe suite, which at seven hundred square feet was perfectly adequate for the two of them. It was beautifully appointed, with a bedroom, a living room, and a balcony overlooking the front of the hotel. Isobel, however, was very unhappy.

"Explain to me again, Daniel. Why did Patsy not book us into the Belvédère Suite as I had instructed?"

"Isobel, we've been over this. I told you. It was already booked. She couldn't get it. This one is fine."

"She left it too late. That woman is incompetent. You should get rid of her. Fire her, or if you're too timid, pass her off to some low-life VP and get someone who's worthy to serve a Chairman and CEO. Why didn't she offer the hotel some money to bump whoever took our room?"

"Isobel, she tried. It's a sheikh from the Gulf for Christ's sake. We may be in the stinking rich category, but there's no winning a spending war with an oil billionaire."

Isobel screwed up her face to show her displeasure. She picked at her plain omelet and sipped her water while Grauermann enjoyed a generous plate of cold meats, cheeses, and hot croissants and savored his new morning beverage of choice, a strong, spicy Bloody Mary.

"Well, sheikh or no sheikh, I still blame Patsy. She should have made the booking earlier. Make sure she gets it sorted out for next year as soon as we get back."

"Yes, dear, I will. Is that before or after I fire her?"

"Oh, don't start trying to be funny, Daniel. It doesn't suit you."

They were now into the fifth week of the trip and were tired of each other's company. Hotels, irrespective of how luxurious they were, became irritating eventually. The tension of their row in Singapore still hung in the air. Although Isobel liked to needle Daniel about his long-standing assistant, she could only blame herself for their exhaustion and the small suite. At the last minute, when everything was arranged for the visit to Australia and Singapore, she had read about the Davos World Economic Forum and decided that they just had to fly from Singapore to be part of the event, rather than head back directly to the US.

They were at the center of things now. A little later they would take their place among the two thousand leading politicians, financiers, and business executives, as well as a handful of respectable showbiz celebrities. Four days of intense, lofty debates. Four nights of receptions, dinners, and seriously powerful networking. She looked forward to adding the finishing touches to her gloating email to her sister.

"So, CockRobin, have you fired that idiot McLaughlan yet?" She resumed the conversation with venom.

"Oh, you heard about my code name then? No. I'm not going to fire him just because you don't like his choice of restaurant. He's doing a decent job. He has some good ideas on where to take his business. And besides, I had a great day out with him at that golf club in Indonesia."

"Have you forgotten everything we talked about in Singapore, Daniel? I know that you drank way too much whiskey that night, but remember Jebby. I meant what I said. Besides, think of your position. You do not have 'great days out' with your employees. It undermines your authority. If you want a 'great day out,' try spending some time with me, not some ill-mannered opportunist. Fire him before your 'great day out' is the talk of the company." She drove her point home relentlessly with each repeated phrase.

"All right, Isobel. You win. I'll get Pearson to take care of it. We'll give him a good payoff to keep him quiet. Please can we drop all talk of the Jebby thing too?" Grauermann replied.

"Duly dropped." She smiled magnanimously. "Now that you mention Pearson, have you done anything about all those messages you got in Singapore? I told you that Patsy called you about them while you were out with McLaughlan."

"No, not yet. There's nothing out of the ordinary there. I don't know what all the fuss is about. It's just the usual operational grind. The guys just need to step up and deal with it."

"Daniel, I read some of the messages. They seemed a bit more serious to me. You'd better know what you're doing. You can't let things slip now."

"I'm on top of it, OK? Just leave things alone."

They finished their breakfast in stony silence.

■

On their return to earth from their stay in Davos, Grauermann's first priority was to navigate through a quarterly Board meeting. Inevitably, the news of the competitor's moves had bubbled up to some of the members. Grauermann knew that they would have questions. He didn't have the patience to listen to their sanctimonious claptrap. They'd just waste time on their irrelevant theories and pet projects. What did they know about running this business? He planned the agenda carefully. The morning session would be spent on the usual formalities and status briefings. Some thorough preparation would paper over the cracks, leaving the impression that all was running smoothly. Then for the main piece of the afternoon, he arranged for Christina Drago to give an update on the eLite venture.

■

Drago had known that the day of reckoning was approaching. She was looking for a substantial investment for eLite to get sufficient scale to flourish as an independent company, or the unit would have to fold back into another Lassiter division. The former outcome would be a big feather in her cap, the latter a major setback to her career. This presentation would be critical.

The day before the big event, she arranged a private meeting with Kathryn Gerrard to get some final coaching. She ran through the presentation material as Gerrard listened intently.

"That was good, Christina. I'm sure it will go very well with the Board tomorrow. I've made a few notes on the charts for you."

Drago looked through the deck. "Yes, thank you, Kathryn. Some good points here. I just don't have all these details to hand. I didn't really cover this aspect myself—Knight dug into it for me. I'll check with him before the meeting."

"Knight? Really?" Gerrard exclaimed.

"Yes, Knight. Everyone says he's the best strategist around here, so as this is my make-or-break time, I decided to get his input. I put that approachability plan to the test." Drago smiled.

"Let me guess, you convinced him that you're struggling with starting up the new business unit and needed some new ideas, and he couldn't resist offering coming to your rescue?" Gerrard speculated.

"Yep, pretty much. I bought a couple lunches at the local Vietnamese, and he delivered."

"Wow, that was a bold move, Christina. I like it. Did he bring anything useful?"

"Yes, many of the key recommendations in my presentation were his ideas. He was very helpful. We just have to make sure he doesn't find a way to get any credit."

"Christina, there's no worry there. He'll never get the opportunity. I know that Grauermann doesn't like him at all. Thinks he's flaky and disrespectful. You're all set. I'll be there to support you. This is your chance to shine."

■

Drago's presentation proposing the expansion of eLite went very well. Deferential and a little nervous at first, she ran through the prescribed charts with just the right balance of serious intensity and engaging humor. She concluded, "We've come a long way in this area the past year. We've still got a long way to go, but we're making progress. Now is the time to invest in the separate business so we can capitalize on the great foundation we have built." Her closing received a round of applause. She answered a few questions on her goals for the startup, deftly avoiding any specific commitments that would have needed Knight's detailed understanding, and then left to further applause.

"She's a pistol, Daniel. What a great prospect. All credit to you for bringing through," Howard Lyons said, a little too enthusiastically. He was intimidated by Grauermann. He hadn't recovered from his role in the meeting in New York, and harbored guilt over the Hastings takedown.

"Hear, hear, she's a breath of fresh air. There's some serious potential there. We need more like her," Gerrard added. Several others piled on the general acclaim.

"Thanks, folks. She's definitely a keeper," Grauermann responded. He paused, waiting for them to settle, then took a quick look around the table before continuing. "And that's why I've decide to promote her to report directly to me. I'm going to make her an Executive Vice President too. We are going to implement her recommendations. Set up the subsidiary. We need to encourage her and get that business unit leading our growth. Giving her the additional status will show everyone how serious we are."

Grauermann smiled as he watched his announcement sink in. He had discussed this move the previous evening with Isobel. She thought it was a masterstroke—secure Drago's loyalty, keep the Board focused on something new and sparkly. Isobel was hugely impressed with her pupil's progress.

"That's wonderful news, Daniel." Gerrard led the charge. "Bold. Imaginative. Well done."

"I agree, brilliant, Daniel," Lyons added, more sycophantically than ever.

The conversation swirled around for several minutes. The Board members stated and restated their praise for the significance of this move and then tried to outdo one another with their knowledge of the core lessons of Clayton Christensen's book *The Innovator's Dilemma*. Grauermann sat back, doing his best to suppress his self-satisfied grin. What had Isobel called it? Magpie Management?

■

The announcement of Drago's promotion to EVP, reporting directly to Grauermann, took many people by surprise. Grauermann hadn't discussed it with her boss or with the HR leader, Pearson. Isobel's endorsement was all he needed.

Pearson was disappointed. Not with the promotion itself, but with the breakdown in the career-management framework he was trying to enforce. Grauermann's lack of consultation with him also said something about Pearson's declining importance as a senior influencer. Gene Farris would never have made such a move without getting Pearson's opinion first. Pearson's exclusion would have significant consequences.

Drago's new role was an elevation in the organization—literally, as she moved upstairs to an office along the corridor from Grauermann. With the new resources at her disposal, she was soon hitting her stride—hiring new people, flying around the world, meeting potential partners and acquisition candidates. She was consumed in a whirlwind of activity, and she loved it. The status, the power, the visibility.

A floor lower, George Knight was despondent. When he read the announcement of her promotion, he was initially ambivalent. A little envious, yet fair enough; she'd worked hard for it. He thought they'd been getting along quite well, despite the persistent rumors of their rivalry. He'd been pleased to help her with her business plan. But then he learned that she'd presented to the Board with all of his ideas. He saw that she was implementing all of the things he had suggested, and even recruited a couple of members of his team. When he tried to object, his boss, Julie Dreiser, told him not to bother, he'd just be portrayed as a dinosaur blocking the way of progress. The thing that distressed him the most was that Drago didn't say thank you. In fact, she didn't acknowledge his role whatsoever. As soon as she became an EVP, their relationship imploded.

Frustration and disappointment ate away at him. He'd been working for Dreiser for several years. Although he enjoyed it, he had expectations of something more, especially following his move to HQ. But his old qualms about climbing the ladder—or being seen to be climbing it—had caused him to stall. Now Drago was moving to the sixth floor, and worse still, she'd used him to do so. He stewed over it for a month. The final straw was seeing Drago's smiling face on the cover of the Lassiter magazine, and an article in which she mentioned several other people who had helped her career yet said nothing of him. In the article, she explained the derivation of the name eLite: the *lite* for "Lassiter lite," as it would be serving consumers, not businesses, and the *e* to suggest more modern content, with the whole thing pronounced as *elite*. It was brilliant . . . and all his idea. One night, after knocking back most of the contents of his beer fridge, he wrote a letter of resignation to Dreiser and

CC'd Pearson. The letter was polite and respectful. Knight's mood was "Fuck the whole stinking lot of you."

Pearson and Dreiser shared his pain. They both felt bad for him: Pearson because he'd promised Knight that the HQ move would work out well, and Dreiser because she despised Drago. They wanted him to stay at Lassiter; the place would be so much worse without him. They got together to work out a plan to turn his head around.

"If we're going to change his mind, we need to find him a new challenge, Julie. Any ideas?"

"Let's think about it. It seems to me what he really likes doing, apart from kidding around, is one, being with customers; two, selling; and three, leading a team." Dreiser had Knight well fathomed out. "And he doesn't like HQ politics and what he sees as the 'infernal, internal bullshit.'"

"Yes, he loves to be out there on the front line, doesn't he?" Pearson agreed. "Have you got any current accounts that need a fresh face?"

"He wouldn't see that as a challenge, though. Been there, done that. To get him fired up, it needs to be big new deal that he has to sell."

"Let's get Ralph on the phone and see what's in the pipeline," Pearson suggested.

A short conversation with Varella found a possible solution. Lassiter had been asked to bid for a big new contract with a huge multinational corporation based in the Netherlands. They would need a leader for a team of around forty people working on the proposal. The post would be for at least six months and would involve intense long hours and not a lot of downtime.

"I'll talk to him about it, Julie. I expect he'll go for it. He usually takes my advice." Pearson was relieved.

"OK, Stewart. Let me know when you've met with him. I'll follow up with some reassuring words about keeping his day job open, et cetera, et cetera."

"Great, and we'll see where we are when the dust settles on this deal. It might be a whole new world by then."

CHAPTER ELEVEN

A Tale of Two Dinners

October 2011

"Welcome back to the Bowden Steakhouse, Mr. Grauermann, Mrs. Grauermann. We have your usual table waiting for you. Please bring your cocktails and follow me," the maître d' greeted them. The Grauermanns were at the Half Moon Hotel in Palm Beach. They'd arrived on Saturday afternoon so that they could enjoy dinner together and Daniel could have a round of golf before the Lassiter Board Retreat began on Sunday evening.

"Thank you. Nice to see you again," Isobel replied cheerily, looking elegant as ever in a beige mohair jacket, white blouse, and white trousers. Grauermann was a little more casual in khaki pants, a light blue open-neck shirt, and a navy blazer. They took their seats at a table by the window overlooking the golf course. It was a pleasant warm fall evening, the setting sun casting long shadows on the fairway.

"What time are you playing golf tomorrow?" Isobel asked.

"I have an eleven o'clock tee time. I'm not sure if I'm going to play, though." Grauermann was feeling under the weather, with a heavy cold and irritating cough.

"Who are you lined up to play with?"

"I haven't pinned that down. Stewart Pearson for sure. Then we'll make up a four with a couple of the other Board members or maybe some of the guys who are here to present. Livingston, or Jake Wiles-Sheridan, the Phillip Strand Group guy. There's a whole host of them arriving to-morrow. If I still feel crappy, I'll blow it off."

"I think it would better if you played. Helps you to relax. You need to be on top form for this Board session, Daniel. If you don't play golf, maybe you should get a massage at the spa. I'm going for a full day's pampering." To Grauermann, her suggestion of a trip to the spa was an insult to his masculinity. It got the response she desired.

"No, thanks. I'd rather golf with a fever than go in there with a bunch of metrosexuals." He finished off the last of his gin and tonic.

"Suit yourself, dear. I'm sure golf will be good too. The fresh air will help clear your head."

They chose their meals: jumbo shrimp cocktail and the loaded New York strip with parmesan-truffle steak fries for Grauermann, a simple grilled salmon with vegetable risotto for Isobel. A bottle of Australian Shiraz, a favorite from their trip to Adelaide, completed the order.

"You said Jake Wiles-Sheridan is going to be here? What's he doing?"

"He's helping to facilitate the sessions. Keep everything on track. We used to use Harold Griffith, my Chief of Staff. Although he's a li-ability these days. It's sad. He's totally disconnected from the business. The Board is really enamored with this PSG guy too. They think having him around adds some outside validation to everything. So we'll give the Phillip Strand Group five thousand a day for a management consultant to write things on flip charts and pass around Post-it notes."

"And Griffith is done? You'd better not keep him around then. He'll drag you down. Your Chief of Staff needs to be feared and respected, not a lame duck."

"Yes, you're right. But he's been with me for years. Him and Patsy. I have to take care of them."

"Oh, don't get me started on her. I've told you before she's incom-petent. You're just too soft. Just ditch them all."

"I can't. I've been working on my emotional intelligence." Grauer-mann laughed.

"What on earth is that?"

"It was some bullshit HR thing that PSG brought in. We got all this feedback about our leadership styles and how they affected other people. They all said I had to be more touchy-feely. Show more empathy."

"That sounds ridiculous. I hope you aren't serious."

"No kidding. I've been having one-on-one sessions with a coach to help me get it, another consultant. You'd like this one, though. He's an Aussie."

"An Australian coach? Is he teaching you how to speak without a stammer too?"

Isobel's movie reference went over Grauermann's head.

"No, no. I've got another guy for that. Wolf Becker. Used to be a TV reporter. He writes all my speeches now too."

"Let me get this straight, Daniel. You have a consultant writing your speeches and telling you how to read them, another consultant telling you how to manage your people, and another one running your meetings?"

"You missed one. As part of the new, approachable me, I'm doing all this social media stuff too. I've a blog, and Twitter. They got me a ghostwriter, the same one Ralph Varella uses. That seems a bit much to me. Having a ghostwriter is one thing—no one in my position actually writes themselves—but sharing one with someone else is just . . . kinda inauthentic. Don't you think?"

She ignored his ludicrous question.

Seeing a lull in the conversation, the waiter took the opportunity to serve the wine. He skillfully uncorked the bottle and poured Grauermann a small taste. After receiving the customary nod of approval, the waiter filled their glasses, put the bottle on ice, and left them again. Up until this point the conversation had been lighthearted, almost playful. Now it took a more spiteful tone.

"Do you do anything yourself these days, Daniel? Is this why Lassiter is struggling to respond to your competitor's moves?"

"Oh, that's unfair," Grauermann replied defensively. "I still have to make all the big decisions on the deals, the customers, and the team. Anyway, what are you hearing about the competitors?" Grauermann took a large gulp of the wine.

"I just pick up a few things from people. It seems that your technology is becoming obsolete." She sipped her wine, recalling the messages she had read in Singapore.

"Well, you shouldn't listen to rumors. We're responding. Our new technology is coming. The customers and employees are really excited with our plans."

"All of the clients are happy with things, then? They're all sticking with you?"

"Not all of them, no. Not 100 percent. It's impossible to keep everyone happy, you know that. There'll always be a few issues, that's just normal."

"What about this big customer dropping you in England? Sabbi sent me an article she saw in a newspaper there."

"Well, it's true there have been a few issues with that account— it's just their negotiating tactics to try to get a better deal. We've got Houston, our top Quality Management guy, in there now. We'll get it under control."

"That's not very reassuring, Daniel. I hope you don't have our future prosperity, and your reputation, resting on that boring little man."

"Come on now, Isobel. He'll turn that decision around, you mark my words."

"Well, I'm glad you have so much faith in him. If he doesn't resolve it, just make sure it's him that takes the fall, Daniel. That's the reason you have these people. They protect you."

"Let's change the subject, shall we? My head is aching anyway without you loading up all this operational crap to fire at me. How's the salmon?"

"It's actually very good. You know, I like this place. I've told you we should have the executive retreat here. Much more convenient for us than those places out west."

"Yes, I'll see what we can do. Probably not next year, though, as we've already booked the Bourne Canyon again."

"I'm surprised you keep agreeing to that. That was Farris's favorite venue. His influence should be dead and buried by now."

"Well, it is in most things, Isobel. There are just a few little traditions that we keep on. How are things going with your business these days?" He tried to change the subject.

"It's doing really well."

"You don't seem to spend much time there anymore."

"With all the traveling that we've been doing, I haven't had time. Besides, I was getting bored with it all. I don't get involved in the day-to-day now. I leave it all to the team. I've got plenty of time on my capable hands. Maybe you should hire me as a consultant too."

"What does that mean?"

"My business is growing and making some good profits. It seems you could use a little of that."

Grauermann reacted sharply. "Well, it's hardly comparable, is it? Your small business turning over, what, a few hundred thousand? And Lassiter."

"It's $2.7 million actually. Not in the Lassiter league, I know. But at least our numbers are headed in the right direction."

"Do you never rest? You have to rub it in, don't you? Yes, we've had a bad spell. There have been a couple of bad quarters. We'll get out of it. It's just getting things settled back down. We'll get the share price back into the twenties again soon."

"You'd better. Or you'll be out. And all those options in your retirement plan won't be worth very much."

"Now you're going too far, Isobel. I told you, it's a bad spell. Nothing more. We're going to fix it. And besides, no one's going to fire me. Not that bunch of directors. They've not got the guts. There's no one there capable of replacing me anyway."

"Don't be naive, Daniel. No one is irreplaceable. What about your team? All those succession plan candidates?"

"My team? No way. They've all reached as far as they can go. Flaky sales guys, most of them. And as for the succession plan people, two of them are promising. But they're still too green. No need to worry about them."

"What about an outsider?"

"The Board won't pay the freight. They're too conservative. Anyone capable of running this company would want two or three times what the compensation committee would agree to."

"So that's it then. You're fireproof until one of these long-term people is ready?"

"Yes, that's how I see it."

"What will you do?"

"I think we have a good strategy. We just need to execute it. The Phillip Strand Group is working on a whole new program, Project Break Out 2. I've got the little card we're giving to everyone here." He pulled a small plastic card from his wallet and read the bullet points to her in a deep, dark TV-commercial-voice-over style. "'Point 1. We are improving our emotional intelligence.'" He reverted to his normal tone. "I've told you about that.

"'Point 2. We are managing by walking around.' We are going to do much more of that. I'll be doing more town hall meetings, lunches in the cafeteria, that sort of thing . . .

"'Point 3. We are focused on our core competencies. Point 4. We are reengineering our business processes. Point 5. We are embracing Six Sigma.' We're going to get green belts so we can isolate and eliminate the cause of defects."

Isobel's incredulity finally compelled her to interrupt. "Green belts? Why on earth would wearing a green belt make any difference?"

"I don't know. Something to do with the methodology, I think. Houston's running that one. And here's the last one. The best of the lot.

'Point 6. We are having fun at work.' We're acting on the feedback from the employee-engagement survey, and we want everyone to have fun at work. We're getting all modern with open-plan offices, lounge areas, and table tennis tables."

"Fun? At work? My goodness. Don't these people understand the idea of work-life balance? Work is work. It's not meant to be fun."

"Well, that's not the way the PSG guys see things these days, Isobel."

"Yes, I can tell. It's truly a management consultant's dream. Anyway, I don't care about all that. What I meant was what are you going to do to protect yourself from those succession plan candidates you say are the only ones who could replace you? Who are they?"

"Oh, right, them. Drago and Knight. They don't worry me. I'm not as naive as you think. I've dealt with them too. I promoted Drago—she reports directly to me. She's running that start-up eLite business unit, selling our current technology to consumers. With the other changes in the market, it's a lot less important than she thinks it is. Besides, none of the other people in my team like her much. She's quite aggressive. She's too busy scoring points off them and stepping on them, so desperate to climb the last few rungs, that she's forgotten the good qualities that got her there in the first place. She'll flame out."

"And Knight?"

"Oh, he had a meltdown when I promoted Drago. Threatened to quit. Pearson talked him out of it. He's off leading some new deal in Europe. But he's done. Not a serious contender. Probably never was."

"That's very clever, Daniel. You've dealt with those two. I guess they'll lose their other sponsors and fade away. I'm excited. I've taught you well."

"So let's enjoy the rest of our dinner, Isobel. Maybe I'll have a brandy later too. This meeting's going to be a breeze. There'll be some griping tomorrow about the results and the share price, then on Monday we'll present the strategy decks and the new Project Break Out 2 program. Over dinner, Jake Wiles-Sheridan will quietly give his 'independent'

opinion that it's a great plan, while he calculates the price of the thousands of billable days for him and his colleagues. Then first thing on
Tuesday, I'll introduce two shiny new succession candidates, really young
folks in their early forties, as evidence of my new emotional intelligence
and commitment to prepare the next generation. We'll do a bit of the
formal approval business, and they'll all go home happy. I think we have
a contingency plan to cover every possible twist."

Meanwhile, a few miles down the coast, a larger group gathered for
dinner. Pearson had invited his guests to celebrate his thirty-fifth year
with Lassiter. He had also asked all of them to keep the meeting and
their involvement confidential. They thought it a little unusual, but he
explained that he did not want to offend others whom he had chosen
not to invite. They had kept their promise, and the meeting was taking
place in complete secrecy. Pearson had arrived early to ensure he was the
first there and to check on the arrangements. He greeted everyone as
they arrived with a discreet conversation to reconfirm their commitment
to confidentiality.

As they gathered in the small private bar area, the seniority of the
group was apparent: there were both of Lassiter's former CEOs, Clay
Stevenson and Gene Farris, who remained two of the largest individual shareholders; former Board member Bennett Gallagher; two current
Board members, Gerrard and Lyons; and Edmund Patten III, the reclu-
sive chairman of Collateral General. There were no partners, no party
favors or other decorations. As they all had privately surmised, Pearson's
milestone was not the primary item on the agenda.

Once the hors d'oeuvres had been served and the waiters had left the
room, Pearson addressed the group, his voice betraying a little nervousness.

"Firstly, thank you all for coming. I'm really pleased you could
make it. Clay, Gene, Bennett, Edmund, Kathryn, Howard—thank you.

I'm not usually the conspiratorial type. Normally, I put what I'm thinking right out there. And I will tonight. But I needed to discuss things with you all before others have a chance to respond. Frankly, I feared I would be fired if news of this meeting came out, so thank you again for your secrecy."

There were a few groans as he mentioned his fear of reprisals, which they knew would only be carried out by one person.

"No issues, Stewart. Why don't you tell us what's on your mind? I think we can all take a good guess, but it would be best to hear from you." Clay Stevenson, the elder statesman now in his eighties, put Pearson at ease.

"Thanks, Clay. As you all know, I've been with Lassiter for many years and yes, we've had some great times and some lean times. Guys, I've never seen it like this. We are really in trouble."

Pearson looked around the table. His eyes were filled with tears, his usual matter-of-fact style overwhelmed by his outrage.

"Everyone is writing us off; our ratings are abysmal. And you've all seen the results. And then there's the share price. When it went below twenty dollars, I knew it was time to do something."

He paused again, seemingly inviting a reaction. Lyons was the first to speak.

"We've all seen the poor results and the share price, Stewart. It's cost us all a lot of money. And I suspect we've all heard Grauermann's analysis of why we've been overtaken and how to respond. Are you suggesting that we take some other action?"

"Yes, I am, Howard. I'm afraid I am."

"Then what are you proposing, Stewart?"

"What you say is true, Howard. There are a lot of changes in the market, and Grauermann has a plausible strategy. But he can't implement it. You—we—have to remove him and get someone new, before the company goes under or is swallowed up for loose change by a competitor."

"That's a pretty bold statement, Stewart."

Lyons played his role as Pearson's apparently skeptical inquisitor so well that no one would have any inkling that the two had spent that afternoon rehearsing this scene.

Lyons was about to say his next line when Edmund Patten raised a hand. "May I join the conversation?"

"Yes, please, Edmund. We'd be glad of your insight," Lyons deferred.

"As the largest holder of Lassiter shares, Collateral General is obviously very concerned about the company's recent performance. Grauermann has regularly reassured us that he has a plan to catch up with the competition, refresh the technology, and make sure we don't become obsolete. His investor-relations guy also briefed us just last week on financial projections they'll use at your Board meeting. He made a good case for us to hang on and trust him and Grauermann. They're all confident that they can steer Lassiter out of the current slide and get the share price back to a respectable level."

Pearson and Lyons were crestfallen. Pearson started to sit down, his shoulders slumped. Their plan had been to get through all of their arguments and then engage Gene Farris and Clay Stevenson in the crusade before hearing from the more neutral Patten and the Board members. Without Patten's support, their move to oust Grauermann would be dead on arrival. Momentarily they assumed all was lost, before Patten continued.

"However, C-suite execs and investor-relations people always tell a good story. And I mean always. But I look to get a deeper insight. I cultivate a few contacts. Nothing improper, nothing financial, just a feel for the companies we invest heavily in. I've been hearing from people inside Lassiter. Senior people, good people, who tell me things will not improve while Grauermann has the job. I'm interested to hear what you propose to do about it, Stew. If it is a good plan, it will have the full support of Collateral General."

Pearson stood up proudly and looked around the room. He was

suddenly surprised, delighted, and scared all at once: his coup was on. He still wanted everyone's approval and buy-in to the plan. It would make it much easier to execute if they acted as one publicly. And that required their private resolution.

"Although it's a confirmation of my bad news, I'm pleased to get that endorsement, Edmund. I think we all appreciate the significance of what you just said . . ." He paused to ensure that they did. "However, I'd still like to hear from you all."

Pearson asked each of the others their views. Clay Stevenson was very concerned about the state of employee morale. He'd always been a great communicator and in his time was very popular with the staff. He asked Pearson some questions about the latest employee survey, and when Pearson had revealed the dreadfully low scores, he said calmly, "For that alone, we have to make a change."

Gene Farris was more cutting and to the point, yet also more cryptic. "Listen, Stewart, it's very simple. I was always taught 'he that lives by the sword, shall die by the sword.' It's time for him to go."

Bennett Gallagher also kept it short and characteristically candid. "I watched him and supported him. Then my friend Dalton Hastings took up his cause and put him in as CEO. We made a bad mistake. I'll be glad to make amends."

Gerrard saw things through her own experience. "Lassiter is in the ditch, cutting corners, funding cheap events and that cycling team—no company with serious ambition sponsors a cycling team, for God's sake. I agree it's time for a change."

Last was Howard Lyons. "You know I'm with you, Stewart. I have been since the day he bullied his way into the Chairman's job, much to my chagrin."

Lyons shook his head ruefully and then returned to the script he and Pearson had prepared. "So, we are unanimous. He has to go. Stewart, do you have a proposal of who replaces him? Is there someone you've lined up?"

"No, Howard. This time we should get a proper selection panel and get one of the exec search firms to help us."

"Aren't we making one big assumption here? That he'll agree to all this? Who's going to tell him? And when? What happens if he says no? Or wants to negotiate?" Lyons set up Pearson to lay out the last part of the plan.

"I think we can be confident that he'll agree to it. We'll give him a generous package—Drake Devonshire can negotiate that for us."

"OK, great. Last question. Who's going to tell him? And when?"

"I've arranged to play golf with him tomorrow at eleven. I'll tell him then. I'm ready to do it by myself. The other two slots are still open. I'd appreciate the moral support . . ."

"I'll join you, Stew," said Lyons. "I was going to try to play tomorrow anyway."

"Thanks, Howard. Much appreciated."

Clay Stevenson rose to his feet and stood behind Pearson, hands resting on his shoulders.

"Stew, I really applaud what you've done here tonight. You've shown the sort of leadership that made this company great. I may be the old guy here, but I still care deeply about this company. My company. And I can still get around a golf course too. So I'll be there with you. Daniel will be very surprised to see me. He'll know something is up."

Pearson looked up over his shoulder with a proud, shy smile. As a younger manager, he had craved Stevenson's attention and sponsorship. Now he had his respect too. "That's fantastic, Clay. Thank you."

"Guys, promise me just one thing," Stevenson added. "We don't get fooled again. Please select wisely. A smart, farsighted person that gets the best out of our people. That's the way we put this company back together again."

"We will, Clay. We will," Pearson replied. "Now, let's enjoy the rest of our dinner, shall we? I think we have a contingency plan to cover every possible twist."

CHAPTER TWELVE

It's Not What You Know

October 2011- February 2012

The final chapter of Knight's journey began on Halloween with an un-expected call from Pearson. Knight had just collected a new car, ordered over the summer with a very precise spec and loads of extras. Fortunately he'd set up the Bluetooth connection before leaving the dealers as, while he was cautiously driving home, he got the call from Pearson.

"Hi, George. How are you doing? I haven't seen you for months. How's the bid going?"

"I'm doing great, thanks, Stewart. I've just got back. We're waiting for the client decision. Fingers crossed."

Knight had been away for most of the previous six months, pur-suing a big deal. It had been great therapy for him, assembling a team from all over the world—some of whom had worked together before, many who had not—and a real challenge getting them to all collaborate. Knight was called upon as a social worker, agony aunt, peacekeeper, and occasional disciplinarian. He didn't complain, though. It was part of the job; understanding people was essential to getting the best out of them.

"Yes, I heard you did a fabulous job leading that team, George. Well done. How's the family?"

"They're fine, Stewart. Pleased to have me home. We won't hear the outcome on the deal for a few weeks. I'm taking a bit of time off."

"Very good, George. Well-deserved after all that travel. Did you see any soccer over there? I believe those Dutch teams are pretty good?"

Pearson was going through the usual pleasantries, although Knight could tell he had something else on his mind. Then Pearson hit him with it.

"George, the reason for the call is that tomorrow we'll be announcing Daniel Grauermann's retirement."

"Oh, OK. Thanks for letting me know, Stewart." He was a little surprised, but not totally shocked. He was more puzzled why he was getting advance notice. Then Pearson dropped the real bombshell.

"George, I wanted to let you know that you will be considered as a candidate to replace him. Your time has come."

Knight swerved into another lane, narrowly avoiding wrecking his new car on its first trip.

"Wow, Stewart. I'm astonished. I'm driving right now, let me pull over so I can call you back." His mind was racing as he parked at a Starbucks. He'd assumed he was out of the running once Drago had been promoted. Everyone expected her to be Grauermann's successor. He called Pearson back.

"Is this trick or treat, Stewart? You're putting me on, right?'

"Surprised, eh, George? Well, you shouldn't be. I told you that taking the HQ job would be a good move."

"Yes, you did, Stewart. Good job I took your advice." *Even though I hated it and had to head to Holland to recover my sanity,* he thought, but didn't say.

"So, George, let me give you a little more. The company needs a new CEO with a big change in leadership style to get us back to our old values."

Pearson spoke softly as if to underline the significance of the coaching he was conveying.

"In the formal succession plan, you're considered 'Ready with Development,' although that reflects Grauermann's view that no one is 'Ready Now.'"

"Right, Stewart. I'm taking this all in."

"By Grauermann's definition 'Ready Now' would mean you were solely focused on financial results. 'Ready Now' means you've lost track of the needs of customers, are detached from employees, and, above all, appreciate the trappings of the CEO role. I hope that you will never meet that definition of 'Ready Now,' George." Pearson said this last phrase slowly and deliberately, underlining the guidance and his strong emotions about it all.

"The Grauermann announcement will be made public tomorrow. You aren't to discuss the CEO selection with anyone. We have to keep it confidential. You'll be in competition with some internal candidates and some external ones." He was back to his normal snappy style.

"Right, Stewart. I get it. How many candidates are there? Can you tell me who they are?"

"No, I can't tell you that, George. As part of the evaluation team, I have to be professional about all this. You'll have to stick to the rules." Pearson had gone all formal on him. "You'll get some details on the process from the external recruitment firm that we're using to run the selection. I've got to go now. Good luck, George."

Knight left the call elated, convinced that Pearson would be pulling for him. After all, he'd been the beneficiary of Pearson's coaching and sponsorship for years. And there was nothing the HR folks liked better than a risen-through-the-ranks story. Besides, they were soccer buddies too.

Following his call with Pearson, Knight went into the Starbucks to compose himself, straying from his usual no-coffee-in-the-afternoon rule, a self-imposed restriction that usually assured a good night's sleep and was now abandoned in favor of a triple-shot venti latte. His immediate consideration was whether to mention this news at home. He usually shared the big news from work with Carole; keeping her in the know was important to family harmony. But he decided not to tell her about this right away. One step at a time. He went home and showed off the new car. Fortunately the car and then the trick-or-treating ritual provided him with plenty of distractions.

That night, he paid dearly for the abundance of caffeine in his system. He could not get to sleep. He tried all the tricks he knew: soccer clubs recounted alphabetically, Springsteen songs, even the usually successful blank-mind, still-body Zen Buddhist meditation routine. Nothing worked. His mind was racing about the news from Pearson. What would he do if he became CEO? Some of his thoughts were not good ones. First there was his "up against the wall" list. Who would he fire? Who had crossed or slighted him? Who might undermine him? He didn't come up with much of a list, though. He didn't bear any grudges—disappointing really. He did think about all the people that had helped along the way. He also thought about other things he'd do, where he'd focus his time, the type of people he'd hire and promote. He imagined meetings, rehearsed speeches for town halls, composed tweets and blogs, and planned conversations with customers. He was wide awake, his thoughts so vivid it was as if he were dreaming. Eventually he gave up trying to sleep, got up, and went to his study. Using the half-light thrown off by the screensaver on his computer screen, he scribbled in his notebook the ideas that had been running through his head. Then he picked out a book from his large unread pile. *30, 60, 90 Days*. A thoughtful HR person had given it to him at the time of another move. He couldn't comment on its business value, although it certainly proved a great cure for insomnia. He got a couple of paragraphs into the preface and finally fell asleep in the chair.

The announcement about Grauermann's retirement came out the following day as Pearson had said it would. There was not much surprise within the company. They all knew that they were due for a change. Everything was on the slide; going to pot, down the tubes, or to hell in a hand basket; turning to worms; hitting the skids. Whatever the individual's choice of phrase, an insidious sense of inevitable decline shrouded every collective activity, and there was an apathetic futility present at every meeting. Grauermann had tried to pull off a belated personality makeover. It was as if he'd had counseling; the new man began publishing a chatty weekly blog and using Twitter to promote Lassiter. Even if this had all been genuine, it would've been too little too late. But it was so obviously ghostwritten that it simply opened up the G-man to ridicule. Many also scoffed at his town hall meetings and new routine of walking the corridors at 3 p.m. each Thursday. The biggest scorn was reserved for the table tennis table bizarrely set up outside his office. Occasionally he would wander out and challenge people with a "Show me what you've got." The sight of seasoned Lassiter execs, with their jackets off, ties loosened, and sleeves rolled up, scurrying around the floor for a stray table tennis ball, was as much fun at work as anyone could take.

That all changed the day after the announcement came out. The table tennis table disappeared. Grauermann's blogs and tweets stopped. The members of his mysterious security detail, two-ton Bud and his sidekicks, were laid off. The Phillip Strand Group contingent dwindled and then disappeared completely within a few weeks. Without Grauermann to sponsor them, the other executives quickly dispensed with their services. In their place came a group of attorneys from QPQ. They all sat together in the canteen at lunchtime like nerdy undergraduates, with their partner, Chip Chambers, and Lassiter's Robert Livingston. Knight had preferred the PSG guys. At least they were ostensibly trying to do something positive with their extensive decks of flimsy, formulaic prescriptions.

Knight learned that Lassiter hadn't won the big deal. He was very disappointed; all of that effort from the team, the team that he had built, had been in vain. He begrudgingly made a last trip over the Atlantic for the formal debrief. The client's lead executive gave Lassiter lots of praise about their strong proposal, great team, and competitive price. Sadly their main competitor had beaten them with their new technology. It offered a more "innovative solution" and allowed for a much more "aggressive" implementation program. In the informal version over a beer later, Knight learned that the winners had committed that their technology would do things right out of the gate that Lassiter had said would take eighteen months or more to develop. He knew—he suspected that the client even knew—that the competition would fail to live up to their promises, yet the decision was made.

Is it better to win with a lie or lose with the truth? He consoled himself that it must be the latter. All the same, it hurt. He would never get a liking for the bitter taste of defeat.

For a few days, he fretted about the impact the decision might have on his chances at the CEO role. On the one hand, if Lassiter had won, it would have been a big plus for him, a significant success for the company at a time when a lot of other things weren't going too well; on the other, he'd been nominated in the proposal to be the lead executive on the deal and, while Lassiter could have found a suitable replacement, it might have been a reason to exclude him from the big job. Now he would be available, which was often a major determinant of internal promotions.

His anxiety grew when by mid-December he'd still not heard from the recruitment firm. Maybe they'd had second thoughts about including him? The process was certainly being kept watertight. He was musing to himself one morning when Christina Drago came into his office, unannounced. They'd exchanged cursory nods to each other in meetings and in the canteen, but they hadn't spoken for several months. He considered several different melodramatic reactions. Sarcasm: "To what do we owe the privilege?" Hostility: "How dare you barge into my office?" In the end he settled on his natural one, affable optimism.

"Christina, this is a surprise. How are you? I don't seem to have seen you in ages."

"I'm well, thanks, Knight. Busy, busy, busy. I guess we all are with all the changes going on."

"Yes, strange days, indeed. What can I do for—"

"I'll keep it brief, Knight. I'd like to get your ideas on something. Can you meet me for lunch today?"

"Sure, OK. Sounds intriguing. Canteen? Twelve thirty?"

"No, not there, Knight. I'd like to go out somewhere. Talk off the record. How about we meet at the Vietnamese place again?"

"That's fine with me, Christina. See you there then."

She headed out as abruptly as she'd come in. He spent the rest of the morning on a conference call listening to the lessons learned from the failed deal, but with his mind focused on what on earth Drago could want.

They had been to Saigon Pho Nomenal several times during their brief collaborative phase. He took it as a good sign that she wanted to meet there. It was a very basic spot in a strip mall. The food was tasty and the service quick, and it was certainly well out of the way of the usual Lassiter executive lunch crowd. Drago had taken a table and was waiting for him. They both ordered the seafood pho lunch special with fried spring rolls and made a little small talk about the weather and holiday season plans until the food arrived. Lacing his soup with a very large splurge of Sriracha, Knight asked with a contrived nonchalance, "So, what's up then, Christina? You wanted to run something by me? Do you need another eLite idea?" He couldn't resist the barb. Although time had passed and the circumstances were now very different, Knight still bore the scars of his last entanglement with Drago. *Tread warily. Don't be drawn,* he told himself.

"Ouch. I guess I deserved that. It wasn't my best moment, was it? I guess I could tell you that it wasn't all my fault, but I guess you don't want to hear it."

"All that guesswork—that's not like you, Christina. Usually so certain, so precise. Don't worry, I'm fine. Water under the bridge," he lied.

"Great, because I've got a much bigger idea for you to think about."

Knight visibly winced. He sensed danger. More significantly, he'd severely overdone the Sriracha. He squeezed a wedge of lime and dropped in another sprig of the fresh basil, hoping to calm things down. He didn't pick up the invitation to ask about her idea.

"The food in here is terrific, isn't it?" he squeaked, then gulped some soda, letting the ice cool the inside of his mouth.

Drago pressed on, determined not to be distracted from her mission. "Knight, as you may know, I'm being considered to be the next CEO. I hear that they've put you on that list too."

He couldn't hide his surprise. "Yes, you're ri—" He was cut off by a giant-sized hiccup that was heard all around the restaurant. The spiciness of the soup had sent him into a spasm. "Sorry about th—" *Hiccup*. He gulped some more soda. "Shit, sor—" *Hiccup*. "It will go in a min—" — "Sorry, what were you—" *HICCUP*. The more he tried to stifle them, the more violent they got. *HICCUP . . . HICCUP . . . HICCUP*.

"You really can't make this shit up, can you, Knight?" Drago rolled her eyes, no trace of sympathy or concern. "I'm trying to put a serious proposition to you, and you can't listen because you've got the fucking hiccups? Jesus. Let me know when you're back with us, would you?" she snarled, her sarcasm as stinging as the Sriracha. She ate her own soup dismissively and checked for messages on her iPhone while Knight composed himself. After several more hiccups and a serious amount of soda consumption, he was finally able to speak without interruption.

"There we go. So, yes, Christina. The CEO job. You're right. But I thought that it was meant to be confidential."

"I have a good source. Don't worry, I'm not going to tell anyone else."

"Good. Although I still don't get where you're going with this. What's your big idea?" Knight asked, his attempt to play things cool totally ruined by his overindulgence in hot sauce.

"You probably also heard that I'm the strong favorite to get the job."

"Well, that's your opinion. I think I've got just a good a shot at it."

"Oh get real, Knight. You've got no chance. As far as I hear it, they only put you in there to make up the numbers and keep Pearson happy."

Knight was silent, doubt in his mind. He had been surprised when he'd learned of his inclusion. His only contact had been with Pearson. Maybe it was all just a charade?

Drago sensed that she had him just where she wanted him, and quickly pressed home her advantage. "George, lots of people tell me that we make a great team. We both have our strengths, and we complement one another. So I've got a proposal for you." She had his full attention. "If I get the CEO job, I'll give you a big role in my team. Direct report."

"Interesting idea, Christina. What were you thinking?"

"You'd be my Chief of Staff, George."

"Your Chief of Staff?" His cool had now totally evaporated. "Thanks, but no, thanks. I'm no one's chart bitch. You'll have to do better than that."

Of course, following her three *P*s methodology, Drago had expected this reaction and had her next card perfectly positioned at the top of the deck. She dealt.

"How about EVP of Sales and Marketing? That's your real sweet spot, isn't it? You'd be great in that role."

"And what about Ralph?"

"He can retire. Time he did anyway. I know you call him Benny the Ball behind his back, by the way."

Knight smiled although he could not hide his surprise at her insight. He replied as calmly as he could, "I'll think about it. If I don't get the CEO job and you do, this could work."

"No, no, no. You don't get that option, George. If you want to guarantee the Sales job, you have to drop out of the CEO process and help make sure they choose me. Tell your buddy Pearson that you've decided it should go to me, that it's too soon for you—young family, whatever you want."

"And if I don't?" Knight asked, dreading her answer.

"If I get the CEO job, you'll be the first one out of the door." She smiled her *All's fair in love and war* smile, then took twenty dollars from her purse and placed it on the table. "I'll give you until the New Year to decide." She stood up and calmly departed, leaving Knight shell-shocked.

■

Knight agonized for several days over Drago's ultimatum. It would feel bad to drop out, but it did seem to make a lot of sense. She had the right profile. And where was she getting all of her information? She must have had the inside track. He decided that he'd talk it over with Ball, only to let his friend know that he was going to take the bird in the hand. He'd let her win. He felt relieved and excited. EVP for Sales and Marketing would be cool.

It didn't take long for him to change his mind again, his ambition rekindled by fortunately avoiding misfortune. His mailbox was stuffed on Christmas Eve, filled with dozens of holiday cards of adorable smiling families in matching sweaters, the obligatory annual letters that no one read, and the usual mass of brochures and junk mail. He'd been preparing some of the Christmas Day food and, fortified by a couple of glasses of red wine, had carelessly assumed that the one standard white envelope was his personal, pre-approved offer of another prestigious, indispensable credit card that he could do without. He tossed it into the recycling bin and only then noticed the Doolittle Associates logo. He opened it up at the kitchen counter, eagerly unfolding the crisp letter. He read the first formally worded paragraph confirming that the Board of Lassiter had retained Doolittle to identify and select their new CEO and President. Knight had been nominated as a candidate for the process. Almost two months on from the call from Pearson, it suddenly felt real.

"Yes!" He pumped his fist.

"What are you all excited about?" Carole had joined him in the kitchen.

It was time to tell her about this. He couldn't keep it to himself any longer.

"It's something I've been meaning to tell you."

"Uh-oh. We're not moving again, are we?"

"No, not at all. It's better. I told you about G-man retiring, didn't I?"

"Yes, good riddance to bad rubbish."

"Well, I'm one of the candidates to replace him."

She took this news in her usual calm way. "Oh, that's good, George. Well done. I knew there had to be a silver lining to all this moving," she said with an unemotional smile. "What's the timing? When do you find out?"

"That's all in this letter." He sat at the kitchen table and read the letter out loud. "'The process will comprise of a series of interviews, simulations, and other assessments with a selection panel. The panel will reach a decision by the end of February, with an anticipated start date of April 1.'"

"You better start doing some preparation. Do you know who else is in the running?"

"No. I've been trying to get Pearson to tell me, but they're playing it very close. And I'm not allowed to tell anyone else. It says . . ." He read from the letter again, "'Please complete the form confirming your wish to participate in the process and adherence to a strict nondisclosure agreement. All correspondence will be sent to your home address. The form must be returned to Doolittle Associates by January 5 with a copy to Drake Devonshire.'"

"What about the selection panel? Do you know who they are?"

"No. Oh, hang on . . ."

It was then that he saw the second page. It had a list of the panel members. He read it with astonishment.

"This is fucking crazy. It's someone's idea of a joke."

"Why? What's the matter?"

"Carole, I know all these people. Look." He handed her the list, which she read to him.

"'Ms. Jacquelyn Crawford, Corporate Executive, FRSC.' Didn't you used to have them as a client?"

"Yes, and she was the main customer. I helped her get the job. I saw her a few months back too. We're still on really good terms."

"'Mr. Stewart Pearson, Corporate Vice President, Human Resources, Lassiter.' I know him, the guy who went to Japan with you and Dunc?"

"Yes. That's him."

"'Ms. Kathryn Gerrard, Chairman Elect, Lassiter.'"

"Yes, it seems that they're making her the Chairperson. That's a surprise."

"Have you met her before?"

"A few times, off and on. She's always been very friendly. Her becoming Chairperson should be good for me."

"'Mr. Conrad Konetski, Managing Director, Doolittle Associates.' I recognize that name. Who's he?"

"You know him too. That's Con Konetski, my CELF buddy. Remember that auction? The crazy dinner party when his wife was all spaced out? We thought he was screwing her sister."

"Him? Really? You're kidding me."

"No, that's him. He's a real big shot at that headhunting firm apparently. Who'd have thought it?"

"'Ms. Moira Kenney, Distinguished Analyst, Deep Insights LLC. Surely you don't know her too, George?"

"I do, seriously. She was at uni with me. She was practically married to one of my friends." He suddenly remembered that he was meant to get in touch with her following their chance encounter in NYC, but he'd never gotten around to it. Oh well. At least they went back a long way. He doubted that Drago or any of the other candidates knew Kenney back in her wilder days.

"And the last one is 'Mr. Edmund Patten III, Chairman, Collateral General.'"

"That's the one that I really don't get. I think that's Cindy's dad."

"Why on earth is he on there? What's Collateral General?"

"I don't know. Let's google it and find out."

Carole grabbed her MacBook and searched "Collateral General."

"George, it's a major private investment fund, registered in the Cayman Islands, with its main office in New York."

With a little further digging, she found out that Collateral General was huge, with over three hundred billion dollars under management. One of their biggest investments was in Lassiter Corporation, of which they were the largest shareholder.

"Look here. Edmund Patten is listed as Collateral General's Chairman."

It began to make sense. He'd met with Patten two or three times since Cindy's Christmas party. They'd shared a coffee and chatted about Lassiter's woes. Knight felt a little cheated, disappointed that Patten's friendship perhaps had an ulterior motive behind it, yet at the same time he was elated that he would have someone else helping him.

"These are the people who are going to pick the new CEO. Jacquelyn, Stewart, Kathryn, Moira, Con, and Edmund. I already know *all* of them. Actually, I don't just know them, Carole; they're supporters. And I've helped them. In some cases like Jacquelyn's it was a long while back, but still, all that goodwill has to put me in pole position."

"I'm really pleased that you're included, although don't count your chickens, George. Are you sure you aren't deluding yourself? Just seeing the positives with these people? They can't all be on your side."

"No, I'm not deluding myself. I'm convinced. I've networked my way to the top!"

Knight was wholly convinced of his advantage, his enthusiasm affirming his positive interpretation of events, several of which, were he not confusing memories with aspirations, could be seen in a very different light.

"Well, even if they are your supporters, you still need to work the process." Carole still wasn't taking anything for granted.

"Yes, good advice. Don't worry. I'll make sure it goes well. I'll sign the form, make the copies, and put them in envelopes ready to mail after Christmas." He would also take great pleasure in telling Drago where to put her offer, very politely of course.

"Then let's forget about it for a while. Cindy is due over for a Christmas drink any minute."

∎

The Knights anticipated a fun occasion with their friend. Cindy was great company. Given the earlier news, Knight hoped that he might be able to ask Cindy a couple of subtle questions about her father to confirm their googling. It didn't turn out that way. Cindy was in a dreadful state, very distraught. She had a brief, animated conversation with Carole and then left within a few minutes.

"What was wrong with her?" Knight asked his wife.

"It's her boys. They've both been expelled from D'Ayncourt."

"What? How did that happen?"

"She was told about a week ago. She assumed it was a mistake as neither of them had any discipline issues," Carole explained, also getting a little tearful.

"Yes, they seem good lads to me," Knight said.

"She went into the school earlier this afternoon for an appeal hearing. But the decision was upheld. It wasn't about the boys at all. Apparently some serious irregularities with their original application had just come to light and the school had to abide by its honor code and expel them."

"I can't believe it. It just seems bloody vindictive. Did they say what the irregularities were?" Knight asked.

"Cindy got all the details, but she wouldn't tell me. She was in a real stew. She was ranting that she was going to kill her father and some bitch called Isobel. I don't understand the connection. I'll have to let it go for now."

∎

Knight's first step along the selection process came in mid-January, a hush-hush initial interview downtown at Doolittle Associates with Conrad Konetski. It was a very gentle discussion, mainly about Knight's prior roles and responsibilities, a pre-screening to check that what Knight had on his résumé was accurate. Konetski did the same with all the candidates to make sure it was a level playing field. Knight mentioned his role at CELF as an example of his wider community commitment. At that point, the penny dropped, Konetski finally catching on as to where they'd met before. Sensibly, Knight steered well clear of the disastrous dinner with Konetski's sister act. They were both very professional about the whole thing, not letting their prior relationship have any place in the discussion. Knight tried to get his interviewer to open up about the other candidates. How many were there? What were their backgrounds? He wanted to know who he was up against, especially the external ones. But Konetski was very tight-lipped. Knight thought it went well though and set a good basis for the bigger tests to come.

The next installment was a full-day session at Doolittle. He spent the morning enduring various tests of his personality and leadership style, a whole battery of deep and meaningful analysis. Then, in realty-TV style, he was given two hours to prepare a presentation—a forty-five-minute pitch to the panel, passionate and persuasive—on why he should get the job, what his priorities would be, how he would change things to improve company performance. Then there would be a further sixty minutes of questions from the panel. He was given the option to use PowerPoint charts, but decided to go without. He'd been convinced years ago that charts get in the way of a sincere and compelling presentation. This was the perfect opportunity to follow his own advice and talk from the heart.

He casually prepared some notes, scribbled a few quotes that he wanted to use, and then was done. Why would anybody need two hours to prepare this? It took him about ten minutes. In truth, he'd been preparing for twenty years. Every event, every meeting with a client or a coworker, every proposal or presentation, indeed, every *day* had been preparation for this. He was ready now. He headed out of Doolittle and found a Starbucks nearby to relax. As he sipped his latte, he thought about Christina Drago, the one other person that he knew for sure was on the candidates list.

How will she be approaching all this? Probably very differently. Diligent preparation, data. PowerPoints up the wazoo. Maybe I should put some charts together. Do I have time? Oh fuck it, I can't be bothered. Besides, who cares about Drago? She doesn't have my connections to the panel, does she? She doesn't have my network. She's got no chance.

He was so pleased that he had rejected her deal. She must have been desperate. He read the newspaper for a while.

When he went back to Doolittle, he was asked into the main conference room and for the first time saw all the panel members together. It was a strange, unnerving sensation. He knew each of them and felt totally relaxed with them individually, although he was intimidated by them as a group. He told the George Knight story with plenty of conviction, self-effacement, a little humor, several anecdotes, and a few appropriate quotes about leadership and how to get the best out of people. He thought it seemed to go well, with lots of appreciative head nodding, smiles, and note-taking on their yellow pads.

The question session was good too. Edmund Patten dominated the initial discussions. He was quite brusque and asked a lot of detailed questions about strategy, target markets, profit margins, and risks. Knight's mind kept sensing déjà vu; he'd answered these questions for Patten before. It took great concentration not to fall into the trap of saying, *As I told you before, Edmund, I think we should . . .*

Seemingly satisfying Patten, Knight then took a few softballs from Crawford about how things would change for Lassiter's customers under his leadership.

Then it was Gerrard's turn. She was very interested in his views on marketing, strengthening the Lassiter brand, and dealing with the media. He felt this was an open invitation to show off, so made a reference to the race in Philly, when he'd confidently handled the live TV interview.

Moira Kenney completed the sequence with questions about the future of the industry, how he saw their key competitor and its new technology. She was also very serious. Knight smiled to himself. How far she'd come from the carefree student he'd known way back when. He used his recent experience with the Dutch opportunity to highlight the significance of the threat and reflect on how Lassiter could overcome it.

Konetski didn't ask any questions. He was the moderator. His job was to manage the session, giving each of the other panelists their allotted time for questions and bringing things to a close strictly on schedule. Knight was politely shown out.

He found it difficult to read them. They were all being so impersonal about it all. Even Pearson was doing a convincing impression of someone who had scarcely met Knight before. Not his soccer-crazy buddy. Despite their noncommittal reaction, he went away confident that he'd given it his best shot and still convinced that they were all on his side.

■

He found his final involvement with the process rather squalid. He got an email with a draft contract and a request to submit a markup to Drake Devonshire with any changes that he considered necessary. The email explained that he would be invited to a negotiation session with Dale Dobbs to finalize the draft agreement ahead of the panel's decision. Knight read through the document and was once again in shock. He couldn't believe the compensation package, the retirement benefits, the health care, the perks—the jet, golf club, health club, car and driver, and entertainment allowance. There was even a dry-cleaning allowance. *You have to be kidding me. They pay a fucking dry-cleaning allowance for someone making millions?*

But really, what was there to negotiate? He just sent it back and said it was all fine with him. No big finale, no last test of his competence or commitment. He just hit the Send button. Later, he worried that he'd made a mistake by being straightforward. Perhaps he should have had it reviewed by his own attorney and then marked up some things just to play along with the process? He hoped it wouldn't count against him. With everything else going for him, he doubted that it would.

◼

A week after the final curtain fell on Grauermann's career, the Lassiter team gathered in the auditorium at corporate headquarters. They had been invited to hear a "major announcement" at 2:30 p.m. It sent everyone into a flat spin of speculation. Most assumed it was the news on the new CEO. That seemed the obvious thing. The timing was right. Grauermann hadn't been seen since the retirement party. He'd just disappeared, faded to black, like a bad dream. The office was crazy with the "Who's getting the job?" rumor mill.

There were about 120 people in the room. There also would be a live webcast for the people who weren't based here in HQ. It would be a pain for the folks in Asia and Australia to get up in the middle of the night, but there was so much interest they would all do it, with differing levels of disgruntlement. Knight recognized most of the people in the room: the usual HQ folks, Varella, Houston, and Dreiser; the remaining members of Grauermann's erstwhile inner circle, Griffith and Myer; Elliot, who was pacing around nervously, concerned that everything went smoothly as the auditorium was part of his empire; Livingston, with his buddy Chambers; and a couple more QPQ types. *How'd they get invited to this?* He turned and caught sight of Christina Drago. Her presence unnerved him. *God, I hope I've got it.* As the moment of truth drew near, his confidence began to waver, just a little.

At 2:28 p.m., Elliot set out the chairs on the stage very precisely, six together in a row. Knight realized it was going to be the members of the selection panel. Why hadn't he seen it earlier? None of the panel members were there yet. They would all come in together and then announce who had the job. Knight wondered why they hadn't let him know. It seemed a bit odd. His anxiety grew. For a brief moment, he considered defeat. Had he missed out? *No, of course not,* he reassured himself. *It must be part of the new authentic leadership style.* They wanted the new CEO to be surprised and excited. They wanted him to go up there and make spur-of-the-moment and emotional comments, to send the right message about the changes coming to the way Lassiter does things. This had to be Gerrard's influence. They wanted a live communicator, not someone reading calculated, prepared remarks precisely crafted by a ghostwriter. Once again, he shut out the possibility of defeat.

2:29 p.m. Knight was becoming increasingly nervous, his palms sweating. It was a good thing he had a dark suit on as his shirt was soaked. What was he going to say? He'd have to thank them all of course. All the panel members. Lots of other people too. How much should he say about his ideas for changing the company? He needed a good quote to end on. How about that Churchill one? "Not the beginning of the end, but the end of the beginning"? No, too old-fashioned and military sounding, it needed to be new and forward looking. Crap, why could he never remember these things when he needed them? Perhaps he could google something? No, fuck, there was no signal in here. Maybe the lines from a song then? That one by Yazz, "The Only Way Is Up," kept coming into his head. That had been used though. "My Way"? Regrets he'd had a few, yes, but today wasn't the time to discuss those.

2:30 p.m. There they were. As he'd guessed, it was the panel, led by Gerrard. Conrad Konetski said a few words of introduction about the process, how Doolittle had been delighted to assist, blah, blah, blah. *Get the fuck on with it, Con.*

2:31 p.m. And finally, Gerrard had the microphone. She was about the make the announcement. Knight had just hit on the song to quote: "Never Forget," Take That. Perfect. One of his favorites. *Why did I come up with that one all of a sudden? Does that mean that it's me or not me? She's almost there. Any second now. We'll see.*

"Thank you, Conrad. Yes, ladies and gentlemen, I am honored to have been asked to serve in the role of Chair of the Board of Directors of Lassiter. My first responsibility is to announce our new CEO. After an extensive process, I'm pleased to say that the selection panel came to a unanimous decision . . ." Gerrard paused, then announced proudly, "Ms. Christina Drago will be the CEO of Lassiter. Congratulations, Christina. I look forward to working with you."

The audience applauded, initially slowly then growing to an enthusiastic crescendo, rising to their feet, cheering.

"Well done, Christina. Brilliant choice!" Varella shouted.

"Hear, hear! Way to go, Christina," Houston echoed.

Meet the New Boss

Three days later

Although the selection panel's deliberations and final vote were never made public, the following version of events has been pieced together from "inside sources."

Early on in the process, Gerrard had made her play to become the Chairman, happy with the gender-specific title. She argued that this power-sharing model was the most effective way to ensure that the company couldn't be brought down by one person again. Her checks-and-balances rationale was convincing, and she quickly secured Patten's support. The rest fell into line, and this was soon ratified by the full Board. Gerrard would assume the role with the appointment of the new CEO.

Despite Konetski's singled-minded focus and Doolittle Associates' vast network, it was difficult to attract well-qualified external candidates. Lassiter's perilous market position was a big deterrent. Their reputation as being penny-pinchers didn't help either; Grauermann's prediction that they wouldn't pay the freight had been right on the money. Konetski did manage to include a couple of midlevel executives, journeymen who had spent most of their careers with Lassiter's competitors, never coming close to anything on the Lassiter scale.

From the initial round of interviews, it was clear that the internal candidates were superior. They were by far the more knowledgeable, more experienced, and more inspiring, offering insightful visions for the future of the company. It became a two-horse race. Knight and Drago's dif-ferent styles were very apparent in their pitches to the panel. His oratory stoked their emotions and made them all want to work for Lassiter. Her presentation was packed with detail and precise analysis. Both were bril-liant in their own way.

They each had two strong supporters.

Patten and Pearson were for Knight. That had never been in doubt.

Kenney would only consider Drago. She appreciated her data-driven approach. Crucially, Knight had seriously overestimated Kenney's fondness for him and their shared university experiences—carefree, bohemian days of which she wanted no painful reminder.

Gerrard had supported Drago this far; she wasn't going to let her down now. And as the new Chairman, she wanted her choice next to her in the executive suite. Her preference soon became a necessity—she herself would only be successful alongside someone with true CEO potential. Only one met that definition: it had to be Drago.

Konetski was also inclined to go with Drago. He had no idea about her true potential as a CEO, or Knight's potential as a CEO, or anyone's potential to be a CEO, truly clueless about anyone's potential for anything. He paid no attention to any of the psychometric analysis, Myers-Briggs mumbo jumbo. He knew what he needed to know, and that was that she was Gerrard's choice. And that Gerrard had told him that she would send a lot more business his way if the panel came to the right result. Fortune favored the undiscerning, so it would be a no-brainer for him, a state with which he was very accustomed.

Crawford struggled with her decision. She liked Knight and had misgivings about Drago's overzealous hyperintensity, a concern only slightly improved by their ski-trip bonding. Eventually she was swayed by other factors: she was very concerned about Gerrard's new hostility toward cycling, and her threat to end the sponsorship. At a private dinner with Gerrard on the evening after Grauermann's retirement party, still aglow from her encounter with Dusty Rhodes, Crawford explained that she wouldn't be able to maintain her involvement in L-SAC without Lassiter's commitment to the team. Seizing her chance to seal the outcome, Gerrard offered her a deal; Lassiter would guarantee continued sponsorship for the next two years, with a higher fee and more frequent customer events, and in return, Crawford would support Drago and continue to head up L-SAC. They were both very satisfied with the plan.

With Konetski and Crawford's votes secured, Gerrard arranged the final selection panel meeting for 10 a.m. on the day of the announcement. She wouldn't allow any time for second thoughts, scheduling a fifteen-minute conference call at noon with the full Board members to secure their formal approval of the panel's recommendation. She also asked Elliot to put out the email invitation for the 2:30 p.m. session. She lined up one of the PR people to wordsmith the announcement and Dale Dobbs from Drake Devonshire to take care of all the legalities, regulatory notifications, and so forth. It was all teed up perfectly.

At their final meeting, the panelists reiterated their commitment to abide by the majority decision, stated their choices and gave their rationales, sticking to their critiques of Drago's and Knight's capabilities, rather than revealing any of their own personal agendas. The result was in: 4–2, Drago.

It took a few days for the news to sink in. Knight had convinced himself he'd get the job. In a bout of wishful thinking, he had molded every piece of evidence to fit his foregone conclusion. So much for the precious network.

Drago did as she had threatened. Knight was let go, as the HR eu-phemism goes. He took it phlegmatically. He packed his office, loaded his car, turned in his badge, and turned the page on his Lassiter career, "Never Forget" playing as he drove away.

It was time for him to move on. Could he bounce back? Had

he learned enough along the way to handle the setback in a mature productive way? The answers to these and many other questions would determine Knight's future. It would prove to be an exciting new adventure for everyone.

www.ingramcontent.com/pod-product-compliance
Lightning Source LLC
Chambersburg PA
CBHW022154170626
46807CB00005B/2204